Riptides

Riptides

Sherry Comstock

CONTENTS

To my husband, Keith, my children, James, David, Kenny and Sarah, as always.

Riptide defined: "A strong current caused by tidal flows in confined areas...presenting a hazard to swimmers and boaters. (Oxford Languages)

Riptides pull the swimmer out to sea, away for the storm.

How does a swimmer get out of a riptide? The common advice is to swim parallel to the shore until you are free of the current.

1

Callie April 1997

Her wicker rocking chair moved slowly in the ancient, comforting rhythm known to all who enjoy sitting in such chairs. Callie sipped her morning coffee on the front porch while looking over her yard. Every now and then the chair added a small squeak to the sounds of the herons taking wing. She inhaled deeply, relishing the sweet, citrusy scent of magnolias in the light breeze, and then let her breath out slowly. The majestic, old magnolia was only a shadow of its former self after hurricane Henry mangled its major leads. Still, the arborist had done a good job salvaging the tree. She and Luke had planted two more magnolias, several live oaks, and a few redbuds and dogwoods once they completed renovations for the house.

She watched Kim's car drive away until its taillights were hidden by the dense foliage along the roadside. As it disappeared, her thoughts went back to 1993. When after getting her masters' degree and landing her first job, Kim brought home her new boyfriend, Jake, a tall muscular young man. Her daughter's face was aglow with newfound love.

"Hi, Momma, Luke." Kim called as the couple climbed out of the car. A huge grin spread across her face.

Callie hurried down the steps to hug her daughter. "Hey, sweetheart," she said as she held her daughter close. "Come on inside and get something to eat."

She turned to give Jake a hug, but he had already gone to the back of the car. Hiding her disappointment, she slipped an arm around Kim's waist as the two women headed up the walkway. Once everybody was on the porch, Luke gave Kim a big hug and managed to get Jake to shake hands.

Jake remained taciturn during the visit. He did open up enough to let them know his family had moved to Charleston from New Jersey when he was six. Even though he was a Registered Nurse and worked at one of Charleston's larger hospitals, Jake did not seem to share Kim's passion for nursing. Kim laughed it off as his being jaded after working several years in the emergency room.

Shaking her head, Callie brought herself back to the present. Luke was already in his studio. *Something feels off. It shouldn't. Over the last ten years, we've all been able to rebuild our homes and the Emporium. Business is good. Kim and Jake married three years ago. Granted, I don't feel close to him, but I guess I can't expect everyone to look at family like I do. Besides, I've always encouraged Kim to handle things in her own way.* Callie continued her mental check-in on those she loved.

Alma seems a bit slower since Carol died, but she still comes into the store two or three times a week. It must be hard to realize that you are the last of your generation and that your family has scattered.

Max and Louise are well. So are Momma and Dad. The same goes for Bobby and his family. Luke's family is good. She smiled thinking of her husband. *Hell, Luke and I are better than ever. It's the spring of 1997 and life is good. So, what's wrong with me? Guess I'll figure it out; I usually do. I'm due at the Emporium at ten this morning. Better get moving. Co*ffee cup in hand, Callie went inside.

After a quick shower, she towel dried her hair. It fell into a dark curtain just below her shoulders as she brushed it out before pulling it into a loose bun. *No gray yet. Guess that's the advantage of not having Momma's auburn coloring.* After pulling on loose slacks

with a sleeveless top and over blouse, Callie slipped on her Keds before going to the kitchen to eat a bagel and have one more cup of coffee. Sitting at the kitchen island, she pulled out her planner and heard the back door open.

"Morning, love," Luke said as he walked up beside her and hugged her before getting his own coffee. Even though there was a coffee maker in the studio, he often took a break to join Callie before she started her day.

"Morning," Callie murmured.

"Do we have anything going on this week?" After grabbing his coffee, Luke pulled out a chair and sat next to her. The hurricane in '87 damaged Aunt Sally's vintage enamel topped kitchen table beyond repair, so they added a large kitchen island.

Callie looked at her planner. "No. Jake is off this weekend and Kim was just here, so she'll be staying in Charleston. And my family's not coming to the island until May."

"That's good. My parents have asked us to dinner on Friday. Not sure what time, but knowing them, it will be six-thirty or seven. Is that okay?" Luke rested his arm on the back of Callie's chair and gave her a light squeeze before turning his attention to his coffee.

"Yeah, that's fine. I should be out of the Emporium by five. It's still early spring so we haven't adjusted to later hours." Nodding, Callie made an entry for Friday's dinner before slipping the planner into her bag. Putting the bag on her shoulder, she stood. "Give me a hug and a kiss. I need to get going." Stepping back from Luke, she began to pick up her dishes.

"I'll get those into the dishwasher before I go back to the studio. I'll call my mom and see what time dinner is."

"Thanks, love. See you tonight."

Parking in front of the Emporium, Callie's chest swelled with pride as she surveyed what she, Max and Alma had accomplished. After hurricane Henry in '87, they rebuilt the store on steel pylons. That made it six feet above ground level to reduce the risk of flooding. The exterior was white stucco. Steps and a gentle ramp led to the deck which now surrounded the building. Black and white striped awning stretched across the front of the structure and around one side. White wicker chairs with cushions to match the awning and a few small tables sat along the deck in front of the store. To the left of the store's display window a glass door opened directly into the store's portion of the building. Further down and to the right of the large window was a set of double doors leading directly into the gallery. *We've really come a long way since our days of selling on the pier.* Callie smiled to herself.

As she walked through the door, Max stuck his head out from their glassed-in office and waved for her to join him. Making her way to him, Callie greeted Sheila, one of the artists working in the store today. "How's it going?"

"Pretty good," Sheila answered. "Michael brought in a few new pieces so I'm shifting things around to be ready once you've checked them in. They're all in the back." Michael, a local artist, had been showing his work in the Emporium since its opening. His

first showing was a big event, drawing customers and the local press. That New Year's Eve gala had done much to cement the Emporium's reputation as a gallery..

"I'll do that once I see what Max needs," Callie said over her shoulder as she continued on her way. *Sheila might be the best of the artists working in the store.*

"Morning, Max. What's going on?" She asked as she put her bag down and joined him at the worktable. They still did all their planning as well as the Emporium's paperwork at a long table, although they did upgrade to comfortable office chairs and an actual rolling lateral file cabinet.

"Hey, Callie." Max looked up from the ledger. His smile enveloped his entire face. "It's nothing big. Louise and I are thinking about going on vacation, maybe take a cruise."

"Really? That's great. When are you going?"

Max shrugged and grinned. "I'm not sure. Louise is checking everything out. I just wanted to give you a heads up that I'd be out for a while this summer."

"I hope you can book one that gives you a few days in the Bahamas. Luke and I really enjoyed our honeymoon there. What brought this on?" Callie looked down at her lap. She had grown even closer to her partners as the years went by and struggled with the idea they would eventually retire or possibly develop some terrible ailment.

"I asked her what she wanted for her anniversary this year. You know we've been married for fifty-three years." Max paused and smiled. "Louise likes to wear a bit of jewelry. And as the business grew, I was able to give her nicer stuff. But this year, I wanted to do something special for her. She surprised me with this cruise idea."

"That sounds great, Max. Luke and I don't have any big summer plans so whenever you want to go is fine with me." Callie was happy for her friends and relieved there was no bad news. "You've both worked so hard all your lives. You deserve some fun. Is that Ethel I hear in the store?" She turned in her chair so she could see out of the large window between the store and the office. "It is. Haven't seen her in a while. I'll see what she needs."

"All right, I'll finish up here before heading home," Max said turning back to the ledger.

Callie watched Ethel make her way through the store. Even with her walker, Ethel stood as straight and nearly as tall as she did the day Callie first met her while selling on the pier. *Wow, Ethel has really aged since Jack died. She must be at least ninety. Can't believe she's still here on the island, living alone in that big house.* Callie smiled as Ethel approached the seafood counter. "Hi Ethel, what can I get for you today?" Callie asked as she washed her hands and slipped on a pair of vinyl gloves.

"Well, you know me. I'd like three pounds of flounder," Ethel said with a grin. "The kids are coming to help me go through some stuff at the house for a yard sale."

Callie frowned slightly and then smiled. "You're going to do that and fry flounder? Ethel, you're amazing."

"Well, Stacy thinks she can fry the flounder if I sit in the kitchen with her. We're getting the place ready to sell. Probably should've moved after the hurricane in '87, but Jack had his heart set on staying on the island."

Ethel turned her walker around so she could sit on it while Callie weighed and wrapped the flounder. "Anyway, the place is a lot for me to keep up with. The kids try to help, but they're so busy. It's not right for them to spend all their vacation time working down here." Ethel looked at her lap for a moment before lifting her chin. "And besides I don't like driving off the island in the crazy traffic and that makes shopping hard sometimes."

"Will you go to Fort Mill with Stacy?" Callie slipped the flounder into a bag.

"Yep. When they built the new house, they put in two master suites downstairs. It's big enough for me to have a small sitting area with a TV and I'll have my own bathroom with a walk-in shower. It's real nice, it's where I sleep when I go to visit."

"Next time I go to the mainland, I'll give you a call to see if you want to come along." Callie tossed her gloves in the trash and rang up the purchase. "That'll be five-fifty."

"Here you go." Ethel stood to hand Callie the money. "I might take you up on that offer of a ride into town." Ethel smiled as she placed her bag on the walker's seat.

"I'll call you next time I go to town. Don't forget to get Stacy to call me, maybe I can help out. Getting a place ready for sale is a big job." Callie stepped around the counter.

"I'll do that. Though I expect she'll just come in with her own plan and that's okay. It makes my head and my heart hurt just thinking about what I can take and what has to go." Ethel smiled and made her way through the store. She paused to wave back at Sheila and Callie before she stepped outside.

Callie wiped down the seafood counter and returned to the workroom to get Michael's new pieces into inventory. With any luck she and Sheila would get them out in the gallery before closing.

"So how's Kim doing?" Max closed the ledger and began preparing to leave.

Callie sat down and looked at Max. "She seemed quiet this trip and more tired than usual. Several times I thought she wanted to tell me something, but she only talked about the clinic and how much she likes working with her patients there."

He was thoughtful for a moment, running a hand through his salt and pepper hair. "Did Jake come with her?"

"No. Apparently, he forgot they were coming this weekend and signed up for extra shifts at the hospital." Callie shook her head as she thought about how little she knew her son-in-law.

"I'm sure she'll tell you before long. You guys have always been close." Max put away the ledger. "Alma's in tomorrow, right?"

Callie turned to look at the large wall calendar where they tracked days when they each would be in the store. "Yeah, she'll be here about noon. We don't have an artist in tomorrow. So I'll overlap with her. I should be here about eleven."

"That's good. We all need to look at those applications for a new delivery driver. Lewis has decided to enlist and is working his notice, don't forget." Max paused in the office doorway.

"Oh, that's right. I sure miss Danny, although I do see he visits Alma from time to time. He was so conscientious." Callie waved a hand toward the door. "You get on home. I need to get these things tagged so I can get them displayed this afternoon. See you tomorrow."

2

Kim April 1997

Kim rolled her window down and breathed deeply. *I do love that marshy, salty smell. I don't know why Jake had to pick up those extra shifts this weekend. There really wasn't any reason for him to do it. It's not like we're hurting for money. I wanted to tell Momma about the baby. But I haven't had a chance to tell Jake yet, so I didn't. He fell asleep as soon as he got home Friday night and only told me about the extra shifts while I was packing Saturday morning. I hate keeping things from Momma, especially happy things. She knows I wanted to tell her something.* Crossing the bridge leaving Caines Island, Kim rolled up her window. She put aside these thoughts and focused on Charleston's traffic.

Pulling into the garage of their townhouse, Kim was disappointed to see Jake's car wasn't there. *I thought he'd be home by now.* Before leaving for her mother's Saturday, Kim had told him she had some good news. She had wanted to tell him then, but he seemed out of sorts. With a deep sigh, she got her suitcase from the trunk and went into the house. Stopping in the kitchen, she checked the answering machine and listened to a message from Jake telling her he was going to a friend's after work and to eat without him.

With another sigh, Kim picked up her suitcase and went upstairs to unpack. A quick check of her closet made sure her uniform was ready for tomorrow. *So glad I'm not having any morning sickness. I'd like to work as long as I can. I'm needed at the clinic. I know Jake loves me and I want to be a mother, but I make a difference in people's lives there. That's important to me, too.* Smiling, she went back downstairs.

Rummaging through the refrigerator, Kim found everything for a chef salad. Putting the eggs on the stove to boil, she cut up the vegetables and some turkey. Slipping the bowl into the refrigerator, Kim turned to the pile of mail on the island. *Just the usual bills. I can take care of that later. Ah, here's my new nursing journal.* She began reading while waiting for the eggs.

After eating her salad, loading, and starting the dishwasher, Kim stretched out on the living room couch with her journal. She tried hard to keep up with advances in the profession. Besides, the board of nursing required her to regularly complete continuing education units in order to maintain her license. She was nearly asleep when she heard Jake come in through the garage door.

"Hey, honey," he called as he came into the living room. Leaning over the back of the couch, Jake kissed her forehead lightly before plopping down in a nearby armchair. "How are your parents?"

"They're fine, but I've got some more exciting news." She got up and sat on Jake's lap slipping an arm around his shoulders.

"Whoa, babe. I'm kinda tired." Jake scowled. Kim felt his whole body tense. *What's that about?*

"I know, silly." Kim shifted so she was sitting more on the arm of the chair, as much to avoid the alcohol on his breath as to make it clear she wanted to talk. "We're pregnant." When Jake didn't react right away, she added. "The way I've got it figured the baby will be here in October."

Jake sat up straighter, nearly unsettling her with his sudden movement. "You're kidding, right?"

She steadied herself on the armrest and hid her regret while tugging at her curls. *We both agreed to stop birth control four months ago.* "No, it's for real. Confirmed with a blood test last Friday."

"Honey, that's great. Sorry about before. You just caught me off guard." Jake pulled her onto his lap. "Guess we'll have to start on that spare room and turn it into a nursery. Does anybody else know?"

"Just a couple of lab people at work, but they won't say anything until I do. I wanted to tell you Friday but..." Her voice trailed off.

"Wow, that's awesome. I'm going to be a dad. I know we agreed but I kinda put it out of my head." Jake shifted in the chair again and Kim got up.

"Did you get something to eat?" As she returned to the couch, Kim cringed inwardly. *How could he forget we made the decision to become parents?*

"Yeah, Lucy puts on quite a spread when the card games are at her place. I think I'll go shower and get some sleep." Jake stood up and stretched. "It's been a long weekend. I'm off tomorrow. Why don't we go to the mall and check out baby stuff when you get off work?"

"That sounds like fun. Maybe we'll just eat out. Then we can call our parents when we get home," Kim replied, but Jake was already halfway up the stairs, leaving Kim alone with her thoughts. *How did we get to this place? Where he doesn't remember decisions or plans we've made. I know he's drinking more, but I don't think it's that much. Or is it?* Kim tugged at her hair and turned her attention to the journal she had abandoned when Jake came home.

The next morning, her coworkers at the clinic showered Kim with all the excitement she had missed from Jake when she announced her pregnancy. Their obvious relief when she said she planned to continue working until her due date let Kim know she had made the right decision.

At lunchtime, Crystal, the registered nurse she worked with most often, came in to remind her to eat. "Did you bring something in today or should I order something for you?"

"I've got a fruit bowl and some yogurt." Kim looked up from the note she was writing. There was a lot of talk about electronic medical records, but providers in the clinic still wrote their patient notes in a paper chart. Some doctors dictated their notes. *Maybe I'll start dictating my notes. Soon, I won't have the luxury of staying until I've written all my notes for the day.*

"You're going to have to do better than that and you know it. You need more protein." Crystal, a mother of two, smiled as she shook her head. "How about I order you a chicken sandwich when I order for the rest of us?"

"You're right. Please order it." Opening a desk drawer, she reached into her purse. "Here's my card. Call me when it comes in. I'll come out then and take a break from these notes."

"Nah I got this one. You get the next. And remember, after lunch you have two new patients. They're referrals from Dr. Abrams."

"Okay, thanks. I'll review his notes before lunch then." Kim followed Crystal as she left the office and stopped to pull the charts for the new patients. After signing for them she returned to her office.

Dr. Abrams was the psychiatrist who worked at the clinic. He referred patients to her for primary care and she often saw his psychiatric patients when he was out of the office. Although patients had the choice of using another provider, several issues made it easier for them to see her, especially since the clinic worked closely with the homeless shelter next door.

With his guidance and some extra study on her part, Kim had learned how to establish a connection with the patients she saw. Many of them had mental health illnesses, like schizophrenia or severe depression, as well as chronic medical conditions. To make matters worse, most of them had had negative experiences with healthcare institutions in the past.

When Crystal returned to let Kim know lunch had arrived, she shook her head as Callie looked up from the chart she was reading. "Are you still going through those charts?"

"Well, yes. I like to see what's already been done. It's helps me make a connection with a patient when I know their history and don't repeat tests unnecessarily."

"That makes sense. I'm so used to the fact that I've seen my doc for years. I forget the system has bounced around so many of our patients and they often don't know who they'll see." Crystal's frown was thoughtful. " Anyway, come eat."

Closing the chart, Kim stood up behind her desk, "I'll stop by the ladies' room and be right there.

Thankful her afternoon patients' needs hadn't been too complicated; Kim was able to change before Jake got home from the gym. Feeling hungry, she pulled some grapes from the refrigerator. She sat at the kitchen island, peeled an orange, and started eating it and the grapes. *Wow, is it my imagination or am I really this hungry already? Guess I'll have to make sure I've got plenty of healthy snacks around. Maybe eat a little more protein. Need to set up an OB appointment with Barbara Jenkins.*

"Hey, babe." Jake came in through the door from the garage.

"Hey, honey." Kim turned to greet him. "How was your day?"

Jake gave her a quick hug before reaching around her to grab several grapes. "Pretty good. Caught up on some sleep and went to the gym. Where do you want to shop?"

"I think we should go to Toys R Us. I'm sure we can find a crib, bassinet and rocking chair there. We can get other stuff along the way." Even though she knew about Alma's difficulties and had heard her pregnant friends talk about waiting until they were further along before setting up the nursery "just in case there were problems with the pregnancy", Kim was excited to set up the nursery and determined to see it take shape quickly.

"Alright. I'll be back down in a few minutes," Jake said over his shoulder as he started up the stairs.

The mall was just a short drive away. It didn't take long for them to decide on a white crib, a bassinet, a dresser that could serve as a changing table. They also found a glider rocking chair and ottoman. Kim spent several minutes gazing at and handling baby outfits, but in the end decided to wait before buying any clothes.

"Hey, babe. Let's get some food. I'm starved." Jake pulled at Kim's elbow. "We can get them to deliver this stuff on Saturday and then spend the weekend putting them together when I get off."

"Do you want to go to Outback?" Kim asked as she put the yellow onesie with the cute, hooded jacket back on the rack.

"Sounds good. You mentioned buying paint. We could still do that after." As Jake made a path through the crowd, the couple headed to the register with the tags for their items.

"I'm getting hungry again, even though I had that fruit before we left and had a chicken sandwich for lunch." Kim grimaced. "I can't eat like this for nine months. I'll turn into a whale." *He is so into body building. Don't think I'd like going to the gym. Besides where would I find the time?*

"Nah, you're active and while we know you don't really need to eat for two, you do need a few more calories. Don't sweat it." Jake countered as he quickly handed the cashier his credit card. Kim gave him a tiny smile. *He makes such a show of paying for things when we're together. I don't see that it makes much difference who pays. But then, he's always been sensitive about the fact that I earn more money than he does.*

At the restaurant, they discussed how long Kim felt she could continue working. Jake agreed with her plan to work until her due date as long as there were no problems with the pregnancy. He also liked Kim's idea of using Barbara Jenkins, a midwife, for her obstetrics care. After serving Kim's shrimp, the waitress placed Jake's steak in front of him. It was rare and the meat's juices ran across the plate, pooling around his baked potato and asparagus. Kim swallowed convulsively. *Ugh, that's almost enough to make me sick. I never developed a taste for beef after all the seafood and chicken we ate while I was growing up, but his steak never bothered me like this before.* As the waitress left their table, Kim kept her eyes focused on her plate.

"Hey, you feeling okay?" Jake looked up from his food, glaring at his wife's pale face.

"Yeah, but for some reason the steak is making me feel a bit off." Kim smiled, trying not to give offense.

Jake's brow crinkled. "I know you don't care much for beef, but making you feel sick?" He asked doubtfully.

"Never happened before. I just won't watch you eat it." Kim looked down at her plate again before taking a bite of shrimp.

"Okay. What color do you want to paint the nursery?" Jake cut into his steak again.

Kim looked toward the ceiling as she thought a moment. "I'm leaning toward a pale yellow, something neutral. I mean we don't know if we're having a boy or a girl. Something soothing, no primary colors."

"I don't have strong feelings one way or the other. Whatever you want to do is fine with me." Jake returned to eating with renewed zeal. After a moment he added, "If we hurry, we can make it to Lowe's before they close."

Kim nodded as she kept her eyes focused on her plate. Her nausea was not getting worse, but she didn't want to risk looking at Jake's plate. In a few minutes, they both finished eating and the waitress returned with their check. Jake placed his bank card in

the holder. When the waitress returned, Kim put the leftover packs of crackers served with her salad into her purse. *Just in case Jake's steak wasn't the culprit.*

Jake wandered around Lowe's as Kim went through the paint chips. Finally deciding on a color, she gave her selection to an employee. While he mixed the paint, she picked up painting supplies. As she made her way to the register, Jake meandered over to her side.

"You found what you wanted?" He looked at the dot of paint on the paint can's lid. "That's almost white."

"Yeah, it is kind of creamy, buttery. Chiffon, they call it. As baby gets older, we can change or paint the room again." Kim shrugged and giggled. "We've got to decide on a name before long. I feel like I'm back in a hospital nursery when I keep saying 'baby'."

After checking out, the conversation continued as they walked to the car.

"We'll pick one. Just not Jacob for a boy. I've never really liked my name. No sense in repeating it." Jake shook his head. "What was your dad's name?"

"My dad was Joseph. Everyone called him Joe, but if we did that, I'd want him to be Joseph Lucas." Kim shrugged. "But I'm not sure I like that combination. We don't have to decide tonight."

At home with the car unloaded, Jake called his parents to give them the news. They offered the couple their congratulations and hung up after a few minutes. "Now you can call your mom. I'm going to play Grand Theft Auto before bed. See you in a bit." Jake went down the hall and into the game room they had set up in the den.

"Hey, Momma. How's everyone?" Kim asked when her mother answered. She chuckled as she pictured her mother sitting at the kitchen island, much like she was.

"We're all good here. What's up?" Callie wasn't one to worry unnecessarily, but it was unusual for Kim to call so soon after her visit last weekend.

"How do you feel about being a grandmother?" Kim grinned, already knowing the answer to her question.

"Honey, you know I love the idea. Are you sure?" Callie asked.

"Yes, I actually knew Friday, but didn't have a chance to tell Jake before I came out to the house."

"Of course, you would tell him first. No wonder you were so tired. Oh, hold on a minute. Luke wants to know what's going on."

Kim heard Luke's exclamation of joy. Never having had his own children, Kim knew Luke would be excited to be a grandfather. "Okay, I'm back. Luke sends his love and best wishes. When are you due? So, have you decided on names? Have you started on the nursery?"

"Wow, Momma. You sound like those stories you tell on me as a teenager. All these questions at once. Let's see, I think I'm due in October. No, we're still talking about names. We bought paint and furniture tonight. This weekend, I'll start painting and we'll put the furniture together when Jake gets off."

"I'm just so happy for you, sweetheart. You know your highchair, your rocking horse, made by your Grandpa Stevens and the seagrass basket Alma made for you survived hurricane Henry. I suspect we'll have to replace the basket's cushion and liner,

though." Callie was quiet a moment before adding, "I'd understand if you didn't want to use them."

"No, Momma. I think it's wonderful you still have them and I'd love to use them. If you're not in the Emporium this weekend, why don't you and Luke come over for lunch? Then you can see the paint. This shade is called Chiffon, a very light yellow." Kim offered as she moved to the refrigerator and pulled out more grapes.

"Okay. We'll do that. Then I'll know how to coordinate the fabric for the basket's cushion and liner. See you Saturday. I'm so happy for you, sweetie. Love you."

"Love you, too, Momma. My love to Luke." After hanging up the phone, Kim put more grapes in a bowl. Sounds from Jake's video game and his angry exclamations when things didn't go his way filtered its into the kitchen. Kim stretched out on the couch with the grapes and her journal.

When she woke up around midnight and went upstairs to their bedroom, Jake was already there, snoring. Having changed into a nightgown, Kim climbed into bed. After pushing Jake to get him to shift to his side and stop snoring, she soon drifted off to sleep thinking about the little life she carried inside her. *A boy or a girl. It doesn't matter, just be healthy my little one, Momma loves you.*

3

Callie July 1997

Callie walked along the edge of the road, slowly making her way down to the ocean. She never tired of walking on the beach. It helped give her peace of mind, even when there wasn't much going on in her life. A light breeze ruffled the sea oats, filling the air with a rustling sound that registered just below her awareness. Seagulls shrieked overhead as they dipped into the ocean for their morning meal. Turning towards the pavilion, Callie continued to the water's edge and slipped off her shoes. The ubiquitous sandpipers hopped about looking for tiny morsels of food.

Luke's parents had surprised them last month, by announcing they were selling their home in Charleston and moving to a senior living community near their daughter's home in Charlotte. And Ethel's house was up for sale even though she hadn't actually moved to Fort Mill with her daughter yet. *It will be so strange without Ethel in the community. I'll miss her humor and all her tales of island history, especially the hurricanes. At least she'll be in a place where she is loved, instead of struggling here on the island or stuck in a facility. I'm still young at fifty, but what will I do when I can't keep up with the Emporium?* Without an answer to her question, Callie turned and began the walk back home.

Slipping off her shoes in the garage, Callie stepped into the pair of flipflops she kept nearby to cut down on the amount of sand coming into the house. She found Luke already in the kitchen and joined him at the coffee maker. "Morning, love." He hugged her before pouring coffee for each of them. "How's the ocean today? Did you set the world right while you were walking?"

Callie smiled. This little byplay was typical for them and Luke's way of letting her know he understood that the recent changes along the periphery of their life disturbed her. "Don't know if I've solved anything or if there's anything to solve, but I always feel better after my walk."

"Good." Luke handed her a cup of coffee. "I'm a little hungry. Would you like an omelet? I'm going to fix one for myself in a few minutes."

"Sure. Thanks, honey. I'll finish this coffee and get my shower." She looked up from her planner. "I've got to figure out when to do Kim's baby shower. It'll be a while though. Probably won't do it before August. It's better not to have it too early. I'm stopping by Alma's before work. What are you up to today?"

"When you go to Alma's, I'll go to my parents. There are some things they want us to have. Even though they've contracted for one of the single family homes in the community, it is so much smaller and they need to get rid of some stuff." Luke shrugged his shoulders and sighed. "There are a couple of pieces I'd like to keep, but not much. Mostly, I'll just help them sort out what shops to send stuff to."

"Okay, sweetheart. Whatever you want to keep, we'll work it in somewhere." Callie leaned against his shoulder. Even now, ten years later, they still sat side by side whenever possible. "I'll get my shower now. See you in a bit."

From habit formed years ago when she was a single mother, Callie's shower was quick. She pulled on a loose mid-length dress and then her favorite slip-on Keds, she soon re-joined Luke in the kitchen. He had just put her plate with a ham and cheese omelet and toast at her place.

"Am I that predictable?" Callie laughed as she sat down.

"Well," Luke grinned as he turned back to the stove. "You do tend to stick to a routine for most things."

"Guess I do, at that," she said before turning her attention to her breakfast.

His omelet ready, Luke joined her at the island. "Have you heard from Kim?"

Callie put her fork down and turned to look at Luke. "Not since last week. She did say the sight of rare beef is still giving her stomach fits. But otherwise, she's doing fine."

She gave his arm a quick squeeze. *Oh yeah, Myra miscarried several times before their divorce.*

"I've been a little worried. Good to know she's okay. Have they decided on any names yet?"

"No, they can't seem to agree. All I know is any boy will not have Jacob as a name," Callie laughed. "Apparently, Jake really hates it." With her breakfast finished, she loaded their dishes in the dishwasher, before stopping beside Luke. "I'm heading over to Alma's now. She wanted to talk to me about her basketweaving book and I'll go to the Emporium from there."

"I'll be leaving for my parents soon." He leaned over to give her a quick kiss. "So, I'll see you after work."

"I'll see you then, sweetheart." She stuffed her planner into her bag before leaving.

It's hot already. She made the short walk across their yard to Alma's. She paused on the threshold as she opened the back door. "Hey, Alma. It's Callie."

"Come on in. I'll be right there," Alma called. Entering the kitchen, she gave her friend a hug. "Would you like something to drink before we go to the workroom?" *When did Alma start going grey? At least it's a pretty shade, like slate, and no yellow.*

"A glass of tea would be nice." She set her bag down in a kitchen chair.

"I just want to show you some of the baskets I'm going to feature in the book. You remember Macy, her mother taught me to weave baskets. Anyway, she will do the photography for me." She poured two glasses of tea and gave one to Callie. "Okay, let's go look at them. Let me know if you think I should include another pattern or something."

"I will." Callie followed her through the house to the workroom. "Alma these are beautiful." Putting her glass on a side table, she picked up a small basket with a lid. "I don't think I've seen this pattern."

"I haven't done that one before." Alma put a finger by her nose. "It's very close to one my mother used to weave. Not sure I've gotten it exactly right, but I'll call it a variation."

Callie slowly walked by the baskets displayed on a long wooden worktable, pausing now and again to pick one up for a closer look. "I think you should keep all ten of them and I think that's plenty. Do you have to write out the whole pattern for the basket?"

"I'll just show the weave for the design portion of the basket. The historical society is interested in the old designs. And when I talked with their person who's helping with the book, we agreed this wasn't a 'how to weave a basket' book, so much as a book about the old patterns."

"That's good. It's still a big project," Callie put an arm around her friend's shoulder and gave her a squeeze. "Is that a car I hear in the driveway?"

Alma reached up to pat her friend's arm. "Probably Danny. He started stopping in once or twice a week when I had that heart attack and he was still working at the Emporium. His mother was one of the nurses who came in. He comes by now and again to keep me up to date on his family. After his wife passed, his mother moved in with him and looks after his two children while he's at work."

"Ah, I see. Give me your glass. I'll take these to the kitchen and pick up my bag before I go. I'll stay long enough to invite him and his family to the cookout next week. It will be good to see him again."

Alma answered the door as Callie came back into the living room. Danny readily accepted her invitation to the cookout. "I've missed seeing everyone from the Emporium. You guys did so much to help me get my life turned around. It will be good to catch up with everyone."

Callie smiled and made a dismissive gesture with her hand. "You've worked hard. Glad you are doing well now. You guys go ahead and visit.

I've got a few more things to get done today." She gave Alma a hug before letting herself out the back door.

Several hours later, Callie pulled into the garage after closing the Emporium. Making her way down the hall, she called out. "I'm home." She was surprised when Luke didn't answer since his car was in the garage. *Well, maybe he's still in the studio.* She continued down the hall.

As she entered the kitchen, she heard him say "Callie just got in. I'll call you back in a few minutes." Luke hung up the phone and turned to face his wife. His eyes glistened with tears.

She hurried to his side and wrapped her arms around him. "Honey, what's wrong?"

"Oh, Callie. I'm so sorry." Luke rested his head on her shoulder for a minute. "Here sit down." He pulled out a tall chair for her.

What's going on? She sat down and turned sideways so she could see Luke's face. "Honey---" Her face twisted with confusion and fear as she clutched at his hands.

Holding her hands tightly, Luke continued. "That was Bobby. It's your Mom. She's in the hospital. She's had a stroke and isn't responding well." Luke pulled her closer.

Tears burned Callie's cheeks as she buried her face against Luke's chest. "How? When?"

"Your dad came home from running errands and found her on the kitchen floor. She was breathing, but couldn't talk. He called an ambulance and Bobby. Bobby hasn't left Spartanburg yet so he really didn't know anything else." Luke stroked her hair and held her tightly as she sagged against him.

Callie straightened and wiped the tears from her face. "I have to get to Columbia. What time is it?"

"It's four. I'll fix us some sandwiches, while you call everyone. I know you probably haven't eaten since breakfast." Callie moved back from his embrace.

"Okay, sweetheart. I'll go wash my face and make the calls from our bedroom. I'll be back in a few minutes."

Coming out of the bathroom, Callie plopped down on the side of her bed and called Bobby to let him know they'd be leaving shortly, but probably wouldn't arrive until eight or nine tonight. Next, she called Alma. After talking a few minutes, Alma offered to call Max. She agreed and hung up to call her daughter. The clinic staff promptly connected her to

Kim's office.

"Hey, sweetie. I've got some bad news. Grandma's had a stroke and apparently, she's not doing well."

"Oh, no, Momma. Is Luke home with you?" Callie could hear Kim's sniffles.

"Yes, he's here. We're leaving for Columbia once we pack. Do you want to come with us? But I really don't know anything. You could come later if that works better for you." Callie went to her dresser and began putting clothes on the bed.

"No, I think I should go now. I'll ride up with you and Luke. I'm sure Jake won't be able to take off."

Callie sat down again as the fear of losing her mother threatened to overwhelm her. She puffed out a breath and tried not to cry. "We'll be at your place about five-thirty. Will that work? I haven't talked about it with Luke, but I think we'll go to the hospital first."

"Yeah, I'll be ready then."

Kim had been waiting by the kitchen window after throwing a few things in a suitcase. She stepped out of the front door as Luke parked the car and her mother opened her car door. "Don't get out of the car. I'll grab my suitcase and be right there."

Callie watched the pine trees along the side of the road fly by. The sky was a deep purple with a few rose-tinged clouds. *I really should stay awake. I know he's got to be tired, too. I can't seem to focus. I just keep thinking about Momma. We've gotten so much closer since the Thanksgiving I stayed with them. She's going to hate being in that hospital.*

Forcing herself to think about something positive, she turned to face her daughter in the back seat. "Kim, did I ever tell you how your grandmother got me to try yoga?"

Kim shifted around as she tried to get comfortable. "No, I don't think so."

"Well, she started taking yoga classes while you were still in high school. Anyway, a few years ago, we were planting green beans in her garden. When we were done, I complained about being stiff. Next thing I know. we're both on mats and she's showing me different poses. I was skeptical, but told her I'd try it, at least the stretching parts. I still do it sometimes; it does help work out the kinks. But your grandmother, she's really good. She says it helps her stay calm"

"Why did she start yoga in the first place? I wouldn't have thought of Grandma as a yoga-type person." Kim wrapped one arm around her watermelon of an abdomen while leveraging her body with the other as she shifted in her seat again.

"Her doctor suggested it as a way to help her relax and clear her mind after she had that mental health crisis in '86." Seeing Kim shifting around, she asked "Honey would you be more comfortable in the front seat? Luke could pull over and we could switch."

"No, thanks, Momma." Kim put both legs up on the back seat. "I've got more room back here. But I do think I'll try to dose off for a while. Sorry I'm not very much company."

"It's okay, sweetie." She turned in her seat to look at Luke. "How are you doing over there? I can drive, you know."

Luke smiled briefly. "I know. I'm fine. Driving is something I can do to help. I mean, I can't make you feel better." He glanced at her for a minute and Callie noticed the lines in his face outlined by the light from the car's dash.

"Okay, love. Let me know if you get tired." Callie yawned and murmured, "I get so bored being a passenger." In a few minutes, she fell asleep.

Callie woke up with a start as Luke parked the car. "Dang, I really slept hard." She ran her hands through her hair and across her face, hoping she didn't look as rumpled as she felt.

"We made really good time. The new interstate helps." Luke patted her knee before he got out and opened the back door to help Kim out of the car. The sad trio made their way into the hospital.

Visiting hours were over but, as Callie had suspected, her dad and Bobby were still in the ICU waiting room. "Hey, Dad." She leaned over to hug him and he began to stand up. "No, don't get up. How are you doing?" She couldn't help but notice how fatigue had deepened the wrinkles in his face. His eyes were puffy and bloodshot. His body sagged against the chair as Callie released her hug. *Dad's always been so ram-rod straight. Now he's more like a deflated balloon.* Callie closed her eyes against tears.

"Hanging in there. I keep waiting for them to tell me she's awake, but there hasn't been any change since we got here. Your mother's going to come out of this. She's got to be okay." Her dad buried his face in his hands as he leaned forward with his elbows on his knees.

Bobby turned in his chair to look at his dad. "Dad, now that Callie's here why don't you let one of us take you home. You need to rest."

"I should be here in case something changes." He lifted his chin and frowned.

Luke rested a hand on his father-in-law's shoulder as he sat down beside him. "Bob, I know I would feel the same if it were Callie in there, but you've got to rest. You can't take care of Lydia if you're exhausted. Callie and I'll stay here." Luke looked away briefly to catch Callie's nod. "You three go home and get what rest you can. We'll call if anything changes."

Bob slowly shook his head, "I guess you have a point there Luke. I just don't like leaving her here. Lydia's always hated hospitals. I don't want her to get the wrong idea about why she's here. She hasn't had any mental health problems for such a long time."

Callie spoke up, not wanting to give her dad a chance to change his mind. "Dad, I get it. I'll make sure she understands, if she should wake up before you get back." Turning to Luke, she added. "Honey, would you give Kim the keys so she can take our car to the house. She'll need her suitcase. We can sort out how to get Dad's truck back to the house later."

After they left, Callie began pacing along the short hallway. She tried to will her mother into responding to her treatment. Luke came up beside her and put an arm around her waist. "Come on, love. Sit down. It's going to be a long night. I'll see if I can find us some coffee."

"Okay. I guess I might as well." With his hand on the small of her back, Luke gently guided her to a loveseat in the waiting room before going in search of coffee. *Why is there so much blue in a hospital? At least the furniture's more comfortable than it used to be. Looks a little less institutional without all those chrome arms and legs on the chairs. They've even carpeted the waiting area.* She sank into the seat as she watched Luke disappear behind the closing elevator doors. *What would I do without him? Guess, I'd have to survive, but I wouldn't want too.*

She smiled as the elevator opened several minutes later and Luke walked toward her with coffee. "Thanks, honey. I sure needed this." Callie took a sip from the steaming cup. "Can't believe I'm still tired, even after sleeping in the car."

Luke sat beside her. "Well, both of us put in a full day and worrying takes a lot of energy." He squeezed her hand. " Anyway, I think we're both past the age of pulling an all-nighter. So, it's probably a good thing if we doze off once in a while."

Before long Callie was drowsy again, she kicked off her flats and curled up against Luke who was dozing with his head against the wall. Sometime during the night, a nurse brought them a blanket and a couple of pillows. It made resting easier, but there was still no change in Lydia's condition.

Callie's dad, Bobby and Kim were back at the hospital around nine the next morning. Callie and Luke decided to wait for the doctor to make his rounds before going back to the house and trying to sleep. Feeling stiff from her time on the waiting room couch, Callie gave into her growing impatience and began pacing in the hall. She tried sending her mother healing messages and encouragement through mental telepathy. *I don't even know if this kinda thing works Momma, but I need you to hang on a little longer. This fall Kim's little one will be here. I know you don't want to miss that.* Thinking the doctor had to come soon, Callie rejoined her family and took a seat beside Luke.

Within a few minutes, Lydia's doctor bustled out from the nurses' station. His white lab coat was impeccable, without a wrinkle or smudge anywhere. He stood in front of Callie's dad. "Mr. Parsons, I'm Dr. Rogers. An embolism caused your wife's stroke. She's beginning to respond to questions by squeezing my hand. She's moving her arms and legs. Those are good signs. But we're still in a wait and see phase." He removed his glasses to clean them. "You can go in to see her. But spread it out. Only two of you at a time. She needs to rest." A nurse came to the edge of the group and waited momentarily to catch the doctor's eye. He nodded at her briefly before turning back to the family. "I've scheduled some more tests and we'll monitor her closely for a few more days. Excuse me, but I have to go," he continued before following the nurse out of the waiting room.

"Why do they do that Bobby? I didn't get a chance to ask questions," Callie fumed.

"Sis, he's probably really busy right now," Bobby answered. "Dad, did you understand everything?"

"Yeah, an embolism is like a clot, right?" Their dad asked.

"Right, it could be some fat or even a blood clot," Bobby answered. "Why don't you and Callie go in first. Just talk to her, Dad."

Callie put an arm around her dad as they returned to the waiting room a few minutes later. "She's still asleep," her dad told everyone.

"Kim, you, and Bobby go see her. Maybe you two can make some sense out of those machines in there." She took a seat on the waiting room couch. Bone weary, she covered her face with her hands as her elbows rested on her knees. Silently, Luke put his arm around her shoulders.

The time for Kim's and Bobby's visit was nearly up, when Callie and Luke noticed a couple of nurses striding purposefully past the nurses' station toward Lydia's room. Callie gripped Luke's hand and tried to steady her breathing. *How could that be a good thing? The nurses hurrying like that.* Bobby and Kim came around the nurses' station. *They're smiling.*

"Bobby, what's the good news?" Callie asked as they got closer.

"Listen to Kim. She'll tell you," Bobby said with a huge smile as tears rolled down his cheeks while he fumbled to find a tissue in his pocket.

"You won't believe it Momma," Kim said in hushed, excited tones. "Bobby and I were talking to Grandma about whatever came to mind. I wanted to give him a few minutes to be alone with her, so I leaned over to give Grandma a kiss." Kim paused and took a deep breath. "As I leaned over the bed, little one kicked hard. Apparently, Grandma felt it too since my belly was against her hand. She opened her eyes and tried to talk."

4

Callie September 1997

Callie paused to look back at her house while she made her way to the beach. *I'm glad we added the extra space when we did the remodel, even though I didn't envision Momma and Dad coming to live with us then.* She continued to the shore. Sandpipers dancing along the frothy water's edge as they sought their breakfast distracted Callie from her thoughts. The early morning sun promised a warm day as it made its way above the horizon and parted the thinning fog so she could see the boats headed out to sea.

Her thoughts returned to the trip to Columbia she and Luke had taken last week. Her parents had talked as if they'd be returning to Columbia at some point. After talking with Bobby, Callie and Luke felt this would be a permanent situation. *We're okay with that. I just hope Momma and Dad will accept it. We've already moved Kim's childhood mementos upstairs so they can have a downstairs room since we remodeled the bathroom at that end of the house. I'm just thankful we have the space to do this. It would be nice if Luke was going with me today, but he has to get ready for a showing next week.* She turned and began the walk home.

Callie changed her shoes in the garage before going inside. Hearing Luke in the kitchen she hurried up the hall. "Good morning, sweetheart." She gave him a hug before getting a cup of coffee.

"Morning, love. How's the island today?" Luke asked as he sat down.

"It's holding up well." Callie laughed as she joined him. "I don't think we'll have to take any drastic action to keep things settled." They always joked about Callie's walks being her way to address any calamities in their life or her way of working out anything that troubled her.

Luke leaned over to give her another hug. "Going to be awful quiet without you here." He took a sip of coffee.

"I won't be gone long, just a few days." She sat down next to him. "I packed last night so I'll sit with you for a little while before I go. Danny's mother, Linda, called last night and gave me a few names of caregivers. When Dad and Momma get here, they can talk to them and set something up. I think that will help Dad a lot."

"From what your dad said on our last visit, your mom is having some trouble accepting her new limitations." Luke turned to look at Callie.

"I know. I'm trying to think of ways to make accommodations for some of the things she used to like doing. I think if they can settle in here and have someone come a few days a week then Dad won't be so stressed. I'm really glad you agreed to give this a try, honey." Callie reached out and squeezed Luke's hand.

"Of course, what else would we do? They're your parents. We should help when we can. I thought I'd have a bagel before I went out to the studio." He stood up. "Do you want one too?"

"That sounds good. I'll grab my suitcase from the bedroom so I can leave after we eat. I'll be right back."

Picking up speed, Callie merged from I-526 onto I-26 and her thoughts turned to the conversation with her mother about her parents' decision to live with Callie and Luke on Caines Island.

<<<<<<

It had been one of those rare days Callie experienced in Columbia when she didn't feel consumed by a longing to return to the island's salty air. She and her mother were on the back porch, enjoying the warm afternoon sun.

Callie turned in her rocking chair to look at her mother, "Are you sure this is what you want to do, Momma?" She looked briefly at her lap before continuing. "I know the island has never been one of your favorite places." Callie reached over and held her mother's hand as she looked at her.

Lydia held her daughter's eyes for a moment before looking away momentarily. "I've changed my mind about a lot of things, Callie. And besides, it wasn't the island I hated so much as I dreaded the unrelenting anxiety and worry that something might happen to you or Bobby. Anyway, I think this is the right move for your dad and me."

Callie squeezed her mother's hand before letting it go. "Okay, Momma. Luke and I are happy to have you. Lord knows we have enough room. I just wanted to be sure you feel okay about it, given your history on the island."

"Sweetie, I definitely have some conflicting feelings about leaving this house where I raised you children and spent all these years with your dad. And it's sad to think I can't run a household like I used to. Your dad is trying so hard." Lydia squeezed her eyes closed and blinked away tears. Her voice was rough with emotion as she continued. "But I know it's a lot of work to help me and keep up with everything here. He can't do it all and I'm frustrated because I can't help. Which makes me not the nicest person to be around. Besides, if I'm with you, I get to see my great-grandchildren more often." Her dad joined them on the porch and their talk turned to more prosaic plans for making the move.

<<<<<<

Callie pulled into her parents' driveway around noon. As she lifted her suitcase from the back of her SUV, her mother waved from the porch. "Hey, Momma. I'll be right there."

Her dad stood next to her mother's wheelchair. "Need a hand?"

"No, I've just got the one bag," She walked up the steps to the porch. Setting her suitcase down, Callie bent to give her mother a hug "It seems like ages since I've seen you guys."

When her mother released Callie from the hug, her dad said, "Come on in the house. Are you ready for some lunch? I just made a fresh pot of coffee." He turned her mother's wheelchair and moved ahead to open the door so her mother could wheel herself inside.

"Coffee sounds good, Dad. I stopped for lunch on the way up so I'm not hungry right now. Let me get this suitcase put away," Callie said as they entered the living room. "I'll join you in the kitchen in a minute."

Lydia was just getting settled at the table when Callie came into the kitchen. "You're doing pretty well with your wheelchair, Momma." Going to the coffee pot she asked, "Would you like some coffee?"

"Sure, " her mother said as she squared herself up to the table.

"Where did Dad go?" Callie brought two cups of coffee to the table. "I heard him say 'Be right back', but didn't catch where he was going."

"Probably went out to put the for-sale sign in the truck." Her mother looked down into her coffee cup. "We don't need two cars any more. I don't think I'll be driving again. It's too hard for me to get in the truck so, there you go." Lydia looked up and gave Callie a tight smile while slowly shaking her head.

Callie heard her dad open the screen door to the back porch. "How can I help you get ready, Momma?" She sat her mug on a coaster.

"I think we have most stuff together. There's some food I'd like to take so it doesn't go to waste." Her mother fiddled with her coaster. "But we can get that together right before we go."

"Now I'll get some coffee," her dad said as he came into the kitchen. "I've just got to give the post office our forwarding address and a few things like that." He added as he sat down at the table with his coffee.

"Okay, Dad." A small frown played across her forehead as she thought about how she would feel if she had to give up her home. "Momma, do you want to take the spread from your room? And maybe the curtains?"

"Wouldn't that be a lot of trouble?" Her mother picked at her nails, avoiding Callie's eyes.

"No. I could wash and pack them tonight," Callie offered. "Pick a couple sets of sheets so your room looks like home and we'll pack those too."

"That would be nice. I really like the set we have in the bedroom now. I just changed everything out this past April." Her mother's eyes grew brighter.

"Okay, we'll get that together this afternoon. And Momma, think about pictures or things that you'd like to have with you, if you haven't already." Callie got up for more coffee. "I've taken all of Kim's old stuff upstairs so you can decorate the room like you want." She rejoined her parents at the table.

"That sounds nice, Callie, a bit of home." Her mother smiled as she backed her wheelchair away from the table. "There are some things I'd like to take for the built-in shelves in that room. In fact, I'll start gathering some of them now." Lydia was humming as she reversed her wheelchair and continued down the hall to the bedroom.

Callie's dad shook his head as his wife left the room. "Why didn't I think of that?"

"Because we look at things differently, " Callie said smiling. "You were thinking of safety, ease of moving and things like that. Whereas Momma and I think about how to make a place feel like home. Anyway, I know I'd rather have stuff I chose over someone else's stuff any day of the week." Callie stood up and took her cup to the sink. "I'll go take down the curtains and get them in the washer. Do you know if she has any other curtains packed away?"

"I'm not sure. If she does, they're probably in the closet in your room," her dad said as he stood up. "I'll go see if your momma needs any help. She tends to get confused when we talk about making changes."

During supper that night Callie explained she had gotten the names of a few caregivers from Linda. "I don't know any of them, but you interview them and find someone you like. If Linda's recommending them, they'll be good people."

"That kind of help gets expensive." Her mother put her fork down. "That's why we don't have anyone now."

"I know, Momma. But your expenses will be less than they are here." Callie gently took her mother's hand. "And if need be, Luke and I can help."

Her dad sighed. "Okay. I won't argue about it. Your momma deserves the best."

"So do you Dad," Callie said as she squeezed his shoulder. " You both deserve to spend your life with some comforts without worrying about things."

There were a few rough patches when her parents first moved in. At first Lydia kept trying to pack, thinking they needed to return home so her husband could go to work. Lydia withdrew into herself for a while when she realized all over again that they would not be returning to Columbia. Kim's visits and talk of great grandchildren seemed to help brighten her grandmother's mood.

When the ramp leading from the deck to the yard was completed, Callie's dad built raised beds next to the deck so Lydia could plant a fall garden. She seemed to enjoy planning a garden of her own.

Still, Callie was troubled that both of her parents were reluctant to find an aide to assist Lydia during the day. Her dad had just pulled a muscle in his back trying to help her mother get into the car after going shopping. "Dad, I'm glad you're okay, but why didn't you wait until Luke or I was home to go out?" Callie asked as she helped her dad unload the trunk.

"I just thought of a few things I wanted to buy so I went. I didn't want to bother Luke since he was in the studio," he answered with a huff while he sat the bags on the kitchen island and began putting his purchases away. "I'll be fine in a day or so." He stopped talking as he turned to watch his wife go down the hall to their room.

Callie frowned when she saw her dad wince as he turned to look back at her. "See, Dad. That's why someone should be here when I'm at the Emporium. You could just go when you feel like it." Callie folded her arms across her chest. "I hate seeing you in pain. What if you fell while helping Momma?" She shook her head and went to her bag hanging near the door. "Here is another card with the ladies' names and phone numbers. Please call them," she said as she returned to the kitchen.

He didn't answer her then, but a few days later he and her mother were interviewing the women recommended by Linda. The plan was for an aide to come in three days a week. They would help her mother get a shower, get dressed and, in general, be there if her dad needed to leave when Luke or Callie weren't home. An added bonus was that a registered nurse assessed her mother and recommended physical therapy to help her strengthen her legs.

5

Kim-October 1997

Kim put the last of the notes she scribbled during a patient's visit into a folder and put it in a desk drawer. She usually kept them a couple of months before dropping them in a box to be shredded. *That's it. Glad I went to using dictation. It's a lot faster to double check the printed notes than it is to write them out by hand. Let me see if there are any in my box that need checking since I won't be back in the office for a while.*

After picking up the signed notes, she leveraged herself out of her desk chair and checked the folders in the box outside her office door. Finding them empty, Kim went along the hall to find Crystal, the RN who worked with her most often. "Ah, here you are. Are you about ready to close up?" She asked while perching on the edge of a low counter.

"Yeah, pretty soon. What do you need?" Crystal smiled up from her desk.

"Just checking to see if I have any more dictated notes printed. These are ready to go in the charts." Kim shifted her weight as she handed them over. Staying in one position for very long had become difficult during this last trimester of her pregnancy.

"No, I didn't see anything for you." Crystal frowned slightly while she thought about turnaround times with the service.

Kim hesitated a moment. "I've been through everything. So only today's notes are with them. I really should check them before I come back from maternity leave."

"It will be okay for them to wait for your signature a few weeks until you're ready to travel after the little ones are here."

"I guess you're right. If we have an audit, someone could bring my handwritten notes along with the printed ones and I could sign off on them." Kim stood up and began massaging her lower back. "I'll be glad when Avery and Allison decide to make their appearance. I can't seem to find any position that's really comfortable."

"Oh yeah, I remember those days. Just leave today's notes where I can find them in your desk." Crystal waved a hand toward the door before turning to retrieve something from the printer. "You need to get out of here. We'll survive without you for a little while. Go home and put your feet up."

"I will. My handwritten notes for today will be in my upper right hand desk drawer should something come up." Kim gave her a hug before returning to her office, gathering her things, and driving home.

With the car in the garage, Kim grabbed her bag from the floorboard and pushed herself up from the seat. *Where is Jake today? I thought he was going to be home when I got here.* Inside the house, Kim stopped in the kitchen to check the answering machine. *No messages and there are no missed calls on my cell phone. I could call him, but I hate to sound like I'm checking up on him. I'll hear from him eventually.* She picked up her bag and went upstairs.

After changing, she stood in the nursery doorway remembering everyone's shock when she found out she was carrying twins. *Fraternal at that, a boy and a girl.* There was a flurry of activity as they duplicated many of the furnishings in the nursery. Alma even wove another basket like the one Kim used as an infant. Her stomach's rumble reminded her she hadn't eaten since lunch. *Okay, I'll have a snack while I cook. You two are voracious.* Kim chuckled as she rubbed her large belly and felt the babies kick.

As Kim pulled the turkey breast out of the oven, Jake came in from the garage. "Hey, babe. How was your last day in the office?" He sat at the island still in his scrubs.

"Not too bad," she said while placing the food in serving dishes on the island. *I wish he would get home in time to change before we eat. So many germs in a hospital.*

"Good. I know you've got to be ready for a break." He began piling food on his plate." Kim joined him, served herself and began eating.

"Are you keeping your cell phone on?" She looked at him pointedly. 'I know the hospital has all those rules about personal cell phones but, If you leave it on vibrate, I'll be able to reach you when I go into labor even when you're in the hospital." *I'll never get over how it takes so much longer to cook a meal than it takes to eat it. Jake's nearly finished.*

"Think I forgot and turned it off today." Jake grinned while he fished around in his pocket before pulling out the cell phone along with alcohol preps and IV connectors. A few minutes later, he announced. "There. It's on vibrate now. I'll just leave it that way."

"Cool. I think I'll go out early tomorrow and pick up a few diapers. And you're working a 7am to 11pm shift tomorrow, right?" Kim got up from the island, taking her plate with her and putting it on the counter next to the dishwasher.

"Yeah. You won't be working for a while so I figure I'd better pick up a few extra shifts." Jake stood up. "Here, I'll get the kitchen. Go put your feet up."

"You know we've saved for this so you don't have to work yourself into the ground." She refilled her water glass and went into the living room.

Jake joined her on the couch after starting the dishwasher and picked up the conversation they started in the kitchen. "I know, but I keep coming up short on my end so I want to be sure everything's covered."

"What's going on?" *I don't think any of our bills have gone up. I don't understand why he doesn't have enough money to cover his part of the bills without having to work overtime.*

"Don't you remember? I got that ticket last month when I was so tired coming home from the hospital and they thought I was drunk. Even though I wasn't, they still gave me a ticket." He reached over Kim to grab the television remote from the coffee table. "I just paid the fine instead of going to court and then I bought that new game system. Aw, there's nothing on. I'm going to go play for a while before bed." Jake dropped the remote onto the couch.

Kim sighed in frustration as she watched him walk away. *He'll play for hours and there's no talking to him once he gets into a game. For the last few months he's not been able to put his share into the joint account. There's enough in our joint account to cover all the bills so that's not a problem. Still, I just don't understand.*

Knowing Kim was getting antsy as her due date neared, Callie decided to bring her lunch from the little restaurant they frequented when Kim was younger. Pulling into the parking spot reserved for visitors, Callie noticed Jake's car wasn't in its spot in the driveway. She picked up the bags from the back seat.

Kim saw her mother through the kitchen window, opened the door and stepped out on the small porch as her mother approached.

"Hey Momma. Good to see you. Let me take one of the bags." Kim peered into the bag. "Oh, the hot fudge brownie sundaes. How did you know I've been craving chocolate like mad."

Callie grinned and hugged her daughter. "Just had a feeling."

Inside, the women settled at the kitchen island with their lunches. "Thanks for bringing Jake's lunch. He was late heading out to the gym and hasn't gotten back yet. I'll put his in the fridge."

"Sorry I missed him." Callie started eating her salad.

"So Momma, with the babies coming, I've been thinking about my grandparents. We were always so close with your parents. But I can't remember much about Dad's family. Why didn't we spend more time with them? I mean they were in Columbia, right?"

Callie's brow creased and she blew out a breath. "Well, when you were less than two weeks old, your Grandpa Stevens had a major heart attack."

"Oh, no." Kim took another bite of her salad. "I do remember getting cards and presents from Grandma Stevens. I just have trouble remembering them as people."

"Grandpa Stevens was a big, tall man. He loved you to death and would hold you for hours while he was recuperating, just watching you play with your hands. Then when you were about six months old, he had like three heart attacks pretty close together." Callie paused to take a few bites of salad. "He had retired from the mill and was working to make their dairy farm a going concern. Anyway, never one to sit around, he pushed himself working on the farm. He had a fatal heart attack when you were a little over a year old." Callie stared into her plate.

"Aw, Momma, that's awful." Kim pushed her food away. "If you're through with your salad, I'll get the sundaes from the refrigerator."

When Kim settled back in her seat, Callie continued. "Your Grandma Stevens was devastated. She came along with Momma and Dad to see us on the island a couple of times. You were her little darling. She was a petite woman. She was so tickled that you had red hair like hers." Callie filled her spoon with brownie and hot fudge and stared at it before taking a bite. "It was hard for us to get to Columbia since we didn't have a car for the longest time and then I was always working." After taking the bite of sundae, she continued.

"She tried, but wasn't able to keep the farm going. I can't imagine losing your only child and your husband in less than a year. And then she developed her own health problems. By the time we were in Columbia, after the first hurricane, she had sold the farm and moved in with her sister in North Carolina. She sent you cards and presents until she died. I think you were about seven then."

Kim's lips turned downward. "Well, I knew it had to be something because you've always been so big on family." She turned her attention to the sundae melting in front of her.

Her mother thought for a moment. "I know I have pictures of them somewhere and I'm pretty sure I was able to save some of the cards from the hurricanes."

Kim's eyes sparkled. "Really, Momma?"

Callie smiled and nodded. "I'll find them for you. You should really have them now."

"That'd be great."

After cleaning up the kitchen, the two women went into the living room. Kim vented her frustration not working for a while before Callie left to return to the island. Propping her feet up on the couch, Kim dosed off.

A few hours later, the sounds of a video game woke Kim up. *Again, he's avoided my mother.* She sighed as she struggled up from the couch and went to the game room. Standing in the doorway she asked about his afternoon. His answers were short. Obviously, his attention was elsewhere. "Momma, brought salads. There's one for you in the fridge. I'll warm up some leftovers for myself."

"That's fine." Jake paused the game to look at Kim. "You feeling all right?"

"Yeah, just tired. Eat whenever you want. I'm not really hungry right now."

Kim went back to the living room and picked up her book. Early on she used to sit in the game room with Jake, but found the high volume nerve racking. Unable to get comfortable on the couch, she got up again and stopped by the game room.

"Hey, I don't feel like eating so, I'm going to get a shower and probably go to bed. I've had some mild contractions, but nothing consistent." Kim stood in the game room doorway. "Anyway, I'm going to try and get some sleep."

Jake turned away from the game to look at her closely and nodded. "Good. You should rest. I'll be up soon. It's been a long week."

"Jake, wake up," Kim shook his arm. "It's time to go to the hospital."

He groaned and rolled to his side to see her sitting on the side of the bed. His head lay flat against the pillow, his eyes barely open. "No, I'm off today." Opening his eyes more, he looked carefully at his wife. "Oh." He propped up on his elbow. "Are you sure?"

"Yeah, the contractions have been five minutes apart for the last 40 minutes." She started to stand up until a contraction made her sit back down.

"Okay, just take some cleansing breaths, slow and easy. There you go." He got out of bed and hurriedly pulled on some clothes. "What was it you wanted to wear?" Jake opened her closet and began moving clothes along the rod.

"I've got an outfit hanging on my closet door," Kim said. After the contraction passed, she made her way to the bathroom. "Just bring it to me, please."

Jake rushed in with her clothes. "Where's your suitcase? I didn't see it."

"It's in my car," Kim said around brushing her teeth. "Call Barbara's office and our parents, while I finish changing. "Oh, my water just broke." Kim looked down to see the clear liquid running along her legs and pooling around her feet.

Jake tossed a towel on the floor and helped Kim ease herself over to the toilet before drying the floor and tossing the towel aside. "Sure you got this?"

"Yeah, I can get myself cleaned up and changed. Just bring me some clean underwear." Kim began changing as he went into the bedroom.

"Here you go. Sure you don't need a hand?" He asked when he handed her the underwear.

"I'm okay. Just give me a couple minutes and I'll be ready."

Jake had made the few quick calls by the time Kim reentered their bedroom. "Okay, let's get you into the car."

Since it was four in the morning, Jake pulled up to the emergency room entrance. "Do you want me to get a wheelchair or do you think you can walk in?" He turned to look at Kim who was focused on her hands cradling her abdomen.

"Hmm?" She looked up at him briefly. "No, let's just get inside. I can walk. They'll stick me in a wheelchair fast enough once we're at the desk," Kim resumed focus as another contraction started. As it passed, she added, "Okay, let's go."

Her midwife had called the hospital as soon as she had hung up with Jake. Alerted to the couple's arrival, the emergency room staff settled Kim in a wheelchair and escorted her to the labor and delivery floor while Jake parked the car and dealt with the paperwork.

Once there, the nurses helped her into bed. Fairly innovative, this hospital had turned a few of their labor rooms into birthing rooms. This would allow Kim to remain in one room for her both her labor and delivery without having to transfer to another room for the twins actual delivery as long as there were no complications. Barbara quietly entered the room as the nurse finished taking her vitals. *Look at her. Barbara's so calm. Me I just want to get this done. I'm tired of not being able to find a comfortable position.*

Barbara had completed her initial examination by the time Jake made it to Kim's room. Even though this was Kim's first pregnancy, the midwife felt the twins would make their arrival in three or four hours. She stepped out of the room to give the couple some privacy.

"How you holding up?" Jake perched on the edge of the bed.

"I'm doing okay. I'm tired though. I didn't sleep much earlier." Kim reached for Jake's hand. "How about rubbing my lower back? I think one of the twins is trying to dance on my spine." Using the upper bedrail, Kim rolled to her side. "Ah, that's better." *This is so strange. I'm a nurse, I know what's happening and yet I have no control over what my body is doing. I don't think I can lay in this bed until the babies are born.*

"Hey, Jake. Are my slippers nearby? I think I'll walk for a little bit." Kim sat up on the side of the bed and wiggled her feet into the slippers he had put there for her.

"Want me to come with?"

"No, I'll be all right. You might want to doze for a while since you worked yesterday. I think I'll need you more later." Kim shrugged into the housecoat Jake held out for her.

"Well, if, you're sure." He hid a yawn behind his hand.

Kim returned to the room after a couple of tours around the unit and found Jake out cold in the recliner. The nurse had set up two infant units in the room so they'd be ready to assess the twins. Leaving her robe across a chair, Kim climbed into bed and gently rubbed her taunt belly as another contraction rippled across her abdomen. *That's it. Just take nice deep breaths. This will pass. Hey, my little ones, you'll have more room soon. Just a few more hours in that cramped space. Can't wait to hold you both in my arms. Although it will be nice, but strange, to have my body back to myself.*

After knocking softly, Callie slipped into the room first. Kim smiled as her mother hugged her. "Hey, Momma. Where's Luke?" Kim frowned slightly since she couldn't think of a reason for her mother to come alone." He's right outside. He didn't want to interrupt if you were feeding one of the babies." Callie gently hugged her daughter.

"Tell him to get in here." Kim smiled and shifted in the bed. "Allison and Avery just ate and are in the nursery for an examination."

Callie recrossed the small room, stuck her head out the door and motioned for Luke to come in. Carrying a vase of peace roses, he went to Kim's bedside. "How's the new momma doing?" He beamed. Callie took the flowers and he gave Kim a hug. "Where's Jake?" He asked, looking around the room.

"In the cafeteria, getting some lunch. He should be back soon." Kim motioned for them to sit down. "Thanks for the flowers. They're beautiful."

"How did your labor and delivery go?" Callie sat on the edge of the bed and Luke sat in a nearby chair.

"Things went pretty smoothly." Kim smiled. "And twins are a little smaller."

"Glad you didn't have a hard time of it." Callie looked around the room. "How long will they keep the twins?"

Kim chuckled. "Not too much longer, I think. Avery has dark hair. Allison has red hair like me. Too soon to tell about the eyes though. Allison was five pounds and twelve ounces. Avery was five pounds and six ounces.”

“Nice healthy weights for twins.” Callie smiled.

Luke laughed quietly. “At least you had a boy and a girl. No getting them mixed up.”

“I know.” Kim joined in the laughter. “How are Grandpa and Grandma doing?”

“They’re doing pretty well. Grandma seems to have settled in finally and has begun physical therapy, but I don’t know how much longer it will last. She’s not making as much progress as they’d like. Even so, I think she’ll feel better, if she can get rid of the wheelchair around the house.” Callie took off her jacket. “They both send you their love, but decided to wait until you were home to come visit.”

“I’d love to see them, but that’s probably a smart move.” Kim yawned. “Sorry,” she said from behind her hand.

“No need to apologize. From what I understand you just completed something equivalent to a marathon. Maybe we should go.” Luke reached for Callie’s hand.

A knock at the door heralded the babies’ return from the nursery. “Dr. Peterson will be in when he finishes checking the other newborns. We had five deliveries last night. Six babies.” The nurse grinned as she settled the layettes near Kim.

“Go ahead Momma. I know you’re dying to pick them up.” Kim smiled at her mother.

Callie walked quietly to the layette. “Oh, they’re awake. I wasn’t going to bother them if they were sleeping.” She leaned over and talked softly to Allison as she brought the infant up to her shoulder and walked over to Luke. “Here honey, just hold her up to your shoulder.” She handed Luke the baby. “That’s it, you’ve got it.” She returned to the layette and picked up Avery. Cooing to him softly, Callie walked around the room. Luke was soon doing the same thing with Allison.

Jake returned from the cafeteria; his face nearly hidden by the dozen red roses he had purchased in the hospital’s gift shop. But not so hidden that Kim didn't see him scowl momentarily as he spotted Callie and Luke's roses on a table. Recovering quickly, he smiled. "I see we all had the same thought as how to honor Kim today. How are you two doing?" He made room for his flowers on the table.

"We're doing fine. How are you? I know Kim had all the heavy lifting, but I understand you were with her throughout her labor and delivery." Callie shifted Avery to cradle him in her arms. "That's got to be tiring. We didn't do that when Kim was born. Joe had to stay in the waiting room until everything was over. I think this way is better."

"I'm okay. But I'll probably go home and get some sleep after the twins' next feeding." Jake crossed the room to Kim's bedside and belatedly gave her a hug and kiss. "I'll be back later in the afternoon," He added as he sat on the edge of the bed and stifled a yawn.

Callie looked down at the infant who had drifted off to sleep in her arms. "I suppose we should go and let these two have some time alone while the babies are sleeping." She placed Avery back in the layette. After watching her for a minute, Luke did the same. Once they secured a promise from Kim to call if she needed anything and hugging her goodbye, Luke and Callie left.

After they left, Jake began pacing the room, yawning loudly.

"Honey, the roses are beautiful. If you're that tired, go on home. The nurses will help me if I need anything." Kim settled against the pillows.

"I don't want anyone to think I've deserted you with two newborns." Jake ran his hands through his hair. "Besides, doesn't your mother realize I'm here to help? What did she mean? 'Call me if you need anything.' That's why I'm here." Jake plopped into the chair next to Kim's bed.

She turned onto her side to face Jake. "Sweetheart, she didn't mean anything by it. That's just how Momma is. They know you have to go back to work tomorrow." Kim reached out to take his hand, but the chair was too far away from the bed and Jake didn't reach out to her. Kim let her hand fall back on the bed and closed her eyes. *I don't understand why he's so jealous of my relationship with Momma. She's never interfered or tried to tell me how to live. I know they aren't as close as she'd like, but she's never forced the issue.* Startled, Kim reached to her chest and she felt the dampness against her breasts. *Okay, now. Let those negative thoughts go and relax. Take some deep breaths. Wow, my breasts are starting to feel fuller. The twins must be getting hungry if my milk is letting down now.*

Opening her eyes, Kim saw Jake at Avery's layette. "Avery's beginning to squirm around some. Doesn't he get a bottle at this feeding? or does Allison?" Jake asked, looking over his shoulder.

"You're right, Avery gets a bottle this time. Would you ask the nurse for the milk I have stored in the refrigerator? At least that will save them a trip." She got up and brought Allison's layette next to the bed.

"Sure. He's not quite awake. I'll get his diaper when I get back," Jake said as he left the room.

By the time their diapers were changed, the twins were awake enough to let their parents know they were definitely hungry. Kim had decided to introduce bottle feeding to allow Jake to participate and because she planned to return to work within a few months. Judging by her mother's experience, Kim felt she'd have plenty of milk and the newer electric pumps would make the process so much easier.

"How's it going over there?" Kim looked up after Allison latched firmly to her breast.

"Avery's pretty hungry. He doesn't seem confused by the bottle. I squeezed a drop of milk onto the nipple and he got down to business without fussing," Jake looked up from the infant to see Kim settled cozily on the bed. "Is Allison eating alright?"

"She nuzzled a little bit, but then latched on nicely. Both of them seem to have a good suckling reflex. She shifted slightly on the bed. "I'll be glad to get home so I can sit in my rocking chair. This bed's okay, but I think the rocking chair will be more comfortable with its armrests and our firmer pillows. These pillows aren't quite up to the job"

Avery guzzled down his bottle and began drifting off to sleep. Jake managed to coax out a couple of burps and change his diaper again before putting him into the layette. "Is there anything else I can get for you?"

"Don't think so. Everything I need for the pumping session is here. Check the snack basket for me, please. But I don't think I need anything right now." Kim eased Allison to the other breast and shifted her clothing.

"Naw. You seem to have a bit of everything you like. And Dr. Peterson said you guys might be able to come home tomorrow." Jake checked under each layette to be sure there were enough diapers and other supplies for the babies. "It looks like the littles have everything they need, too. I'll head home so I can nap and still be able to sleep later."

"Yeah, that recliner couldn't have been comfortable last night." Kim smiled as Jake kissed her briefly.

"I'll call you later. I'll probably be back before my parents get here." Jake turned and left the room.

6

Kim October 1998

Kim felt relieved as she crossed the bridge onto Caines Island. She rolled down her window to let the ocean breezes fill the car. After several deep breaths, her pounding heart slowed down to something resembling a normal rate. *Why would Jake pick a fight right before he was going to work? How could he call me a snob just because I don't want to put the twins in day care. It would be much better to let Julia continue to take care of them.* Kim let lose another deep sigh. *No sense staying worked up about this. Maybe I'll have time to talk to Momma sometime today.*

Pulling into her parents' driveway, Kim left the car running with the twins in their car seats. She began unloading all the paraphernalia that accompanies anyone with small children: diaper bag, changes of clothes and bottles. Luke and her mother came out to help.

"Hey, baby girl. Let me help." Joining Kim at the back of the SUV, Callie gave her a hug. Going to the rear passenger door, she began getting Allison out of her seat.

Luke walked to the back of the vehicle where Kim was unloading. "You get Avery out of the car. I'll take this stuff upstairs for you. By the way, where's Jake?"

Kim ducked her head for a moment pretending to look for something in the car. "He's at work. He'll be here before we eat." Straightening up, she went to get Avery.

"I see." Luke picked up the bags and headed inside. "I'll take everything except the diaper bag upstairs."

With both toddlers out of their car seats, Kim and Callie made their way inside. "I brought a few toys downstairs so they have something to play with and we've installed a gate on the stairs," Callie said. Released from protective holds once everyone was inside, the twins headed straight for the blocks.

Kim watched for a moment and then turned to her mother. "Thanks for setting up everything in the living room. We can see the twins while we work in the kitchen. I came early 'cause I didn't want you to have to do everything by yourself."

"Thanks, but Max, Grandpa and Luke got outside ready last night. Alma, Louise, Grandma, and I arranged the cut flowers yesterday. The asters hold up pretty well and so do the hydrangeas."

"Well, that's good. So do you have a list of things for us to do today?" Kim asked as she went to get a glass of tea and put packets of breast milk in the freezer.

Her mother pulled out the steno pad she used for planning events. "Here you go." She slid the pad to the seat next to her. "We've just got the deviled eggs and the watermelon boat to get ready."

A small crease formed along Kim's forehead as she sat next to her mother and looked at the list. "So you started the seafood boil already?"

"Sure, honey. You know I always start that early in the morning." Callie looked closely at her daughter. "What's bothering you?"

"Maybe we can talk when the twins take their nap. It's nothing major." She gave a small smile and went to the refrigerator. "How many eggs do we need to boil?"

"Three dozen. I'll get the other big stock pot for you." Callie got up and began to peer into the deep lower cabinet that made up the kitchen island. "Here it is."

Kim left the eggs on the counter, went to her mother's side, and took the stock pot from her. "Are all these eggs from Alma?"

"Yes. They still have the bloom on." Callie pulled herself up from where she squatted by the island, pausing for a minute to check on the children playing in the living room.

"I figured." Kim counted out the eggs, washed them off, put them in the stockpot and covered them with water. "How long do you boil the eggs?" She looked at her mother after turning on the burner.

"Once the water comes to a low boil, set the timer for ten minutes." Callie collected items from the upper cabinets to blend the yolk mixture for the deviled eggs.

By the time they finished the deviled eggs, the twins were pulling on their mother's leg, ready for lunch.

"I'll get the high chairs from the laundry room while you get their lunch ready." Her mother went off on her mission. While Kim gave each of the toddlers a thin slice of cucumber before preparing the rest of their lunch.

Callie put the twins in their highchairs as Kim gave each child a small plate of food and a cup of milk.

"How's the weaning going?" Callie asked as she sat at the island with a cup of coffee.

"Not bad. They get most of their milk in the cup now. Although they take a bottle at night. Once they got teeth, nursing wasn't as comfortable for me." Kim grimaced remembering her discomfort when the twins were teething.

"Oh, I remember. I didn't breast feed you much after a year." Callie made faces at her grandchildren as the twins ate and laughed at her antics. "I probably shouldn't distract them."

"No, you're fine Momma." Kim smiled. "If they are actually hungry, not much changes their focus."

Callie took her coffee out to the front porch while Kim put the twins down for a nap. Within a few minutes, Kim joined her.

"Is this a good time to tell me what's bothering you?" Callie stopped the porch swing so Kim could join her.

"Where are Grandpa and Grandma?" Kim asked, looking at the screen door. "I thought I heard a car while I was upstairs." She didn't want to bring her grandparents into the conversation.

"Taking their own nap. Grandma had an appointment earlier. They got back while you were putting the twins down." Callie started the swing slowly.

Kim tilted her head and shrugged. "Maybe I'm making too much of this. Jake wants to put the twins in daycare. 'It was good enough for me,' he said. And I don't want to. You remember Julia, don't you? She's been the twins nanny since I went back to work. I want her to continue as their nanny. At least for a few more years."

Callie kept the swing's gentle motion going while she waited for her daughter to continue.

"It isn't so much that he disagreed with my choice as much as it hurts that he called me a snob." Kim looked down at her hands before turning to look at her mother. "Just because I want the nicer things doesn't make me a snob. I've worked hard for what we have."

Callie patted her daughter's hand. "I agree with you. You have worked hard and understand that circumstances can change from generation to generation."

"I know I'm fortunate to be able to make this choice. It's not an option for many families. Heck, it's something many of my clients struggle with constantly, trying to find good childcare that's affordable." Kim clenched her fists.

"If you can afford this and it's what you want, then do it." Callie looked closely at Kim. Even though she had relaxed her fists, Kim's neck muscles were still tense. "So is that all?"

"I don't know." Kim slumped against the swing. "I just don't want to be one of those people who make good and then forget where they come from. I mean, I know you kept me near you when you were working. Times were hard then, I get it. You didn't have any choice really." Kim planted her foot and stopped the swing's easy motion as she turned to look at her mother. "I'm sure it would have been so much easier to spend that insurance check after the first hurricane instead of leaving it in my college fund. Now the only debt we have is the townhouse. Not having student loans has been great and allowed me to do more. I'd hate to be in the boat that many of my colleagues are in."

I'm not sure how Momma did everything when I was a kid. From the stories I've heard, she used to carry me and seafood down to the pier before she, Max and Alma bought the Emporium. Momma was quite successful before she married Luke.

"But you're doing what every parent wants for their child. You're building on what I did." Callie put her arm around Kim's shoulder and felt her daughter relax a little. "Now, if you start behaving differently around me because I never went to college—" Callie laughed at Kim's outraged expression.

"Momma, don't you ever…" Kim shook with laughter. "Okay, that was good. You got me. I will probably enroll them in a preschool program before they go to kindergarten. Right now, they can't tell me what happened during the day and I trust Julia. I was going to do it anyway. I just didn't want you to feel I was being all snooty."

Callie waved a hand in dismissal. "Come on, let's get the watermelon boat together. People will start coming before much longer."

Brenda and Lee came down from Columbia. Brenda had moved to Columbia with her sons after her divorce several years ago, but tried to get to the island a couple of times a year. They were staying with Josie and her family. Kim knew her mother relished the times when she could get together with the two women who had played such a pivotal role when she first came to Caines Island.

Jake came just in time to eat and begging off because he had to work in the morning, he was the first to leave. Kim took several pictures of the twins with her parents and grandparents. It was nearly dusk when she gathered their things to go back to Charleston. Callie excused herself to give her a hand with loading the car and Kim was soon on her way.

Crossing the bridge as she left the island, Kim rolled down the window to breathe in the ocean air. *If I ever retire, I think I might come back to the island.* As she entered Charleston's city limits, she rolled up her window. *It's always so good to talk to Momma. I get things off my chest.*

She usually has an opinion, but leaves it up to me to make up my own mind.

7

Callie March 1999

Callie sat on the sand watching the tide roll in while the sandpipers danced at the water's foamy edge. Stretching toward the early morning sun, she decided it was time to go back home. *Yesterday Momma and I bought the plants for the raised beds and we're planting them today. I'm sure she's up by now.* After slipping on her shoes, Callie brushed the sand from her clothes. Seagulls dipped and squawked along her path through the swaying sea oats. *The little beggars. It seems the gulls have gotten used to swiping food from us humans.*

"Hey, Momma," Callie said as she entered the kitchen. "Are you ready to plant all those zinnias, petunias and begonias?"

Her mother smiled as she put down her coffee cup. "Yep. Dad's moved all the plants and potting soil to the deck and I have that cart we picked up that has all my tools in it."

"Alright, I'll bring some tea out on the deck so we'll have it when we're ready and then we can get started." Callie put a covered pitcher of iced tea and two tall glasses on a tray and held the door leading to the garage open for her mother. Putting the tray down, she turned back to her mother and took her walker. When Callie had it settled at the bottom of the steps, Lydia held on the rails and made her way into the garage.

"I had your dad take the zinnia's down to the next level. They're tall and will look good against the deck railing. I'd like to start there." Lydia continued on her way to the lower level with only a few frustrated grumbles at her walker when it veered too close to the ramp's railing. Her silver hair glinted as she emerged from the shadows and into the sun.

"Okay, Momma. I'm right behind you now." Callie paused to look along the raised beds and noticed her mother's hair. *Momma's gray is so pretty. Will I be that lucky?* "Well, the seat on your walker will work for today, but maybe I should add some pavers and a bench so we can sit when we get tired." The women paused to don their floppy sun hats and gardening gloves.

"That's my girl. Always dreaming up some new project." Her mother chuckled and added some plants to the basket on her walker.

"You're right, Momma. I do tend to think one more project of mine will fix anything. Let's get the planting done, first. Then I can talk to Dad about a little sitting area and pavers for you." Callie picked up a flat of flowers. "I'll start at the other end of the deck."

The two women filled the four lower planters with zinnias and creeping jenny to break up the flat surface of the planters. Lydia sat on a chair Luke brought over for her when he stopped by on his way from the studio.

"Callie, this is looking good." Her mother fanned herself with her hat as she watched Callie finish the last planter.

"Thanks Momma. I like the combination you chose. They'll bloom long into fall. Do you want to have lunch before we start on the deck?" Callie noticed her mother's eyes shining brighter than she had seen them in a while. *Maybe this is the ticket.*

"I'm not really hungry. Let's just take a few minutes to drink some tea. Would you bring the cart up with you?" Lydia began making her way up to the upper deck as Callie gathered tools, empty plant packs and put them into the cart.

"I'll be there in a couple of minutes, Momma."

Callie's dad, Bob, joined them on the deck with his own glass of tea. "How's the planting going my beautiful girls?"

"We're done with the raised beds and I've had more fun than I have in a while." Lydia's eyes danced as she smiled at her husband. "Callie's got another project for you. And Callie, what do you call these glasses? They sure kept the tea cool and the bugs out."

"They're Tervis tumblers, Momma." She took a long drink.

The three of them sat discussing Callie's plan for putting pavers in front of the raised beds and adding a few benches so people could take a break for several minutes. "That's definitely something I could do. What kind of material do you want the pavers to be?"

"Well, they definitely need to be smooth, not stamped to look like stones. And something that would blend with the brick skirting. Other than that, I don't care." Callie drank the last of her tea. "I'm going to have a little more to drink. Can I top off your glasses?"

Her parents declined with a shake of their heads. "While you finish that, I'll move the pots near the table here," her dad said. He placed a large, French provincial blue, glazed pot in front of Lydia and a red one in front of Callie's chair.

"Thanks Bob. We'll be able to work from these chairs." Lydia stood and pushed the cart next to the table.

Callie wiped her brow after taking a last long drink of tea. "Oh, great idea, Dad. This will let us get finished today. Luke will be installing the art work under the pergola tomorrow." Settling into her chair, she began planting a white geranium.

"How did you guys come up with the color scheme for the deck? It sure is different from the soft pastels I've seen in Charleston. Almost pastel, but brighter, a little more vibrant." Her dad refilled his glass and settled into a nearby chair.

"It was Luke's idea, really. When he was a kid, his dad took the family to the French Riviera. He saw these colors on a terrace of the house they stayed in there. I like the French provincial colors. They're bright, but a little faded at the same time. " Callie lifted the repotted geranium and placed it on one side of the door leading from the porch.

"Are the geraniums on the steps all going to be in the yellow pots?" Her mother asked, as she swiveled the pot she had filled away from her and pulled another planter in front of her chair.

"No, I want to alternate the yellow and blue on the steps. I thought about using some red ones on the steps, but felt they wouldn't show as well with the red geraniums. The red ones will go by the door with the white geraniums." Callie took off her gardening gloves to push her hair back from her face and settled her hat back on her head before potting the next plant.

"When are you putting up the sailcloth cover for the pergola?" Her dad asked. "I'd really like to see the system for rolling it across the deck."

Callie scrunched her nose up as she thought. "Next week, I think. I'll ask Luke when he gets home."

After watering in the geranium, her mother set the can off to the side. "Bob, would you fill this and move my plants over on the stairs?"

He filled up the watering can and began moving the flower pots. "Does it matter how I start?"

"Start with the yellow one and then alternate them." Callie waved at the swarm of gnats and mosquitoes swirling around her face. Pulling off her gloves again, she reached across the table for a citronella candle and lit it. Then she stepped away from her mother, held her breath and closed her eyes as she surrounded herself in a cloud of insect repellent. "I should have done this when we first came out. Luke always teases me that this is my summer perfume." Callie laughed as she put her gloves back on.

"Do you still swell up when you get bit?" He mother frowned slightly.

"Yep. I'll be putting Benadryl cream on for days. Luckily, none of them got my face." Callie resumed transferring the geraniums from garden center pots into the brightly glazed pots.

"You had such a hard time with mosquito bites when you were little. Sometimes, you'd be covered in bites and scratch so much, the pink dots of calamine lotion nearly ran together. I just knew you'd scar your arms and legs up the way you scratched." Her mother shook her head.

Callie laughed and stuck out an arm and a leg. "Looks like the calamine lotion did the trick. I think the legs turned out okay."

Grinning, her mother agreed. It wasn't long before the geraniums were potted and placed along the stairs. With tools and gardening supplies gathered, the three of them sat on the deck enjoying the slight breeze coming from the ocean.

"Is your sewing machine still set up?" Her mother asked. "I could make some table linens to go out here. What do you think?"

"It is. That would be great, Momma. Let me know when you're ready to start. Maybe we can go choose the fabrics together." Callie flicked her wrist to check the time as she stood up. "Oh, I'd better clean up some so I can get supper ready on time. We just have the begonias for the tables under the pergola to pot. We can get them tomorrow. Thanks both of you for all your help today." She paused at the ramp leading to the garage.

Her mother grinned. "You're welcome, sweetheart. I think I'll go into and rest for a while. If I go to sleep, please wake me before dinner."

"I think I'll join you, Lydia. I'm a bit tired myself." Callie's dad followed her inside.

"Okay, I'll knock on your door, if I don't see you at supper time," she said as she continued to the garage to put things away.

When Callie returned from her walk the next morning, she was surprised not to find her parents in the kitchen. Usually they were drinking their first cup of coffee when she got home. Hearing voices outside, she went out to the deck and saw her mother surrounded by gardening tools, potting soil and plants. On the table in front of her were the pots for the begonias and a cup of coffee.

"Wow, you got an early start this morning," Callie said, grinning at her mother. "Where are Dad and Luke?"

"Oh, they're off to the garden center to pick out pavers." Her mother pushed the brim of her hat back. "And maybe a couple of benches. They brought all my supplies up here before they left. I didn't want to leave the begonias in the garden center pots too long."

Callie began rummaging in the cart. "Let me grab my gloves and I'll help finish up."

Soon plants were repotted and placed on the tables scattered around the deck. "Callie, this looks so good. Luke said he's got a splitter that will let us set up two garden hoses, one for the raised beds and one for the plants on the deck."

"What a cool idea, Momma. I wondered about getting water to all the plants and wasn't looking forward to carrying a watering can around."

"I wanted to be able to take care of these flowers without making more work for someone, to be able to come out here and do it myself." Lydia took her gardening hat off and ran her fingers through her hair.

"Well, I'll surely appreciate your help looking after them. Somedays I barely make it out to the vegetables." Callie began gathering their tools and supplies and put them in the cart. "Did you guys eat before all this started?"

"Dad scrambled some eggs and made toast. I wanted to get started early before it got too hot." Lydia tossed her hat and gloves in the cart. "I guess you didn't eat before your walk?"

"No, just had a cup of coffee. After I put this stuff away, I'll have a bagel and maybe some fruit. Would you like something?" Callie paused before going down the ramp to the garage.

"I'll have a bagel and cream cheese." Her mother stood and went inside. "I'll put the bagels in the toaster."

"Okay, I'll be right there as soon as I take the tools to the garage."

Callie and her mother had just finished eating and were still at the kitchen island when her dad and Luke got home.

"Hey Callie, Lydia," Luke said as he poured a cup of coffee and joined them at the island. "I think we have enough of everything to finish out the raised bed area. You guys will love the benches." Luke gave Callie a quick hug.

"They're a heavier wrought iron," her dad added as he squeezed his wife's hand. "But instead of white or black, they're a bronze color. Wouldn't you say, Luke." Callie's dad looked at Luke for confirmation.

"Yeah, that's pretty close, Bob." Luke sipped at his coffee. "Callie, if you and your mom aren't too tired, why don't you come out and take a look?'

Everyone followed Luke out to the truck. "They'll deliver the pavers on Friday and the chairs should be in next week," Callie's dad said while he lowered the tailgate.

"Oh, I do like these. When you said wrought iron, I was afraid they'd be all filigreed and stuff. This is more like lattice work or a widely woven basket."

Luke and Bob set the two benches on the driveway. "Try it out, Lydia. They're nice and sturdy." Callie's dad moved aside so his wife could get to the bench.

"This is great," Lydia said. "I can get up and down without worrying about it tipping over."

"There are cushions, so it will be comfortable to sit on. I'll just put the boxes off to the side in the garage." Luke took one box and Callie's dad grabbed the other. "Bob, let's put the benches out by the raised beds. I know Lydia will have to water those flowers before we get the pavers set. It'd be good for her to have a place to rest."

"I was going to suggest that myself," Callie's dad said. He and Luke soon had the benches in place. When they returned, Callie suggested they go out for lunch. Everyone easily agreed that the diner on the Isle of Palms would be a good place to go and after lunch they would just relax around the house.

8

Kim September 1999

Kim slumped against the living room wall with her knees bent. She folded her arms across her knees and rested her head against her arms. *I'll rest just for a minute. Man, I'm so tired and I still need to drive to Columbia tonight.* Everything that could be moved from the downstairs was now jammed upstairs. Allison and Avery played nearby with a few of the toys they were taking with them while Kim watched the heavy winds batter the small trees in the yard. Luke had come by earlier to help Jake put all the appliances up on cinder blocks before going back to pick up her mother and Alma. As soon as Luke left, Jake packed a duffle bag and went to the hospital. He would stay there until a decision was made to evacuate the hospital.

The plan was for her and the twins to stay with her mother, Luke, her grandparents and Alma in Columbia. Jake would join them eventually. Brenda had found a four- bedroom house for sale whose owner agreed to a short-term rental. Between the three families, they were able to take enough household stuff to make it practical.

Wish just once Jake would put his family before the hospital. Kim frowned. *He would probably say the same thing about me and the clinic. Don't think he'd be right though. I do a pretty good job of balancing things. Of course, I don't have the lure of overtime and bonuses. Sometimes I think it's more about the excitement and the adrenaline rush from working in the ER than anything else. When he's home, he's great with the twins. Getting up at night when they were younger. It's just that now he's never home.* The doorbell's chimes broke up her thoughts.

Kim smiled at the twins while trying to mask her groans as she stood up. "Who could that be?" Allison and Avery grinned at her and began toddling to the front door.

Opening the door, Kim motioned her mother to come inside. "Eey, Momma, get out of the wind. Does anybody want to stretch their legs before heading out?"

Callie reached down and picked up Allison. "Luke's getting out and will help get the downstairs electric shutters in place. Alma's staying in the car to talk to your grandparents until we're ready to go." She followed her daughter into the now empty living room.

"All right." "I just need to gather the toys and make sure the twins are dry before we go."

Callie swiveled her head around and found the diaper bag. "I'll get Allison changed."

Luke came inside after securing the patio doors with shutters and squatted near Callie and Avery. "Is your car loaded?"

Kim paused while changing Avery. "Yes. I just need to add my purse, these two small bags and that little basket of toys."

Luke stood up slowly. "I got to quit doing that. The knees can't make it anymore. Are your keys still by the garage door?" Kim nodded. "Okay, I'll back the car into the driveway and keep working on the shutters. Shouldn't take long. I'll take the basket of toys out."

With Avery in her arms, she stood up. "Thanks Luke." Looking at her mother, she asked. "How's it going?"

Callie laughed and tickled Allison's belly. The toddler erupted into laughter. "She's a wiggly one, but I got it." After standing, she picked up her granddaughter. "I'll grab the diaper bag and you get your purse."

Okay. I'll get the car started and the air conditioner going. It'll be nice to have Alma to talk to on the drive," Kim said over her shoulder as she walked to the front door.

Hunching her shoulders and pulling Avery close to her chest to shield his face from the stiff wind, Kim got him settled in the car. She was happy to see Luke had left the car running so it would be cool.

Odd for it to be so warm with all this wind. It's so muggy though. "Luke, you are such a prince," Kim called out as he secured the front door behind her mother. The heavy winds bent the wide, leafy branches of the palmetto trees planted throughout the neighborhood and sent wisps of Spanish moss floating as it screeched through the rows of houses.

Callie went back to her car after securing Allison in her car seat. Alma settled herself in the passenger seat as Kim slid in beside her. Luke stopped by the car to let Kim know the house was secure and to be sure she knew the address of the house they were renting. "Alma and I have our cell phones. I'll call when we need to stop."

Luke's brow creased in thought. "The hurricane seems to be moving faster than predicted. Hopefully we'll be well out of Charleston before we need to stop."

Kim nodded. "Oh, yeah. We should be nearly to Columbia before we have to stop. They usually fall asleep pretty quickly in the car." She gave his arm a thankful squeeze before he turned away. Turning to Alma she added, "I'm going to follow them."

"Okay, you're driving. I'm not going to tell you how to do it." Alma grinned and then seemed lost in thought. "Do you remember leaving the island ahead of a hurricane when you were little?"

Kim bit her lower lip as she thought for a moment. "Well, obviously I don't remember the hurricane in '71, but I do remember the one in '87." She shook her head. "I remember waiting for the artists to pick up their work and thinking we'd never get off the island. I've always afraid of being trapped by a washed-out road or something."

"Oh, I know. I remember one year, must have been about 1960, we thought the hurricane would miss the island. So, Nate and I stayed. Man, the water couldn't have been more than two hundred yards behind us as we crossed the bridge. At least this time everyone collected their work from the Emporium without much fuss." Alma readjusted her seatbelt and looked into the backseat at the twins. "Their eyes are fluttering like little dolls. Looks like they'll be asleep in a minute or two."

Turning back to look at Kim, she asked, "What did you say Jake was doing?"

Kim shrugged and sighed. "He's staying at the hospital until they call for it to be evacuated. Seems they offered a pretty good bonus to get nurses to stay." *I really feel he should have come with us. Not like we need the money. I truly think he just likes being the "hero".* Kim shifted her focus to change lanes. Traffic was picking up as they left Charleston.

"Hmph. Think a man would stay with his family to be sure they're all right." Alma looked out of the side window as Kim expertly passed the slower cars. "As it is, even without accidents, we won't get to Columbia until three or four this afternoon."

Kim ignored Alma's comment about Jake. She knew Alma really didn't care for him and only tolerated him for her sake. It was one of those topics they generally avoided despite their closeness. "Allison and Avery will sleep for a couple of hours. When they wake up, we can pull over for some food while I change them. I have their food in the cooler."

"Sounds good." Alma began nodding while Kim followed Luke smoothly as they passed another group of slower-moving cars.

"Alma, get some shut eye, if you want. I'm good to drive without chatting right now."

"If you're sure?" She looked to Kim's nod before reaching down to pull a small pillow out of her tote. Alma settled herself and was soon asleep.

They were about forty-five minutes from Columbia before the twins began squirming in their car seats. Already awake, Alma called Callie to arrange a stop at the next exit where there was a Cracker Barrel. Alma, Luke and Kim's grandparents went to get a table while her mother helped change the twins. "You've managed to keep just enough room for a changing area back here," her mother said as she joined Kim at the back of the SUV after getting Allison out of her car seat.

"You know me, Momma." Kim moved Avery over so her mother could lay Allison on the blanket she had put down earlier. "I really con't like public bathrooms. Besides it's easier to handle the two of them in the car than in a bathroom."

"No, it makes a lot of sense. Bathrooms are germy anyway." Allison and Avery began to play with each other, grabbing at the other twin's hands and giggling. "I've said it before, but I love these new disposable diapers. No matter what I tried on trips you would soak through your diapers about half the time."

"I know. They do work a lot better and there's not all the laundry you had to deal with." Kim looked at her mother briefly and grinned before putting Avery on her hip and going around to the side of the car. "I've got some fruit to put in the diaper bag before you close it up."

Holding Allison, her mother was waiting when Kim walked to the back of the car and put two Tupperware containers in the diaper bag. That done the two women joined the rest of their group inside.

The twins were settled in high chairs with some fruit, when Kim noticed the tightness around her mother's eyes. *Has Momma been having the hurricane dream again. I'm so glad I don't have them.* "Hey, Momma," she said before opening her menu. "Have you been getting enough rest?"

"There's just always so much to coordinate when we evacuate." Callie brushed away a few stray hairs that fell across her face and gave Kim a halfhearted smile. "At least this time, people were pretty prompt getting their work from the gallery."

"I should have come out to help more." Kim opened her menu, but kept peeking over the edge to look at her mother.

"Sweetheart, you had enough to do at home." Callie shrugged before she continued. "And then at work, arranging for people in the shelter to be evacuated and getting all those records and equipment ready to be moved to safety."

"Not to mention the fact that you helped me get ready." Alma patted Kim's hand. "You did plenty, my girl. Now figure out what you want to eat."

Over their meal, they decided where everyone would sleep when they got to Columbia. Kim's grandparents would take the master bedroom with its attached bathroom. Alma would take the second downstairs bedroom. Kim, Jake and the twins would share one of the upstairs bedrooms while her parents took the second one. *At least the house has three full bathrooms so Alma doesn't have to take the stairs for a shower.* Kim took a drink of coffee and stared across the dining room.

Luke's laughter brought Kim's attention back to the table. "What did I miss?" She asked.

"Nothing important." Luke folded his napkin and put it beside his plate. "I was just playing with the kiddos. Does anyone want more coffee?"

"Yes, I do, but I'd like it to go. Would you order for me while I go to the bathroom." As Kim stood up the other women decided to go along with her.

"Dad, looks like you and Luke have baby duty. We'll be right back," Callie said over her shoulder.

Her dad smiled and waved her on. Their waitress returned to see if anyone wanted dessert. Luke declined dessert, but ordered coffee to go for everyone.

Brenda was waiting on the porch when they pulled into the driveway. She hurried across the yard and wrapped Callie in a hug as she stepped out of the car. "It's so good to see you. Come on inside. I called Lee and he'll be over in a few minutes to help unload."

Callie stood back from her friend. "You're looking good. We can catch up some once I help Kim get the twins inside." She walked to the passenger side of her daughter's car.

"I've got the diaper bag, Momma," Kim said as she straightened up with Allison on her hip, Brenda came toward her.

"Can I hold you, Allison?" The toddler smiled and reached for her when Brenda held out her arms. She held her tightly before shifting the toddler to her shoulder. "You're just too precious. Let's go inside."

Kim grabbed the cooler with the twin's snacks and followed. By unspoken accord, they all gathered in the kitchen. "I've brewed coffee and members of my church have dropped off some food and other household items, mostly kitchen things. I know you're not destitute, but we didn't want you to have to run out to the grocery store as soon as you got here. I've left a casserole in the oven."

The tightness around Callie's eyes eased a little as she hugged her friend again. "You've really done too much. I sure appreciate it."

"Hey, I remember scurrying off the island ahead of a hurricane." Brenda turned to Kim. "There are two porta cribs in your room, thanks to the church nursery. They also lent you two highchairs."

"Thanks so much. I was afraid I'd be pushing the bed against the wall and trying to sleep with them." Kim picked up Avery and turned to leave. "Once I get the twins changed, I'll help unload the car." Smiling, she paused to look at her grandparents. "If Grandpa and Grandma will keep an eye on them, that is."

Her grandparents nodded. "I'll fix you a cup of coffee while you do that. I'll get some for you too, Lydia," her grandfather said as he stood up from the kitchen table.

When Lee arrived, the twins were in their high chairs with a snack. The younger adults began unloading the cars. Afterward, everyone regrouped around the kitchen table. They talked about changes around the island, Columbia, and their lives. Lee was the first to leave.

Everyone spent a little time settling their things in the bedrooms before having a quick dinner. Luke and her mother insisted on cleaning the kitchen so Kim could get the twins to bed. When she returned, her grandparents had turned in for the night. Her mother and Luke said good night shortly after. Alma said goodnight right behind them.

After several tries, Kim reached Jake at the hospital. He was just getting off a grueling twelve-hour shift, he told her. The ER was full of people who had injured themselves as they tried to prepare for the hurricane on top of the usual heart attacks and such. Obviously tired, he did ask how the trip went and if the twins traveled okay. Kim let him know everyone had reached Columbia safely. Jake encouraged her to rest after the exertions of helping secure the clinic and their home against the hurricane. As she said, "Good night, I love you," she realized he had already hung up the phone. Feeling a little hurt as she climbed the stairs to her bedroom, she excused his action as a product of his exhaustion.

Slipping into the bedroom she was sharing with the twins, Kim regretted not bringing the light she clipped to her book. She usually read something when she first got into bed on the nights Jake was away. It helped slow her mind down. Cocooning the covers around herself, her last thought was surprise that she was drifting off to sleep.

Things fell into a routine once setting up the household for their blended family was completed. Her mother, usually the first one up, found a nearby park for her early morning walks. Kim and Alma spend the early morning in comfortable silence with their first cup of coffee before the twins woke up. The twins' activity generally roused the rest of the household. Luke normally took on breakfast while Kim prepared lunches. Her mother, grandparents and Alma usually handled supper.

After they finished eating, Luke gathered the twins under his arms and took them into the living room while the other adults cleaned up and then sat around the table. The twins' squeals of delight filled the house. After sitting on the floor, he helped them build small block towers and laughed heartily with them as the toddlers crashed the towers. Kim thought Luke seemed thrilled with the twins antics as they crawled over and around him while the three of them sprawled on the floor. Everyone watched the news from Charleston in between taking care of the twins and doing household chores.

Occasionally, they had supper with Lee's family or at Brenda's. *I hadn't been to my grandparents' old home since they moved to Charleston. It was so weird. I knew the layout but nothing was the same. Grandma's bright yellow kitchen was gone, replaced with a farmhouse look, distressed blues and off-white with lots of silk flowers. The vegetable garden was seeded over with grass. A more modern play yard stood in the backyard where my old metal swing set used to be. I wonder if it was as odd for*

Grandma as it was for me. It was strange for the place where I had spent large portions of my childhood to look so different. Hearing Allison and Avery babbling through the monitor, Kim stopped daydreaming to get them up for lunch.

At the beginning of their second week in Columbia, Jake called to say the hospital was evacuating now. "Great, our room has a double bed and there's plenty of room here," she said. He let her know he had accepted a temporary evening shift position at the hospital in Columbia. He expected to be in town on Wednesday and would begin work on Friday.

Jake slid more or less seamlessly into the fringe of the group when he arrived just ahead of the storm's attack on Charleston. He spent most of his time at the hospital as he picked up more shifts. When he was home, he was either playing with the twins, taking them for walks in the stroller or sleeping.

Hurricane Flynn made landfall in the Cape Fear region of North Carolina shortly after Jake's arrival. Even though the winds did reach hurricane force, seventy-four miles an hour as it passed by Charleston, it was the three-foot storm surge and heavy rainfall leading to river flooding that caused the most damage. Watching the news left the household in a somber mood as they speculated on the damage to their homes.

Kim again slipped into bed after the twins were asleep. Tucking the covers around herself, she opened her book and yawned. She had found one of the small lights and clipped it onto her book. Soon she realized she had restarted the same page three times and closed the book. *How long will it be before we can go home? It's great that we have this safe place, but I'm ready to be in my own space and get back to work. Glad Jake's not drinking much. Hopefully, it will last, this time.* Kim shifted restlessly for a while before finally drifting off to sleep.

9

Callie November 1999

Callie sat on a park bench watching several Carolina wrens peck at pine cones scattered under the trees. *Glad you're in Columbia and doing well my feathered friends. I'm not there yet, but I can see why some people give up on island life. All this disruption and loss after the storms.* She sighed as she stood up, scattering the birds. *Sorry birdies, Luke and I have to check out our island houses today.* Feeling weighed down by her concerns about their homes and realizing she was hunched over, Callie straightened her shoulders and walked back to the house.

When she turned into the driveway, Luke was loading the cooler into the back of her car. He paused as he saw her approach. "Morning love," he said pulling her into his arms.

"I see you've started to load the car already." She smiled and kissed him. "Have you even eaten yet?"

"I just finished. Kim's got Allison and Avery in their high chairs. Your parents and Alma are with them in the kitchen." Luke nuzzled her shoulder. "You always smell so fresh but, I have to admit I miss the smell of salt in your hair."

She laughed, playfully slapping his chest as she stood back. "Don't you just beat all I've ever seen. I'll go grab something to eat. We're still planning to come back tonight, right?"

Luke grinned. "Well, maybe. I left a suitcase on the bed. We do have three houses to check out." He winked. "It might be too late for us to drive all the way back tonight."

Taking his hand, she laughed again as she winked back. "It might take us longer than we thought, at that. I'll throw a change of clothes in the suitcase."

Callie fidgeted in the front seat, leaning it back as she tried to sleep. Then abruptly sitting up again and running her hands through her hair before returning the seat to an upright position. Luke reached over to pat her leg. "You okay over there?"

"Yeah. No." Callie chuckled at her contradiction. "Yes, nothing's wrong, but I'm tired of sitting in the car. The sooner we see the damage; the sooner we can begin working towards getting home."

"We've only got another forty-five minutes or so to go before we get into Charleston." Luke looked at her briefly. "Are you hungry?"

"I'll grab a pack of nabs from the back." Kneeling in the seat, Callie stretched to reach the bin in the back seat and plopped down. "I don't want to stop. Do you think we should see Kim's first?"

"I guess so." Luke focused on the traffic which was getting heavier.

Mindlessly Callie munched on the crackers while staring out of the window. *The pine trees are giving way to oaks and Spanish moss is showing up. We're getting closer. At least, the winds weren't reported to be as strong as Henry in '87. Still, there've been several downed trees along this stretch of road.* Shaking her head she turned to Luke. "Sorry, honey. What was that?"

"I'm going to pull off and fill up at the next exit." Luke grinned at her briefly. "We can get something to eat then, if you want."

"You're always trying to feed me." Callie shook her head. "I'm just nervous and bored. That's why I'm eating." She folded the plastic wrapper over the remaining crackers and set them in the cup holder.

Luke shrugged. "Okay. I just know how you tend to get focused and forget to eat."

She turned in her seat to look at him. "I know honey. But I really just want to get there and figure out a plan. The place in Columbia is nice and it's good to spend time with Brenda, but I just want to be home."

Luke squeezed her shoulder briefly before moving onto the exit ramp. "I know, sweetheart. I want to be home, too."

Callie sighed and she looked out at the swollen creek running alongside the road. Mud and debris marked where it had risen beyond its banks. It still ran swiftly, carrying flotsam from upstream. She shook her head and focused on the roadside signs. "Hey, at least the gas station is close to the highway."

"From the looks of that creek, I hope they're on a hill." Luke flipped on his turn signal and after stopping made the turn. "We're in luck. They're open."

Getting out of the car to stretch her legs, Callie wandered into the store. *Not really much to see here, just a convenience store. I miss some of the Mom and Pop places we used to stop at. Each one had something unique about them. A reason for people to stop there instead of going farther down the road. Might as well go to the bathroom while we're here.* Luke was paying for their gas as she came out of the restroom. "Hey, honey. I'll go outside and wait for you."

"Do you want the keys so you can wait in the car?" He began reaching into his jeans pocket.

"No, I'll just walk around near the picnic table on the side." Yawning, she moved on towards the door.

Within a few minutes, they were back on the road. This time when Callie put her seat back, she drifted off to sleep.

"Sweetheart, we'll be coming up on Charleston pretty soon." Luke gently shook her shoulder.

"Okay." Stretching, Callie rubbed a hand over her face and raised the back of her seat. "Thanks, honey. Didn't realize how tired I was." Reaching into her bag, she pulled out a brush and ran it through her hair. "How far is it to Charleston? Man, the traffic has really picked up."

"About twenty miles." Luke paused as he watched a car darting in and out of traffic in front of them. "Yeah, it has. But it's always a mess here. Still want to check out Kim's place first?"

Frowning slightly, Callie bit her lip. "Maybe we should go to the island, first and work our way back." Smiling, she added. "We'll probably have better luck finding a place to stay once we're away from Charleston."

"I like the way you think." Luke grinned at her before giving the traffic ahead his full attention.

She stared out the window at the swollen river just barely contained in its banks as it rushed over fallen logs. *Lord, it looks like it spread at least three feet from its banks when the river crested. All that mud and debris. Don't know if I'll ever get used to all the mess hurricanes leave behind. That beautiful old oak tree uprooted. Most every house I've seen has missing shingles, siding, or both.*

As they got closer to the bridge leading to Caines Island, Callie grew restless again and she began readjusting her seat belt. "I need to make a little pad for this cross piece. If I don't have a collar on my blouse, they just aggravate me to no end."

"We could probably find one in an auto parts store." Luke shook his head and smiled.

"That would be faster. Think I'll be too busy to sew anytime soon." Haunted by memories of past hurricanes, Callie looked out of the window again.

Large trees had smashed through the roofs of several homes they passed. *At least the houses seemed to be steady on their foundations unlike in '87 when it looked like a giant had tried to knock them over.* As they crossed the bridge onto the island, Callie noticed several small plumes of smoke. People were already cleaning up and burning debris. Cracks and potholes, formed as the raging water washed out the roadbed, made driving precarious, but Luke managed to dodge the worst of them.

"You know we'll probably have to redo the Emporium's parking lot," Luke said as they got closer to the store.

"I know, but I hope we raised the store high enough during our remodel to avoid most of the water." Callie leaned forward in her seat, straining to see the Emporium through a few trees that were still standing.

Luke nodded while continuing to focus on dodging the worst of the potholes. Two barricades barred their passage when they were a block away from the Emporium. Luke pulled over to the side of the road. "Do you have enough room to get out?"

Callie cracked her door. "I've got plenty of room. Let me get my Keds on and I'll be right out. Do you have the backpack with the flashlights and water?"

Luke nodded. Hand in hand, the couple walked the few yards to the barricade and peered beyond it. The water had washed away a section of the road that was at least eight feet wide. The small gulley in between the two sections still had water running through it.

"All right, let's go see the rest of the damage." She let go of Luke's hand and inched her way sideways between the barricades.

He followed close behind, studying the banks of the shallow gulley running between the two sections of the road. Tentatively, he stepped onto the sandy bank while keeping one foot on the solid asphalt. "I think we can get across okay." Turning to look at his wife, he held out his hand. "Hold on to me until you feel steady on the sand."

Reaching for his hand, Callie stepped off the asphalt. "I'll be okay, It's not packed, but it isn't shifty either."

Carefully, they crossed the eight-foot span of sand. Luke used a wide piece of lumber left behind by the storm to fashion a temporary bridge over the water at the bottom of the gully. Once across, they made their way up the small bank, onto the next section of asphalt and continued walking toward the Emporium. As the building came into view, Callie sighed and slipped her hand into Luke's. *Doesn't look as bad as it did in '87 even though the decking is a mess.* "Let's get closer. It's pretty much what I expected."

After walking a hundred yards or so, the couple began picking their way across the potholed parking lot. Like the road, it had several gullies where the force of the water had pushed the asphalt aside. "All in all, it seems to have held up pretty well. And like we thought, the hurricane ripped up the parking lot and it will need to be replaced."

Luke let go of her hand and pushed against a post supporting the deck running along the front of the store. "This seems pretty steady, but I don't think we should be walking around up there, just yet."

Stepping back a little, Callie shielded her eyes against the sun and looked upward. "I can see a few rough spots on the roof. The stucco will need to be redone." She puffed out a breath. "It was a good move raising the level of the building." Turning toward Luke, she continued. "Not much we can do here. Let's go check out the house."

"Do you want to walk or should we try to drive up?" Luke asked as he followed her across the pocked parking lot.

Callie shrugged. "Let's walk." Looking across the landscape, Callie was happy to see grass shoots and briar bushes coming up in the tidal areas.

"Funny how quickly nature reestablishes itself isn't it?" He paused as he stretched to step over a large pothole. "It's going to take a while for them to get this road right again."

"I know. They'll probably do something temporary so people can get home." Turning onto Kiawah Trail, Callie's heart beat a little faster as their home came into view. She increased her pace.

"Okay. I know you're anxious to see the house, but slow up a little bit." Luke grabbed her arm as she nearly stepped into a deep pot hole.

"Thanks, honey."

Not speaking, they picked their way across the cratered asphalt and finally reached the driveway of their home. The surging water pushing under the concrete drive had heaved it up into small hills. Tears pooled in the corners of Calie's eyes. *Not as bad as before, but still, I hate the way the wind strips the leaves from the trees. The old magnolia seems to have survived without too much damage.* Tugging at Luke's hand and then releasing it, she began cutting across the yard. "Let's go this way. At least, I won't turn my ankle here."

Midway through the yard, Callie stopped so suddenly Luke nearly stepped on her heels. "Well, part of the shingles and siding are gone. We'll have to replace the skirting around the pylons again. But the house still seems level to me. What do you think?"

Luke stepped up beside her and put an arm around her shoulder. "It doesn't look like there's been any major shifting." He gave her a quick squeeze before reaching into his pocket for the house keys. "Come on. Let's have a look inside."

After manually opening the hurricane shutters covering the porch, Callie and Luke nodded with satisfaction. "It might be okay to turn on the breakers, but I don't want to chance it," Luke rummaged in the backpack and pulled out the flash lights.

"Right." They followed the porch around the house before stopping by the side door into the kitchen. "It looks pretty good out here. Things have started to mildew already so the porches at least need a good power washing."

Luke unlocked the door, leaving it open to let in some fresh air. Callie wrinkled her nose and sneezed. "Ah, the lovely smell of mold and mildew."

Dust motes danced in the beams of their flashlight while Luke and Callie made their way through the house. There was sand and some tunnels where condensation had run down the walls, but nothing they had seen so far reached the level of devastation from the hurricane twelve years ago.

Back in the kitchen, Luke pointed his flashlight at the floor. "Ready to check upstairs? While we're up there we can open the shutters."

"Sounds good honey. We've got a lot of work to do, but it's not as bad as I imagined." They turned to go up the stairs.

"I'll go first. Just in case." Luke grinned as Callie playfully swatted at him and missed.

"All right then. Although I don't know how I'll get you out if you fall through." Laughing, she waited until he was halfway up the stairs before following him.

"Well, that seemed steady enough. What's so funny?" Luke turned to look at Callie as she stepped into the upstairs great room.

"You, my Sir Galahad, and the memory of the inspector after the first hurricane this house and I went through. He was so alarmed because we had planned to start cleaning before we knew he had inspected the house." Callie's shoulders shook as she erupted into laughter again. *I was so naïve. Had no idea what I was getting into then.*

"I guess he had a point. At least with the wiring." Luke grinned back at her.

Callie sighed deeply looking at the sand on the floor. "Guess the wind swept it up here. Still, I haven't seen signs of high-water in the house." Nodding, Luke agreed with her.

After opening shutters in all the rooms, they made their way downstairs. "Let's go across the back way to Alma's," Callie said as she started out the kitchen door that led to the deck. She stopped suddenly "We won't be going out this way. The deck's a mess and all the raised beds are gone. Let's go out the other way."

Luke locked the side porch door behind them. "I think the azaleas and hydrangeas will come back," she said as they picked their way around fallen branches. "Not sure if the bulbs were washed away or not. Guess we'll have to wait 'til spring and see."

They found Alma's home in pretty much the same shape as theirs. Her spirits buoyed by the lack of horrific damages to the two homes, she waited on the porch as Luke locked the front door. "Let's go by Max and Louise's. Then we can look for a room and dinner."

Seeing Max, Louise and their son, Steve, on the front porch, Callie waved enthusiastically as they walked up the driveway. She noticed branches and other debris piled along the side yard and the smoking burn barrels.

"So glad I get to lay eyes on you," Callie said as she hugged Louise. Turning to hug Max she added. "How's the damage to the house this time around."

"We got off real lucky. There's some damage on the roof over the bedroom we added and some repairs in that room need to be done. The inspectors are moving more quickly this time around," Max said as everyone settled back in their seats. "We called Charles Kingston. You'll remember him from our remodel in 1986. His sons have pretty much taken over the business. They'll be out next week."

"We're just out here today doing some of the cleaning inside and getting the yard cleared." Steve turned to look at his mother. "Momma and Tina did wonders inside the house. Tina's gone into town to pick up a few things. Listen to me just rattling on. Can I get you guys something to drink?"

Louise smiled at her son and reached out to pat Callie's arm. "Guess you've been to you place and Alma's. How did you guys weather the storm?"

"No thanks, Steve. We still have to check out Kim's place in Charleston. Like you, we were lucky. Those new hurricane shutters did a good job keeping out most of the sand. Wouldn't you say, honey? Of course, we're missing some shingles and siding." Callie looked at Luke. *He looks tired.*

Luke smiled tiredly and ran a hand through his hair. Watching him, Callie was surprised by the flecks of gray at his temples. *Guess neither of us are getting any younger. Still, he's everything I need.* "They did work well. We lost a lot of the back deck and the raised beds. Alma's place looks good." Stretching in his seat, he looked at Callie sitting beside him. "We probably should get moving."

She rotated her shoulders to release the tension built up worrying about their homes. "You're right. There's still Kim's place to look at. Don't bother getting up." Callie leaned over to give Louise a hug as Max and Steve stood up anyway.

"You guys be careful on the road," Max said hugging Callie tightly. *Such old Southern politeness.*

"Oh yeah, we plan to stop overnight. Round trips to Columbia are a thing of the past." Callie grinned with a twinkle in her eye.

Steve laughed. "It'll give you two time away from everyone."

"It does at that." Luke grinned, the twinkle in his eyes matched Callie's "Then too we can make calls to inspectors while we're still in the area. We'll talk to you later."

Turning into the entrance for Kim's development, scenes similar to the devastation they had seen on the island: uprooted trees, sand where there used to be grass and, of course, the ubiquitous missing siding and shingles greeted Callie and Luke. Being further inland and on the western side of the Charleston's sprawl, the homes in the neighborhood didn't suffer as much outward damage as those on the island. They noticed trucks owned by several home inspectors parked near some of the homes. A few people were bringing debris to the curb.

While Luke parked in front of Kim's and Jake's townhouse, Callie fished around in her handbag to locate the key to the front door. A quick look around, revealed that the damage to the outside of Kim's home was minimal. Some shingles and siding were missing and the brick and wrought iron fencing in the back yard would need some repairs. *I'm glad her Little Gem magnolia and crepe myrtles weren't damaged too badly. They lost a lot of leaves, but there's enough left for them to come back. Of course, she'll have to replace all her mulch, as well as several of her smaller plants. I know this yard is a haven for Kim much like the ocean is for me.*

Returning to the car, they stopped to talk with an inspector as he left the home of Kim's neighbor. "Hey, do you have a minute?" Callie asked. "Is that your truck? The one with Kingston and Sons on the side? I think your company did an inspection for us after hurricane Henry."

The young man smiled and reached out to shake their hands. "It's possible. I'm Mike. My family's been in the business for over fifty years. We work on the islands as well as in town."

Luke nodded. "We've got four properties that need to be inspected." The young man's eyebrows shot up.

"Not all ours." Callie chuckled before continuing. "There's our place and that of a dear friend's on Caines Island and our daughter and son-in-law's home here. Oh yeah, there's the Emporium on the island."

Mike slipped his clipboard under one arm while reaching into a shirt pocket. "I remember my dad working on a remodel of the Emporium when I was a kid. Here's a couple of our cards. The office would have to schedule the inspections."

Callie nodded. "Yeah, he basically rebuilt the Emporium after the hurricane in '87."

Luke looked up after reading the business card. "We're staying in Columbia until we know the houses are safe to move back into. With enough notice we could come back to let you in."

"It'd be hard to say how things are scheduled." Mike pushed his ball cap back on his head.

"Of course. We might be able to leave keys with friends that are already back on Caines Island." Callie touched Luke's arm. "Let's call the office and then we'll decide whether to leave keys with Max and Louise or make another trip down."

"Okay." Luke smiled. "Thanks for taking time to talk with us."

"Hopefully, we can get something scheduled for you real soon. I'm always sorry about the destruction after a storm, but it would be cool to work on something my dad did. Have a good day." Mike turned to go to his truck as the couple crossed the driveway.

Luke started the car and waited for Callie to get her seatbelt fastened. "Steve told me Dante is doing limited dinner service at the Inn. What do you think about eating there tonight? Maybe he has a room or two available."

"That would be great, but I'm hardly dressed for dinner." She ran a hand through her hair.

"Let me make a call before we get started." He winked at Callie while he talked with Dante on the phone. After hanging up, he relayed the gist of the conversation. "Dante says come as we are and we do have a room for the night."

"Oh, that's wonderful." She beamed. "Have to admit I'm a little tired of the chicken and beef we've been eating lately."

"I figured." Luke patted Callie's thigh before backing out of their parking spot.

After taking a quick shower, Callie called Kim in Columbia to update her on the status of the houses and went downstairs to join Luke in the dining room. As always, dinner at the Inn was superb. Callie had her favorite, flounder with a lemon butter sauce and Luke had a steak.

While they lingered over dessert and coffee, Dante joined them briefly with a cup of coffee. "So glad you guys came in tonight."

"The food is always fantastic here. You and your staff do such a wonderful job. Are most of your people back at work?" Luke asked as he moved his dessert plate to the side.

"No, there are still quite a few people struggling to get back into their homes. But I'm trying to keep a place for them and not hire new staff right away."

Callie sipped her coffee. "Even though this storm wasn't as powerful as predicted, not everyone has the advantage of having top of the line shutters and such."

"Don't I know it. We had to do so many repairs after Henry, I had them put in hurricane straps for the roof and porches, as well as those shutters." Dante drained his coffee cup and pushed his chair away from the table. "It's good to see you two. I'm not

doing a breakfast service right now, but there'll be complementary pastries and coffee when you get up."

"Come on, sweetheart. We'll settle everything in the morning." Luke grinned at her. "I'm ready for bed."

The next morning Callie called Max. She explained about the inspector and to be sure it was okay for them to leave keys for Kim's with them. The three islanders always kept a spare keys for each other. With that settled, Luke called the inspector's office and scheduled inspections for the three homes and the store while sitting on the bed. Closing their suitcase and plopping onto the bed beside him, Callie looked lovingly at her husband. "You know. Last night's dinner and all made me miss the times when there was just the two of us."

Luke held her close. "Me too. We're just going to have to leave home every now and then."

Reluctantly Callie sat up straighter. "Come on. We should get back to Columbia."

"Aw, you're right." Luke shrugged as he stood and picked up the suitcase. "I'll take this to the car and see you in the dining room."

"All right, honey. I'll get us some coffee and a plate of pastries." Callie held the door for Luke and then followed him downstairs.

When Callie and Luke returned to Columbia, they found everyone on the back porch. After hugging her parents, Callie turned to Kim who was holding the baby monitor to her ear. "Are they still sleeping?"

"Yeah, but they'll probably wake up soon." She stood up and hugged her mother. "There's coffee on. Do you want me to get some for you?"

"That would be great. When you get back, Luke and I can fill you in on the details. I know we didn't talk long last night." She settled into one of the rocking chairs scattered around the porch after hugging Alma.

Ah, Alma asked,

"So how much longer are we going to be here?"

"We could probably go back in a week or so to begin some cleaning." Callie paused for confirmation from Luke, who nodded. "Kim, I think your carpet is going to have to come up, at least downstairs. You didn't get much water inside, but still, everything is mildewing."

"There are companies that do restoration after fires and flooding. Maybe we could try one of those." "I'd like to feel sure there isn't mold or mildew in the house especially with the twins being so young."

"Of course. The houses seemed to be structurally sound to your mom and me. Any damage to wiring would be the biggest concern. The inspectors assured me they'd be getting to our places by the end of the week." Luke stood up. "I'll be back in a minute. Just need to get some iced tea."

Callie's dad leaned forward in his chair. "Are you planning on hiring a cleaning crew?"

"I don't think so, Dad. With all the protection stuff we've done over the last few years, there's not as much damage or sand as we had a few years ago." Callie turned to look at Alma. "Luke and I were thinking of making a trip back to the island once we have

the inspection reports. Like we did years ago, we'd get enough spaces clean for everyone to come back and then start on the Emporium."

"I'd like to go with you. Kim, Jake, and the little ones could stay with me, if they want." Alma nodded toward Kim. "What do you think? It could take a while to sort out that carpet mess."

"We might do that, Alma. Let me talk it over with Jake when he gets home." Happy giggling sounds came through the monitor and Kim went upstairs.

"Momma, the only thing that bothers me is until we get the deck and ramps rebuilt, it won't be easy for you to get outside." Callie looked at her mother with concern.

"Well, if I can get out on one of the porches, that'll be fine for now. Not like I have to get out every day for work."

After supper, Alma and Callie sat on the porch enjoying the cool breeze. Callie wrinkled her nose as the acrid smell of smoke from the mills reached them. *They say they've cut down on emissions from the smoke stacks, but man, I miss the smell of the ocean. This breeze is nice but all I can smell is the smoke from the mills.* Startled, she looked at her friend. "I'm sorry. What was that?"

Grinning at having caught Callie daydreaming, Alma repeated herself. "I think maybe I should hire a cleaning crew for my place. I'll want to clean my kitchen, but it'd be tough for me to get the whole house done."

"I could..."

Alma held up her hand. "You've got enough on your plate with your parents. Besides, we'll have to get started cleaning up the Emporium."

A few days later, the women were sitting around the kitchen table. Jake was with the twins at the park. Luke was sketching on the deck and Callie's dad was sleeping.

"Alma, did your niece in New York get back to you?" Lydia asked.

Shaking her head, Alma lifted a shoulder. "No, didn't really expect it, but felt I needed to let them know I was okay." Her mouth turned downward and her jet black eyes glistened. "I used to play with all of them when they were kids. Made little baskets with them. Funny how things worked out after Carol died."

"I can't imagine having family and not talking with them. I know they live in New York and are busy. I think I'd at least call." Kim sighed before drinking her coffee.

Alma patted Kim's arm. "Don't get worked up on my account. You know, I've tried to get them to come down and visit, but there's always something in the way. Their work. Kids activities. But maybe I pushed all the Kiawah traditions on them too much when they were younger."

"Maybe it's just that you guys have lost the threads of your everyday lives so it's harder to know what to say." Kim frowned as she imagined losing contact with her Uncle Bobby's family. "But every family has that one person that's the glue. The one person everyone wants to see. Without the glue they don't relate so well with everyone else." Kim gave a halfhearted smile. "At least that's what Crystal, from work, said happened in her family after her dad died."

Lydia squeezed Alma's shoulder. "At least with Sally's children, I can say we have nothing in common. Although they do touch base from time to time."

"It does make my heart heavy. Knowing people are related to me and don't care to keep in touch." Alma released an uncharacteristic sigh. "Hey, but I'm fortunate, Lydia. Your daughter has always welcomed me into her family like a beloved aunt. And you guys accepted me as well. I try not to dwell on the things I can't change."

Callie nodded and smiled at her friend. "You've always treated me like family from the first time we met." *I'll be sure to ask her nieces and nephews to come to the October celebration next year.*

A clatter on the front porch heralded the return of Jake and the twins. "Go find Mommy, Allison," Jake said as he sat the toddler inside the door. The somber group broke up and began making lunch.

As work began in their homes, the Emporium's partners hired Kingston and Sons to complete the necessary repairs. It took two weeks and a few more trips to the island than they had anticipated for their return to be complete. Kim, Jake and the twins stayed with Alma until their home was ready. By that time, the shelter, and the clinic where Kim worked were open again

Callie October 2000

Callie slowly made her way across the road and began walking along the path toward the dunes. Stately, blue gray herons, feeding in the tidal pools, looked up nonchalantly as she passed by. The herons had apparently cataloged her as harmless during her many walks over the years. Smiling and nodding to them, she continued on her way. Sea oats swayed lazily in the light breeze.

With the gentle, white crested waves in sight, Callie paused to breathe in deeply and let out a slow breath. *That salty ocean smell is so relaxing and invigorating. Don't think I'll ever get tired of it.* As the sand grew firmer, she picked up her pace a little and then slowed again as a flock of sandpipers landed at the water's foamy edge. Smiling, she moved a little further away from the ocean to avoid scattering the birds.

Letting her mind wander without coherent thought, she continued. As always, she marveled at the way the water swelled and turned into small waves as it approached the shore. Seagulls squawking overhead brought her back to today and the laundry list of things she needed to accomplish before the October neighborhood party. Grinning at the antics of the birds, she made her way home.

Leaving her shoes in the garage, she slipped on the Keds she left outside before her walk and went into the hall. "Hi, honey. I'm back home." Callie called as she approached the kitchen.

"Hey, sweetheart," Luke answered. "Alma and I are tasting the banana bread you made yesterday."

She paused by Luke's chair. "Hey, Alma. How are you today?"

"Doing pretty good." Alma smiled and raised an eyebrow. "Have you heard from Francine and William yet?"

"Yes." Callie gave Luke a hug before going to the coffee pot. "Let me get some coffee and I'll tell you about it. Does anyone need a refill."

Alma and Luke shook their heads. As Callie settled at the kitchen island, Luke stood up. "I'll see you about lunchtime, honey. Catch you later, Alma." Kissing Callie lightly on the cheek, Luke went to his studio.

"So, what did they say?" Alma's lips thinned as she tapped her friend on the arm. "Bet they aren't coming."

Callie scowled. "Come on now." She waved a hand at her friend. "Have a little faith." Alma's lips turned downward. Callie leaned over and put an arm around her shoulders. "I'm sorry for teasing a bit. Francine and her family are coming. William can't come because of a work trip, but is thinking about making a trip closer to Thanksgiving."

Alma's mouth and eyes formed small circles. "How did you manage that?"

"I told them a little of the conversation we had last November and mentioned that none of us were getting any younger."

Alma swatted her friend's arm, a little harder than last time. "I'm not some decrepit old woman."

Callie laughed as she rubbed her arm. "Careful, that almost hurt. I never said you were decrepit or anything like that. Just that time gets away from all of us. Francine agreed. William said much the same thing. He seemed disappointed to miss this."

A slow smile spread across Alma's face. "Did she say where she wanted to stay?"

"No, she did say she would call you in the next day or so." She looked at Alma from the corner of her eye. "To see if it'd be okay if they stayed with you."

Alma's eyes shone as she looked heavenward. "Oh, Lord, thank you. How I've prayed for this." She turned and hugged her friend tightly.

"She seemed to want to spend some time before or after the cookout. I expect she'll either come in early or stay later." She turned around in her seat and took a drink of coffee.

"That'd be wonderful." Alma stood, smoothing the front of her pants with her hands. "I'd better get home now. Thank you so much."

Callie ducked her head. "Hey, we look out for each other. She knows you don't always have your cell phone on, so she'll leave a message on your answering machine if you're out."

Francine, along with her husband Henry, and their two children, Lisa and Andrew, flew into Charleston around noon on Friday and rented a car to drive out to the island. Alma greeted them from the front porch and helped everyone get settled in their rooms. Coming out of the bedroom, her niece asked. "What do we need to do today?"

Alma led her towards the kitchen. "I've got to bake a couple of pies later. Other than that, I usually help Callie set up the tables in the yard. Would you like something to drink? I've got iced tea and some sodas."

"No, thanks Aunt Alma. When the kids come out why don't we go over and help Callie since that's what you'd usually do?" Francine put her hands on her hips and twisted her waist a few times. "After sitting on that plane, I really need to move around."

Henry joined the women in the kitchen. "So what's the plan for today? Is there going to be a lot of cooking?"

Alma filled him in on the need to set up tables at Callie's and that a lot of people were bringing food. "Can I get you something to drink before we go, Henry?

"No thank you. The kids and I'll come over and help. Then maybe we'll walk down to the beach."

The group went outside and Lisa looked toward the chicken coop. Her eyes widened. "Aunt Alma, you have chickens?"

"Yes, sweetie. I've always had chickens." Alma grinned at her niece's incredulous expression. "There's nothing like fresh eggs. They taste so much better than store bought."

"Wow." Lisa looked at the remains of Callie's vegetable garden where a few cabbages and carrots were growing. "And they have a garden? Do you guys even have to go to a grocery store?"

Alma could tell the young girl was serious. "Of course we do. But it is nice to eat the things you grow."

With the extra hands, it didn't take long to set up the tables. Henry and the kids headed for the beach while Alma, Callie, Kim and Francine took a break on the shaded portion of the deck.

"Let me get you something to drink," Callie said. She remained standing as the others settled into chairs. "I've got iced tea, sodas and lemonade."

I'll help you, Momma." Kim got up and followed her mother into the kitchen. Within a few minutes, they returned with pitchers of iced tea and lemonade along with several glasses and a dish of cheese straws Louise brought over earlier.

After everyone was served, Callie settled into a chair next to Francine. "I'm sorry to put you to work after your flight."

Francine shook her head. "Think nothing of it. I don't sit well and am usually doing something." She took a sip of her lemonade. "We sure don't get this at home."

"I don't think anyone can make lemonade like Aunt Alma," Kim said. "Just the right balance of sweet and sour."

Francine looked at Alma. "You guys do this every year?"

"Unless there's a hurricane coming through." Alma nodded and sipped her iced tea.

Callie looked at Alma and smiled. "We started back in 1971 using sheets of plywood on saw horses for tables. We were so thankful to have been able to repair our homes and keep the business going after the hurricane. So we held a community celebration. I'd never have gotten through those first years without help from your aunt, Max, and Louise."

The women reminisced about the old days. Callie told the story about Carol coming down for the Emporium's grand opening and giving her a dish of fudge.

Francine interrupted. "Do either of you know how to make my momma's fudge?" She tilted her head. "I have the recipe but, I can't seem to get it right."

Alma chuckled. "Callie does it best."

"Why don't we get together Sunday afternoon. We can make some together," Callie offered.

Alma slowly stood up. "We should probably get back to the house. I've got those pies to make for tomorrow."

"Now pies I can bake." Francine smiled as she stood up next to her aunt. "I still use the same pie crust recipe I learned from you and my momma." Turning to Callie, she added. "I'm really glad to be here. See you later."

Callie stood and hugged Francine. "Stop by anytime. No invitation needed."

The next day, as dusk settled over the island, Callie sat on the deck watching her friends scattered in small groups across the yard. A smile played across her lips as the Carolina wrens warbled their evening song. *I'm so glad Francine and her family seem to be enjoying themselves. I wasn't sure what to expect since they didn't grow up on the island. Alma's definitely happy to see at least part of her family here. I'll just take a few more minutes before I start putting food away.* Footsteps on the ramp alerted her to someone's approach.

Alma's head appeared above the ramp's railing. "I wondered where you got to. Good you're taking a break. Think I'll join you for a minute. Folks'll start heading home soon." Alma sat in the chair next to Callie.

"I was thinking the same thing." Callie looked at her friend for a moment. "How did it go with Francine this afternoon?"

"We're getting reacquainted." Alma lifted her shoulders. "Seems she's been divided about how she feels about being down South."

Callie frowned slightly. "Well, go on."

"It's just when you're brown or black some people make assumptions about you, especially in the South. Said she'd get so anxious she'd nearly make herself sick. So she kept trying to put it out of her mind once Carol died. But there were things about the South that she missed."

"She's not wrong there. This part of the country has a terrible history to overcome."

Alma sighed. "That's for sure. Still, we need to keep trying to understand each other. I don't mean ignoring what is wrong."

"I hear you. If we keep talking to each other, we'll learn we all want the same things." Callie puffed out a breath.

"Oh, you're preaching to the choir. Anyway, she really wants to make fudge tomorrow." Alma smiled in the twilight.

"Okay. You know me. I'll be up early. When should I come over?" Callie squeezed her friend's arm affectionately.

"When we get changed after church. I'll call or send one of the kids over. You got a full house tonight?"

"Yeah, but that won't stop me from making fudge. Call me when you're ready." Looking back across the yard, Callie stood up. "Looks like people are starting to gather their things. I'd better go help."

Alma stood up beside her. "Come on. Let's get started on the clean-up." The two women laughed together as they crossed the yard to begin organizing putting things away.

Sunday, Callie joined her friends in Alma's kitchen. All the ingredients for fudge were set out on the counter along with a candy thermometer.

After pouring a cup of coffee, she sat down at the table. "Hope everyone had a good night."

"Slept like a baby. But I don't remember Momma using a candy thermometer," Francine said as she picked up the recipe card and recognized her mother's handwriting. "But I see you added the temperature, 234 degrees."

Grinning broadly, Alma said, "You're right, she didn't. The old recipe didn't call for one either. Callie and I figured it out because all that 'soft ball', 'hard ball' stuff was so hard to judge."

"Your mother tried to teach me, but I never really got it until we started using the thermometer. Should have seen some of the messes I made." Callie laughed thinking about some of the gooey confections she had called fudge.

In short order, they made a batch of fudge. Lisa went on to make a second batch while the adults sat around the kitchen table reminiscing. "Aunt Alma, didn't I hear that you wrote a book about traditional Kiawah basket weaving patterns?" Lisa asked as she began washing the few items dirtied by their fudge making.

"Yes, ma'am. Selling my baskets years ago really made a difference in my finances," Alma answered with a smile. "I'm sure I've got a couple of copies around here. I'll get one for you and one for your momma."

"Maybe you can show me a little bit of basket weaving before we go back to New York?" Lisa smiled at her aunt. "The ones you have in the bedroom are beautiful."

"Be glad to," Alma told her grandniece.

Callie stood up and took her cup to the sink. "I'll head back home. See you guys later."

Kim October 2000

Kim stood on the far side of her office, admiring her diploma from the psychiatric-mental health nurse practitioner program at Charleston University. *It was tough with the children, but I did it.* She paused on her way to her desk when she heard a knock on the door.

"Come in."

Crystal stuck her head. "When you didn't stop by the office, I wasn't sure you were working today. Thought maybe you and Jake were doing a little spontaneous celebrating."

Kim rolled her eyes as she sat behind her desk and Crystal sat in one of the chairs facing her. "Fat chance. You know how he is about me making more money than he does or having more degrees. He came to the ceremony. We went out to eat with my mom and Luke. I just wanted to add the new diploma before I started seeing patients today."

"What's his problem? Is he upset because he didn't get to go back to school?" Crystal threw her hands up. "Sorry, I just don't get it."

Kim shrugged. "You're okay. We've talked about him going back to school, but he isn't interested. "Anyway, it's water under the bridge. I'm just glad to be finished."

"I bet you are. I'll grab your patient list and charts in a minute." Crystal leaned forward conspiratorially. "Don't be surprised by anything coming down the pike, all the docs were in a meeting yesterday and they were still there when I left. I'm telling you something big's up."

"I heard something about a meeting. I can still get my own charts." A knock on the door interrupted their conversation. "Come in."

Crystal stood up as Dr. Abrams entered the office and sat in a chair facing Kim. "I'll leave your charts by the door. Let me know if you want something from Tony's for lunch."

"Thanks, Crystal." When the office door closed, Kim looked back to Dr. Abrams. "So, how are you? And what's happening to bring you here so early this morning?"

Dr. Abrams' broad smile showed his bright, white teeth which were usually somewhat hidden by his full beard. "Just wanted to offer my congratulations." He paused and looked down at his well-manicured nails. "And to let you know a couple of things before they're announced at the staff meeting on Wednesday."

"Thank you. I heard you were in a meeting until late last night." Kim leaned forward. *He's not usually so hesitant. What's going on around here?*

"You know, I've wanted to retire for some time, but none of the psychiatrists interviewed have accepted the position." He loosened one of the buttons on his blazer before resting his hands lightly on his knees. "We did agree you could take over my patients."

Kim leaned back in her chair in disbelief. "That's going to be one hell of a patient load."

"It took a while to get them to agree, but they'll take over your strictly medical patients until they can hire another nurse practitioner. In fact, they'll start shifting your patients to their care this week." He shrugged. "Even after I retire, I'll still be your supervising physician, if you want to continue our agreement."

"Of course, I do. We've always worked well together." *That's still a pretty heavy patient load.* She shook her head slowly. "Have you set a retirement date?

"I'll be here until the first of the year." He flashed a brief smile. "They've agreed to a significant pay raise for you, above whatever you got at your last review."

"Well, that's nice, but it's going to take me a while to get up to speed on your patients."

"I haven't taken a new patient in a couple of months, so you know most of them since you've covered for me several times already. I'll be here if you need me for a few months, but I don't think you will." He flicked his wrist and looked at his watch. "I'd better get going before I'm late for my first patient." They both stood and walked to her office door.

Kim pulled the chart rack into her office as Dr. Abrams continued down the hall.

Tossing her tote over her shoulder, Kim grabbed her dictated notes from the printer and hurried to the mail room where she put her notes in Crystal's box. *Whatever is in my box will have to wait until Monday.*

Her phone rang as she buckled her seatbelt. "Hello? Oh hi, Jake." She listened a minute. "No, I'm still in the parking lot at work." She stopped talking as he rushed on. Exasperated, she tugged at a handful of curls. "You were supposed to pick up the kids. Oh, never mind. I'll get them. Bye."

She hung up abruptly without waiting to hear what new crisis had befallen one of Jake's coworkers in the ER. *Well, that's that. He's pulling another double. Guess we won't be celebrating my raise.* Tossing her phone onto the seat beside her, Kim took a few deep breaths as she made her way through the parking lot and eased her SUV into Charleston's late afternoon traffic.

By the time she reached the center, where Allison and Avery went when Julia was on vacation, Kim managed to get over her frustration with Jake. Seeing the twins' grins as she stood in the doorway of their classroom made her forget all the hassles at work and their father's distancing behaviors of late. She squatted so she could give them a hug.

"Mommy," they cried as they reached out to hug her tightly.

"Easy there. You're both so strong you'll knock me over." With a final squeeze, Kim stood and led them to the hooks where their book bags hung near the door. "I'll sign you out while you get your bags."

At the car, both children climbed into their seats. Once she had them buckled in, Kim got in the front seat and looked over her shoulder at the still smiling toddlers. "Okay, what should we eat for dinner tonight?"

"Pizza, pizza." Avery clapped his hands.

"Yeah, the pizza lady." Allison chimed in.

Kim smiled into the extra mirror pointed at the backseat. "How about this? When we get home, we can order pizza and make a salad."

Both children nodded and began playing with toys they kept in the car.

Shortly afterwards Kim pulled into the garage and got out of the car. "Okay we're home again." When she opened the car door, Allison's head was bobbing as she fought to stay awake. "Hey, sleepyhead." Kim kissed the top of her daughter's head. "If you go to sleep now, you'll miss the pizza lady." Allison reached out to be picked up. Settling Allison on her hip, Kim went to the other side of the car and began unbuckling Avery's car seat. "Can you climb out, sweetie?"

"I'm big. I can do it." Avery slid out of his car seat, but hesitated as he perched on the car's runner.

"Hold Momma's hand and take a big jump." Kim held his hand tightly as Avery jumped out of the car.

"I did it." The little boy ran to the garage door leading inside and began jiggling the doorknob.

"I'm coming." By the time Kim led Avery into the playroom, Allison began sliding down Kim's leg. "Okay, missy. Play with your brother while I order pizza and make a salad."

Kim April 2001

Kim sat outside on the patio. Lost in her thoughts, she didn't notice the cluster of fireflies blinking on and off as they winged their way across the yard. Kim had put Avery and Allison down for the night after another supper where Jake came breezing in at the last minute. He had played with the twins for a while, before grabbing a shower and heading for the game room. *I don't really understand how he could do this. He's acting like nothing unusual happened today. Didn't he realize the bank would call me?* Kim closed her eyes, squeezing them tightly against her tears. After the bank called, she had locked her office door and cried silent, angry tears. Then she called a lawyer. *Well, there's no getting around this. I've got to settle this tonight.* Bracing herself with several deep breaths, she went inside.

Leaning against the door of the game room, Kim looked in disbelief at the man she married. *I don't understand him at all anymore. Maybe I never did. Maybe I only fooled myself.* With a small shake of her head, she said, "Hey, Jake I got a call from the bank today. I think we need to talk about it."

His eyes never left the television screen. "Sure, just a minute. I've almost beat this level."

Kim stepped in front of him blocking the screen. "No, this can't wait."

"Damnit, Kim. What's the problem?" He tossed the controller onto the table in front of the small couch. "It's been a rough day."

Kim perched on the edge of the coffee table. "I'd say so. What's with taking all the money from our joint account?"

Jake puffed up. His eyes widened. "Well—"

Kim rushed on; fearful her anger would take over. "I know you tried to access my account. The bank called me. What's going on? You're drinking again."

He seemed to visibly shrink before her eyes, resting his elbows on his knees. "I know. I know. I promised to stop, but it's hard." Jake held his head in his hands.

"I'm sure it is." Kim clenched her fists as she fought to keep her voice level. *I don't want to wake up Allison and Avery.* "But that doesn't necessitate emptying our joint account." Not wanting to give him any edge, she waited silently.

"I've gotten into trouble gambling." He dropped his hands, but avoided Kim's eyes.

"What happened to the friendly games with the people from work? Gambling is illegal in this state." Kim stood up and shook her head in exasperation. She paced for a few minutes before plopping in a chair across from Jake.

"Well." He grinned, but his face fell as he looked up to Kim's stony expression. "It got too easy to win with them. It wasn't exciting. One of the docs brought me into a bigger game."

"We don't have the income to sustain that kind of thing, even if it were legal. What were you thinking? Are people going to come pounding on our door for money? What if the Board of Nursing finds out?" Kim searched his face, trying to find the man she married.

"No, it's not like that. But I was winning for quite a while." He grinned then shrugged. "I hit a streak of bad luck."

Kim blinked back tears. "We can't go on like this. You didn't tell me anything. Just tried to forge my signature."

"Kimmie baby—"

"No, not this time. Are you scheduled to work tomorrow?" He shook his head. She stood up and walked to the door of the game room.

"Babe." Jake turned to look at her.

"I'm going to bed. You can sleep downstairs. We'll talk more in the morning."

Once upstairs, Kim showered and then called her mother, asking if she and the twins could stay with them a few days. Not wanting to go into everything on the phone, she didn't give any details. *I need to have a plan first.* Unable to sleep, she made a few notes before exhaustion finally overtook her.

Up before the twins, Kim made her way downstairs and started coffee. She went to the window, staring out at her sun caressed neighborhood. *Hmph. How can everything look so peaceful while my life is falling apart?*

As she was pouring her first cup of coffee, Jake made his way into the kitchen carrying several empty beer cans with him. After dropping them into the trash, he asked. "So, what do you want to do?"

Kim bit her lip. "The twins and I are going to Momma's and Luke's for a while."

"Babe, we can work this out." Jake stood beside her at the counter and reached for her.

She walked away and sat down at the kitchen island. "I'll never be able to trust you again and I won't spend the rest of my life wondering if you're telling me the truth about anything." She took a deep breath before continuing. "While I'm on the island, you figure out what you're going to do. Get in a treatment program. Find a place to live."

"And what about Allison and Avery? Are you going to try and keep me away from them? I won't have that." Jake crossed his arms over his chest.

"No. When you're sober, you're a good dad. The kids need for somethings to stay the same. That's why I'm keeping the townhouse." The unspoken truth that he couldn't make the mortgage payment on his own hung in the air between them. "I think until you've addressed your gambling and drinking issues, you should only see the kids at your parents."

Jake's expression changed rapidly from outrage to one of calculation as he leaned against the counter. "I think it's only fair that you pay me alimony."

Kim nearly laughed out loud. "You're kidding, right? And even if you're not, you drained the joint account. I closed it yesterday by the way. I'll help you get into an apartment and you can take the game room furniture, but I will not pay alimony."

He left the counter, leaned over the island, and stared directly into Kim's eyes. Sunlight streaming in from the window glinted off the sweat beading on his forehead. "That's not right. After all the years we've been together."

"Consider my not pressing charges for forgery as any alimony you feel entitled to." Kim stood up. "I hear the twins. Once they're dressed and have breakfast. I'll finish packing our suitcases and then we'll leave."

Jake played with Allison and Avery while Kim packed and loaded the car. He hugged each child tightly and helped buckle them into their car seats. He shook his head as Kim backed out of the garage and closed the garage door leaving Jake inside.

13

Callie April 2001

Callie walked down to the shore, hoping she could settle her thoughts. Herons called out as she startled them from among the cattails growing in the tidal pools. The early sun warmed her back as the breeze tugged at her hair and swept it across her face. *Always forgetting my hat.* The ubiquitous sandpipers danced along the foamy water's edge searching for another morsel. Seagulls soared on wind currents, squawking as they too sought a morning meal.

Callie's thoughts turned to her telephone conversation with her daughter the night before. *Kim asked if she and the children could spend a few days with us. She sounded upset, but didn't want to get into it on the phone. It has to be something about Jake. We've seen less and less of him lately. He's always working or at a friend's when we visit.*

With the Emporium out of sight, Callie sat on the warm sand and watched the ocean's white foam-crested waves roll in toward the shore. *Just breathe, nice deep cleansing breaths. There's no sense trying to figure out how to help Kim before she tells you what's going on. Just focus on enjoying the time with the twins. I know Momma and Dad will be happy to see them. Maybe it will give Momma the boost she needs. Sometimes she just seems to be slipping away since she had that second stroke.*

Callie shook her head as if to shake away the thoughts that kept whirling through her mind. *All right, this isn't getting anywhere. Might as well go back home and get ready for the day. Momma and Dad are up by now and Kim will be here around one. Maybe I'll make some pimento cheese. It's one of Kim's favorites.*

Callie slipped off her shoes in the garage and put on the flipflops she kept by the door to help keep down on the sand tracked into the house. She could hear her parents and Luke in the kitchen as she walked up the hall. Smiling, she joined them. "How's everyone this morning? Hope you all slept well."

Lydia, Callie's mother, reached out for a hug. "Not too bad last night. Was up only once." She stopped to give her mother a hug before getting some coffee and dropping a bagel in the toaster.

"Hey, Callie. Your dad and I were talking about getting tickets for opening day at Turner Field. Will you be able to go with us?" Luke asked as he stood up from the kitchen island.

"I'm sure I can. Go ahead and get the tickets. Maybe later in the season we can go again when the Mets are in town." Callie spread a thick layer of cream cheese on her bagel.

"Sounds good to me." Luke crossed the kitchen and hugged Callie. "I'm heading to the studio. When are Kim and the kids coming?"

"Sometime around one." Callie leaned into his embrace.

"Call me when she gets here. I'd like to see the twins."

"Thanks, honey." Callie sat up. "I'll eat this and go to the Emporium for a few hours. Max is there and Alma's coming in later so I shouldn't be long."

Luke left and Callie joined her parents at the island. "So what are you two up to today?"

"Think I'll go to Columbia once we're through here. The house is empty again since the last renters didn't renew their lease. It's been cleaned, so if I can take some bed linens, I'll probably stay a few days." Her dad looked at his wife.

"Sure, Dad. Take whatever you need. Do you want to take some groceries, so you don't have to shop while you're there?" Callie looked at her parents. She knew they had been talking about the trip to Columbia, but didn't know any details.

"I don't think so. I want to talk with the real estate agent since we're thinking about selling. I just don't know if we should begin selling off the furniture that's there or what," Callie's dad put an arm around her mother's shoulders.

"You and your brother already have all the good stuff from the house," her mother added. "I'm in favor of letting the stuff go with the house or selling it if the buyer doesn't want it. Amy's working a couple of extra days while your dad's away. Amy and I are going over to Alma's once he leaves."

Callie was loading the dishwasher after making pimento cheese spread when she heard a car in the driveway. She went into the garage to see Kim unloading the twins. Luke had seen them from the studio and was helping her with their bags. "Hey, sweetie, can I help with any-thing?" Callie asked as she reached the car.

"Thanks, Momma. Could you just get Allison and Avery inside? They might need help with the steps into the house," Kim said with a tight smile which didn't quite reach her eyes. "Luke's helping me with the bags."

Each of the children latched onto a finger as Callie held out her hands and led them up the steps. Once inside they dropped to their hands and knees to climb the longer set of stairs to the upstairs den where they knew they would find their toys.

With a diaper bag on her shoulder, Kim entered the kitchen. "Come here. Let me hug you." Callie opened her arms wide and held her daugh-ter close. "Allison and Avery are already upstairs. I've childproofed everything so they should be all right. Can I get you something to drink? Are you hungry?"

"Maybe some tea after I..."

"I'll get your bags upstairs and hang out with the littles for a while, so you two can talk." Luke picked up their suitcases.

Callie poured two glasses of iced tea and handed one to Kim. "Your Grandma is at Alma's with Amy and Grandpa is on the way to Colum-bia. Come on into the living room. We'll be more comfortable in there." She patted the couch. "Sit down, honey. I see you're upset. What can I do?"

Kim plopped down by her mother. After staring into her tea glass for a few minutes, she let out a deep sigh. "There's no easy way to say this. Jake and I are getting a divorce."

"What? Why?" Callie's mouth hung open in surprise for a moment before she collected herself and closed it.

"You know he's struggled with a drinking problem for quite a while now. I thought he was making progress with that, but there was so much I didn't realize or was too stupid to see."

Callie pulled her daughter close and wrapped her arms around her as tears ran down Kim's cheeks. "There, there, baby. There's not a stupid bone in your body. Sometimes it's hard to see the flaws in someone you love. Take your time. Cry it out."

After a few minutes, Kim moved away from her mother and fumbled in her pocket for a tissue. Wiping her eyes, she continued, "I knew he liked a poker game now and again, but apparently, he got into some high stakes games. He says he won for a while. But then he lost a lot and when he couldn't cover it from his account, Jake drained our joint account and then tried to get into my account after forging my signature." Kim put her head in her hands as she stared at the floor.

"That's awful, baby." Callie rubbed small circles between Kim's shoulder blades.

"The bank called me at work because the signature looked off and because Jake wasn't authorized to make withdrawals from my account."

"What was he thinking? He had to know you would realize the money was gone," Callie's voice rose a little as she became angry about Jake's treatment of her daughter.

"Obviously, he didn't think. He told me gambling was like an addiction with him. That he was always looking for that rush when he won. This is too much. I don't believe I can ever trust him again." Kim got up and began to pace the room. "Anyway, I'd like to stay with you for a few days while he and I sort some things out. I'm not giving him the townhouse. The twins need to have some kind of consistency. At least we agree on that. He's supposed to be figuring out where he's going to stay while we're here."

"How's he going to do that? Won't he lose his job at the hospital?" Callie shifted on the couch so she could see Kim as she paced.

"Well, since he hasn't gotten into legal trouble with anyone else, he should be safe there. I can't do anything about him emptying the joint account and I'm not pressing charges over the forgery. It's not like he actually got into the account."

Kim held up her hands to forestall her mother's comments as Callie sputtered. "But...but that was illegal."

"Yeah, but I don't want the hassle. We'll work out an agreement. If he gets himself together, he can have the kids for overnight visits." Kim stopped pacing to look at her mother. "Until then he can see them for supervised visits at his parent's."

Callie took a deep breath and let it out slowly. "Okay, you've got a plan. What do you want us to do?"

Kim plopped beside Callie on the couch again. "Just let us stay here a while. I'm pretty sure Julia will come out here to watch the twins while I'm at work. I'll offer her gas money since it's out of the way. Is that okay?"

"Of course. Luke and I talked after your phone call last night. Stay as long as you need to. There's plenty of room." Callie put an arm around her daughter's shoulder and gave her a tight squeeze.

"I know I'm doing the right thing, but I feel so sad." Kim rested her head on her mother's shoulder.

Callie stroked her daughter's curls. "Of course you do. You married with the intention of being together forever. It's a loss, ending the relationship and probably losing some innocence." Kim nodded and sat up.

Callie gave her daughter's arm one last squeeze. "Come on. Let's get some lunch."

"Do you have any pimento cheese? As corny as it sounds, your homemade pimento cheese is one of my favorite childhood foods." Kim smiled and although her eyes were red, Callie was happy to see that the smile reached her eyes this time.

"As a matter of fact, I do."

Eating breakfast a few days later, her grandpa told her, "I'm sorry about the way things went between you and Jake, but I have to admit I'm glad you're with us for a little while. It seems to have given your Grandma a new lease on life."

"I'm glad something good is coming from this mess I've made of our lives." Kim shook her head. "I just hope I can manage everything as well as Momma did after Dad died."

"Remember you have family and friends to help you. Make up your own mind and then tell us what we can do to help." Her grandfather squeezed her shoulder. "Your mother is an amazing woman, but she'll tell you herself she had help along the way."

"Aw, thanks, Grandpa." Kim hugged her grandfather. "I'd better get upstairs and check on the kids before I head into work. Julia will be here soon, but I like to have them dressed before she arrives." Kim began stacking breakfast dishes to load into the dishwasher.

"You go on upstairs." Bob laughed as he stood up and gathered dishes from the island. "Now that I'm retired, I've gotten pretty handy loading the dishwasher."

"Okay Grandpa, thanks." Kim hugged him again.

Max and Callie sat in the Emporium's office having a quick lunch before Max went home for the day. "When's the next time Alma's in the store?" Max asked. H

"I can't really read that calendar from here."

Callie swiveled her chair to get a better view of the calendar. "She'll be in tomorrow. Why? What's up?" She asked, turning back to look at Max.

"Remember she finally approved the proof copy of her book. We need to do something when it comes out," Max said with a grin.

"Oh, man. Why didn't I think of that." Callie shrugged. "I love having everyone with me. But four generations in one house. I don't know whether I'm coming or going." Callie laughed and shook her head.

"You do seem to find a way to keep things interesting." Max chuckled. "But it's got to be tiring."

"Everybody does their share. It's not that. Still going from two to seven people takes some adjustments." Callie laughed again. "I wouldn't have it any other way. I always wanted my home to be a place of respite for family and friends."

"How's Kim holding up?" Max began clearing the remains of his lunch and preparing to leave.

"She's doing okay. I think it'll take some time for her to trust her instincts again, but that's normal. It's got to be awful for someone you love to betray you like that." Callie shook her head to clear her mind. "Anyway, I think they'll be going back to the townhouse pretty soon. She's having the locks changed next week."

Max stood up and smiled, "You and Luke should come to supper one evening, maybe Thursday. Give yourselves a break. I'll talk to Louise and let you know. Maybe Alma will come, too. Be like old times."

"That does sound good. I don't think I can wait until summer to have a big get together," Callie said as Max left the office.

Callie took her coffee to the front porch. Settling into her rocking chair, she took a deep breath savoring the heavy perfume emanating from the magnolia trees spread throughout the yard. A Carolina wren perched on the banister, warbling his "good morning" for all to hear. Herons took wing with mighty whooshes. Seagulls squawked as they headed seaward. *The house is so quiet today and there's no little one in my lap. Allison especially liked to sit on the porch with me. Avery did too, but he got restless pretty quick. I hope Jake doesn't make things difficult for Kim and gets his act together for the kids' sake. Only time will tell.*

Momma and Dad got an offer on the house in Columbia already. Apparently, Brenda's son, Lee, has decided to buy it. He still works at the same mill Dad did. How cool is that? There's something in the back of my mind. I feel like I've forgotten something. Picking up her coffee cup, Callie realized it was empty. *Well, I wanted to check my planner anyway. Might as well go inside now.*

Luke was the only one in the kitchen as Callie refilled her coffee. "Morning, love." She stopped by his stool at the island to give him a hug. "What are you up to today?"

"Working on a painting is about all." His arm slid around her waist to pull her closer for another hug and kiss. "Are you scheduled to go into the Emporium? I kinda lost track while Kim and the twins were here."

"Yeah, at twelve. Think I'll see Alma before I go though." Callie sat beside Luke. "She's been so busy with the proof for her book, I haven't seen much of her the last while." Callie began thumbing through her calendar and frowned slightly.

"What's up?" Luke looked over at her planner. "You forget something?"

"No, at least I don't think so. There's just something in the back of my mind and I don't know what it is." Callie closed the planner and pushed it away.

"Honey, just relax and stop thinking about it. Whatever it is will come to mind soon." Luke rubbed her back gently.

"I guess you're right." Callie sighed. "Hey, have you seen Momma and Dad this morning?"

"Come to think of it. No, I haven't. They both seemed a little more tired at dinner last night," Luke stood up from his seat and stretched. "I need to get started or I won't get anything done today."

Callie reached up for another hug. "All right, I'll get ready and see Alma before I go to the Emporium. See you after work."

As she crossed the yard, Callie paused a moment to look at the flower beds full of tulips and daffodils. She always enjoyed the brilliant yellows, vivid oranges, and deep reds of their blossoms. Callie gathered a bouquet for Alma and continued her walk across the yard. The roosters crowed and began posturing aggressively as she passed their coup. *Silly birds. I won't hurt your ladies.*

"Hey, Alma. It's Callie," she called as she opened the kitchen door.

"I'm in here," Alma answered. "Come on in. Do you want more coffee? I can put some on. Won't take but a couple of minutes to brew." Alma met Callie as she entered the living room.

Callie hugged her friend. "No don't bother with coffee, but a glass of tea would be nice. Max told me you approved the final proof of your book."

After putting the flowers in a vase and getting some tea, the two women moved to the armchairs in the living room which looked out a window with a perfect view of Alma's front yard and her hydrangeas, sporting big blue, snowball-shaped blossoms. "Yeah, I sent it back yesterday. I certainly appreciate the opportunity, but I'm glad it's done."

"That was a mountain of work you did. Glad I could help out by reading some of the early drafts."

"Thanks. Even though someone from the historical society helped with the writing, I trust your opinion. I figured if someone who didn't do basket weaving could follow what I was saying then we were on the right track. Did I see that Kim and the twins have gone back to Charleston?"

"Yeah, they went back yesterday. It's eerily quiet at the house right now." Callie shifted in her seat. "I appreciate the house being quiet again, but I miss them already."

"I bet you do. I loved the way they'd run across the yard when they saw me and babble to me about the things they saw. Avery would grab my finger and drag me off to show me the flowers in the yard or where they had found toads." Alma's face broke into a grin. "You certainly wouldn't have to worry about staying limber with those two around. They'd keep you moving."

"You should have seen them helping me put the tomato plants in this year, digging the small holes, patting the soil around each plant, and applying the fertilizer. Now they've got their own gardening gloves and tools for helping." Callie smiled, picturing the twins digging in the dirt.

"Bet that was something. They showed me their tomato plants. Labeled with their names. I was surprised they recognized their own name."

"Kim and Julia read to them all the time, not just books, but whatever signs might be around."

"Tell me, when does your first shipment of books come in?"

"The first shipment will come in next week. I think the historical society wants to do some kind of promotion, but I'm not sure what they have planned. Dang, I thought we'd just get them out on the shelves, but apparently there's more to it than that." Alma shook her head from side to side slowly. "Like you I don't care for much hoopla, but guess I got to play this out."

Callie grinned as she stood up. "I get how you feel. Max and I would like to feature you for a book signing and sale at the Emporium. Maybe we can team up with the historical society. I'd better get going since I'm due in the Emporium at twelve."

"Yeah, I need to get on with my day, too. You and Luke are going to Max and Louise's tonight? We can talk about it then." Alma stood up and followed her friend into the kitchen. "Thanks for the flowers."

"Think nothing of it." Callie paused to hug her friend. "I'll see you at Max and Louise's, if not before."

Callie joined her mother on the front porch when she got home from the Emporium. "Hey, Momma. How are you feeling today? Missed you at breakfast." Callie hugged her mother.

"I'm feeling okay. I just don't have enough to do. I can't drive. The flower boxes are all planted. I've never been one to sit around."

Callie reached out to take her mother's hand. "You started out at such a young age, working with your Aunt Flo. I don't know how you could take Aunt Sally and go to Charleston."

Her mother squeezed Callie's hand. "I didn't have much choice in the matter unless I wanted to end up like Aunt Flo. Married too young, popping out babies and scraping by."

"But you did it and took along your sixteen-year old sister. Then you went to school to become a secretary. Momma, that's amazing, especially back then when things were much harder for women on their own."

"It was what I had to do." Her mother let go of her hand.

"You still take care of all the flowers out back. I'd never be able to keep up without your help there." Callie reached out to pat her mother's arm. "And I love all the table linens you've made for us."

Lydia shrugged. "That never takes much time. Luke said something about you two going to Max and Louise's tonight?"

"Yeah, I haven't seen Louise in ages." Callie got up and turned to her mother.

"Maybe I'll see what's in the kitchen for dinner." Her mother grabbed her walker and began muttering under her breath as she stood up. "I don't like this thing. It makes me feel so clumsy."

She held the door until her mother made it inside. "I'm going to change now. Love you, Momma," Callie said as she kissed her mother's cheek. *I wish I knew how to help Momma. I've got to think of something. But what?*

14

Kim June 2001

Kim pulled into the garage and turned off the engine. Tired from her day at work, she rested her head on the steering wheel for a moment. *I gotta perk up. Allison and Avery need a mother that's not exhausted. Jake wasn't a lot of help, but at least he would play with them while I cooked. Maybe I can make helping with dinner a playtime. But then there's a gate on the stairs so the only places they can go to are downstairs. They don't need to be in my sight all the time.* Shrugging her shoulders, Kim grabbed her bag and went inside.

Peeking around the corner, she took in the scene. Julia, Avery and Allison were sitting on the floor in the den, building block towers. Avery saw her, squealed loudly, and ran to her with open arms. Kim knelt to the floor to give him a bear hug. His sister was right behind him and squirmed into her mother's embrace. All three of them landed in a heap on the floor. "Oh, I'm so happy to see you, too. Did you have a good day today?" Kim asked the children.

"Went to park," Allison said as Avery spread his arms and ran around in circles. "Avery likes airplanes," she added.

"I know, " Kim said. "Let me talk to Julia a minute and then I can start on supper. Are you hungry?"

The twins' heads bobbed up and down vigorously before they returned to their toys. Julia gathered her purse and bag before the two women paused at the kitchen island. "They had a good day. Both of them seem to be adjusting to being back home. Allison asked where Jake was a couple of times. I told her he was at work," Julia said digging in her purse for her keys. "I didn't really know what to tell her and didn't think to ask you before."

Kim reached out to squeeze Julia's shoulder. "No that's fine. It's how I usually respond. Sorry, I didn't tell you that. I dropped them off at his parents' for them to visit with him last Saturday. I imagine eventually they'll ask why he doesn't stay here. I'll cross that bridge when we get to it. Hey, don't let me hold you up. I know you want to get home."

After seeing Julia to the door, Kim joined the twins in the playroom. "Hey kiddos," she said as she sat beside them on the floor. "That's a pretty tall tower you're building." They paused to smile up at her and continued adding blocks to the tower. "I'm going to start dinner. I'll be in the kitchen. Okay?" Focused on their task, both children nodded.

What was I going to cook? Kim stared into the open refrigerator. *Oh, yeah, pepper steak and rice.* By the time Kim had the peppers, onions and meat cut up, Allison and Avery wandered into the kitchen.

"Hey, you two, want to help cook dinner?" Kim asked squatting to the children's level.

There was a chorus of "Me help, me help," from the twins.

"Okay, let's get the stool. Avery can help get the water for the rice, put it in the pan and Allison can put the rice in. How's that?"

"Me do it," Avery said clapping his hands.

"Me too," said Allison as she began to twirl.

Kim pulled the stool out of the pantry. "I'm so lucky today. Two assistant chefs. Remember the stove is hot so don't dance too close to it." With the rice cooking, she

began adding items to her electric wok. Each child took turns stirring the mixture of peppers, onions, and beef.

"Great work, kiddos. Thanks for all your help. The rice will be ready soon. Why don't you go play while I get the table ready." She gave them each a hug before they toddled off to the playroom. Kim set their places at the island and put the food in serving dishes before calling the twins to eat.

After dinner, she cleared the island, leaving everything on the counter so she could load it into the dishwasher later. *Just a few minutes before it's time for baths and stories. I'll finish the kitchen after that. Then maybe I can get some laundry done before I go to bed. I'd like to take the kids to Momma's this weekend so I need to stay ahead of things here in the house.*

While the twins splashed in the tub, Kim gathered everyone's laundry and left the basket near the top of the stairs. She really didn't like of leaving them in the tub and stuck her head in the door frequently just to make sure they were safe.

Now she sat on the bathroom floor and helped them make funny hats with the bubbles. After a few minutes Kim said, "Okay, time to get out, brush your teeth and have a story before bedtime."

"Stay in tub," Allison said, frowning and hitting the water hard with her small hands.

"It's time to get ready for bed," Kim said firmly. Letting the water out of the tub, she asked, "Who's turn to pick a story?"

"Mine," Avery announced. Allison's pout turned into a smile. Both children loved for Kim to read to them.

"Okay, let's get you both dried off." Kim wrapped each child in a towel after she lifted them out of the tub. " After you're in your pajamas, you choose a story while sister brushes her teeth."

"Okay, Momma," Avery grinned. He liked to choose the bedtime story.

Soon both children were ready for bed. The three of them curled up on the pile of over-sized pillows Kim had placed in a corner of the room. With the story finished, she tucked them into bed with a kiss before turning out the light.

Although each child had a bedroom and a toddler sized bed, not wanting to sleep alone in a room had become an issue for both of them since they returned to the townhouse. *I don't know if it's because of the separation or because they slept in the same room at Momma's. Kim picked up the laundry basket and went downstairs. They were okay in separate rooms before. Oh, well. They each have their own beds and they're still young. If it makes them feel comfortable, then I don't see a problem. They'll figure out when they need privacy.*

With the laundry started and the dishwasher loaded, Kim called her mother to be sure she'd be home this weekend. "Hey, Momma," Kim said when her mother answered the phone. "What are you doing Saturday? Thought the twins and I would come over in the afternoon." As Kim expected, her mother was delighted. "Okay, we'll come over about lunchtime, stay for supper, and then come back home. I'd like to keep the twins bedtime routine the same." They talked a little longer before hanging up. *It'll be good to talk to adults away from work for a change. Avery and Allison aren't great conversationalists yet.*

Kim's heart nearly stopped as she pulled into her mother's driveway and saw the ambulance with its back door open. *Who's sick? Why didn't Momma call me?* She

wondered as she drove around the ambulance and parked beside the garage. She took a few deep breaths to steady her breathing and racing heart before turning to look at the twins buckled in their car seats. "Momma will be right back, okay?" Both toddlers nodded.

Kim ran to the front door, let herself in and found her mother crying on Luke's shoulder. *Okay, they aren't here for Momma or Luke. Grandma? Grandpa?* The thoughts flashed through her mind as she sank to the floor in front of her mother.

"Kim, glad you're here. Where are the children?" Luke asked as Callie dried her eyes.

"They're still in the car. Who—" Kim began to ask.

"It's your Grandma," Callie said. "She laid down for a nap after lunch and then---" She dissolved into tears again.

"She died," Luke said as he finished Callie's sentence. "Because she was at home, the coroner has to pick her up and determine cause of death. I'm not sure when that will be. Do you want to take the twins back home?" Luke asked while he continued rubbing small circles between Callie's shoulder blades. "We can call you later."

The paramedics entered the living room, settling the large bags of gear on their shoulders before Kim could answer. "Mrs. Barnes, your dad is asking for you. We'll be on our way now. Dr. Wilson from the coroner's office should be here within the next half hour or so. I'm sorry for your loss." Settling their bags on their shoulders once more, they left, softly closing the door behind themselves.

Kim spoke up in the emptiness left in their wake. "I'm sure there's something I can do here. I'll take the kids over to Alma's. We can watch from there to see when the coroner leaves. I don't want them to see her going into the van. As much as I want to see Grandpa, I need to get the children settled first."

Callie nodded, accepting Kim's plan as she gave her daughter a hug before going to see her dad. Standing, Kim reminded Luke that her cell phone was on and to call as soon as the coroner left, just in case she missed seeing him leave.

Alma came out onto her front porch while Kim was getting the children out of the car. "What's going on, honey? Do you need some help there?" Alma started down the porch steps.

"No, I've got it. We'll be right there. Let me grab a bag," Kim answered as she pointed the twins towards Alma. "Go see Aunt Alma."

"Come on inside, you two. I think I have some cookies and milk in the kitchen. Can you help me find them?" Alma led the children into the house. Giving Kim a concerned look, she added, "And you can tell me what's going on over at your Momma's. I saw the empty ambulance leave."

When they had settled the children around the kitchen table, Alma and Kim stepped into the living room. With tears in her eyes, Kim explained her grandmother had died and they were waiting for the coroner to come for her.

Alma hugged her tightly. "Oh, baby. I'm so sorry. What can I do?" Alma frowned thoughtfully. "Why don't you let Avery and Allison stay here with me? You can go and say goodbye to your grandmother. I'll keep an eye out and when everyone is gone, the children and I will walk over."

"Are you sure Alma? They can be a handful," Kim asked as she stood back and dried her eyes.

"Sure, I've got a couple of VHS tapes they can watch, Sesame Street, and there's a whole batch of chocolate chip cookies in the kitchen," Alma insisted. "I'll get the tape set up while you say goodbye."

Kim found everyone sitting around her grandparents' bed when she slipped back into her mother's house. She sat on the floor next to the bed before taking her grandmother's hand. The tears she had held back when she was at Alma's flowed. *Ah, Grandma, Grandma. I'm going to miss you so much. I'm glad you got to know Avery and Allison. I'll tell them all the stories you told me. And how you guys baked cookies and worked in the garden together. I know you've been frustrated since you haven't been able to get around like you used to. You're at peace now.*

The doorbell rang loudly through the silent house. Luke answered the door.

"Hello, I'm Dr. Wilson. Sorry to meet you under such circumstances." He held out his hand.

After they shook hands, Luke stepped aside so the doctor could come in. "Her family is with Mrs. Stevens right now."

"Okay, my assistant is getting the gurney out. I do need to do a very brief examination. Could you lead the way?" Dr. Wilson asked while Luke stared into space.

Luke frowned, then shook his head. "Of course, this way. I'll come back to let your assistant in."

After Luke introduced the doctor, everyone except Callie's dad left the room and gathered around the kitchen island. Kim busied herself making coffee. Callie stared out the kitchen window looking at the peturias her mother had planted in the raised beds.

"Hey, Momma. How about some coffee? It'll be ready in a few minutes." Putting mugs on the counter, she grimaced as she asked, "Has anybody called Uncle Bobby?"

"Dang it," Callie said. "I'll go into the bedroom and call him. I'll get my coffee when I come back out."

"Honey, let me call him. Your dad's going to need you nearby in just a few minutes." Luke stood and kissed the top of her head.

"Are you sure?" Callie asked, looking up at him with puffy, red eyes.

He nodded slightly. "Yeah, let me do what I can do. I'll be back in a few minutes."

Alma brought the children over shortly after the coroner left. Pulling Kim into the kitchen she said, "Don't worry about feeding anybody for the next few days. I'm frying chicken and pulling a few things together for tonight. Later the rest of the community will be stopping by. This is going to hit your momma hard. They got closer over time, but I know she regrets it didn't happen sooner."

Kim gave Alma a hug. "You're the best aunt a person could wish for. Thanks."

"You guys are my family. Let me go see your momma, before I go back home."

Around six o'clock, Alma slipped into the kitchen with a basket of food. "Now, you should have everything here," she told Kim. Despite Kim's protests, Alma wouldn't stay for supper saying she would see them tomorrow.

Kim and Luke set Alma's meal out in the dining room. When Luke called everyone to the table, Callie's dad said, "I don't think I can eat tonight."

Callie gave his shoulder a squeeze. "I don't feel much like eating either, but the twins have to eat and they'll do better if we do things the way we usually do. So at least, let's go in together and try."

The mood was subdued with little of the conversation that usually accompanied their family meals. Callie noticed the twins were fidgeting and looking at the adults with confused expressions. She forced herself to give them a smile. "You two seem to be having trouble sitting still. Would you like to take a walk with me on the beach?

The twins nodded vigorously. "Can we get in the water?" Allison asked.

"We'll have to ask your mother, but let's finish eating and we'll go after the kitchen is cleaned up." It wasn't much longer before everyone finished their meal.

As usual, everyone helped clear the table. Even the twins helped by carrying napkins and their plates to the island. "Kim, when did Avery and Allison start clearing the table."

Kim laughed. "It started as a way to keep them near me while I was cooking dinner. Now they 'help' me cook and clean up after dinner most nights."

"Well, it doesn't hurt for them to start learning how to take care of themselves," Callie began loading the dishwasher.

"Of course, at home we're just going from the island to the counter by the sink. They're doing real well tonight. Hey, I can get this while you take them for a walk. My car keys are on a hook by the garage door," Kim said as she began loading the dishwasher.

"Okay. About the water, I know they have a change of clothes up-stairs so I'll let them wade, if they want to. If that's okay with you."

Kim smiled. "It's fine. Whatever makes this night easier."

Callie took Kim's keys from the hook as she began a search for the twins.

Hearing their excited chatter, she went onto the front porch. "Who's ready to go to the beach?"

"Me, me." They called out together, dancing around with excite-ment.

"Let's get in the car then." Callie looked at Luke and her dad. "We won't be gone long. They're going home tonight." She gave Luke a kiss and her dad a hug before following the children to the car.

She parked the car near the pavilion and got the twins out of their car seats. "Don't get too far ahead of me now," Callie called out as the chil-dren made a headlong dash across the sand. The sun turned the ocean into a dazzling display of pink, orange, and gold glistening jewels as it sank closer to the horizon. Sandpipers bounced just ahead of the children as they sought their evening meal along the water's edge.

A few seagulls squawked and dipped toward the sand as if they expected the humans to have some food. Disappointed, the birds soared upward. Catching sight of them, Avery called out, "Look, Grandma. I fly." He flapped his arms and then held them perpendicular to the ground as he mimicked the dipping and soaring birds. Allison stopped digging in the sand and joined him in flight. It wasn't long before the children grew dizzy and fell to the ground in a giggling heap. Callie helped them stand up and brushed damp sand from their clothes.

"I think we should go back now. Your mother wants to take you home tonight," she told them as she took their hands.

Avery pouted. "Don't want to go." Allison watched silently as she hung back, forcing Callie to stop.

Callie knelt down so she could look into her grandchildren's eyes before speaking. "I know how you feel. I have so much more fun when you're here. But I do have a lot to do the next few days. And we really should listen to your mother."

She gave them both a hug before standing up and placing her index finger in the palm of each child's hand. Their small fingers wrapping around hers made Callie smile, despite the day's events. "Let's go now. I think there might be a treat at the house." Both children grinned and soon let go of Callie's hand to race to the car.

It was nearly dark when Kim pulled into her garage. "Hey, guys we're home," she said to the drowsy twins. "Let's go inside and play for a while before bathtime."

Released from their car seats, the twins ran and waited at the door for Kim to unlock it. While they headed to the playroom, Kim went upstairs to refresh the bag she still carried for them. Although the twins were potty trained, there were still a number of things she liked to have as backup when they were away from home.

Downstairs, she hung the bag on its hook near the garage door. Checking to see that the twins were still playing, she called Jake. *I really don't want to talk to him. But he is their father and needs to know what's going on in their lives. Maybe he won't answer and I can just leave a message.*

He answered on the third ring. "Hey, I know you'll see the twins tomorrow, but I wanted to give you a heads up that my grandmother died suddenly today," Kim said. She listened as he expressed his condolences before going on to explain the twins saw the ambulance, but nothing else. And she had told them great grandma had died. "Anyway, we can talk more tomorrow. I'll bring them to your mother's after breakfast," Kim said before hanging up.

Returning to the playroom, she sat on the floor. Leaning against the wall, she watched her children play together. *I'm glad they keep each other company. Although I don't remember being lonely as a child. I had everyone who came into the store as a playmate. Better get this bedtime routine going.* "Come on you two. Let's put away the toys and get a bath," Kim said as she began picking up toys from the floor.

"No bath," Allison said, standing with her hands planted on her hips.

It was all Kim could do to keep from laughing. *That sure looks like me when I'm mad.* "We need to make sure there's no sand stuck to you," Kim told her daughter. "You can put the bubbles in the water."

Allison squinted as she looked at her mother. "Okay, Momma," she said and begin putting away toys along with her brother.

With the twins in bed, Kim began getting ready for bed herself. The emotional impact of the day left her feeling exhausted, but not sleepy, so she went downstairs to brew a cup of tea. Although she didn't grow up drinking hot tea, Kim started drinking it while she was pregnant because the peppermint tea eased her nausea. Now it was just part of her wind-down ritual before bed. She leaned against the counter, waiting for the water to boil. *I'm going to miss Grandma. Poor Grandpa though, she was his world. Good thing they had already moved in with Momma. I should call her in the morning to see how I can help with any arrangements.* Noise from the kettle broke into her thoughts and she poured the hot water into her cup. After a few minutes, she sweet-ened the tea with honey and picked up her book. Settling into her fa-vorite armchair with her feet on an ottoman, Kim began clearing her mind of extraneous thoughts and opened her book.

15

Callie June 2001

After a restless night, Callie gave up trying to sleep around four o'clock. Quietly she slipped on her clothes, went into the kitchen, and started coffee. After a short time, armed with what she knew was the day's first cup of many, Callie went onto the porch. Chirping crickets, croaking frogs, and buzzing winged insects interrupted the early morning stillness. The heavy citrusy scent from the magnolia trees filled her nose. Standing near the porch's railing, she thought about her mother and worried for her father. *Is that the light from a false dawn? I'm not sure when sunrise is. Oh, Momma, I miss you so much already. We've been so much closer these last few years. I'm glad you got a chance to play with the twins. You always wanted great grandchildren. And thankfully, whatever took you, at least you didn't have to be in a hospital. I've got to pull myself together here so I can help Dad.* Callie wiped the tears from her face and went inside.

She sat at the kitchen island with her planner, a legal pad, and a fresh cup of coffee. By the time the sun was up, Callie had made a list of people she needed to call and had written her mother's obituary for the newspaper, except for the part about when the service would be. That couldn't be decided until the coroner released her body.

"Hey, Callie-girl." Her dad went to get some coffee. "Were you able to get any rest?"

Callie looked up and gave him a small smile. "Hardly slept at all. Finally got up around four." Callie pushed her hair back from her face. "How about you?"

"I tossed and turned most of the night." He grimaced as he sat beside his daughter. "Kept waking up because I had so much room in the bed." Shaking his head he continued. "Except for her being in the hospital a few times, your momma and I always slept in the same bed. Nearly sixty years, you know." Her dad pulled a handkerchief from his pocket and dabbed at his eyes.

"I bet that was rough. I can't imagine, Dad." Callie hugged him. "I hate to ask you to do this, but when you're ready, take a look at this pad here. I've started some rough planning for Momma's funeral. We can change anything you want." Callie gave him a final squeeze before putting her cup on the counter by the sink. "I'm going to take a walk now. Want to come along?"

"Nah, I'll just stay here and look at your notes." He picked up the legal pad and sighed noisily. "Like you said, it needs to be done."

Callie pulled her light jacket closer to her body. Even in summer, the breeze coming off the ocean could have a slight chill. Cattails rustled as the gentle wind made its way further inland. Herons with their muted blue and gray feathers stood at the edge of a tidal pool nestled in the cattails. Their heads bobbed down as they looked for stranded fish. They raised their heads to look at her while she passed by, gave her brief consideration, and went back to their fishing.

As she reached the path between the dunes, Callie stopped to take off her shoes. Digging her toes in the sand, she inhaled deeply and exhaled through her mouth a few times until she felt she had replaced all the air in her lungs with the saltier ocean air. *Ah, that's better. The air even tastes salty today. It's going to be muggy later.* Here, on the dunes, sea oats danced in the wind. Sandpipers and seagulls swirled overhead. It was low tide. The small waves with their foamy crests lapped at the hard packed sand.

Sandpipers landed and began their bouncing dance with the waves, a few steps forward to check the wave's offering then a few backward steps as the wave returned.

Making her way along the shoreline, Callie was happy to see no one was on the beach today. The last few houses sold on the island were sold as vacation homes. *I don't really mind them. It just makes it harder to judge when the beach will be quiet. And Lord, please, just don't let us turn into the Isle of Palms.*

Callie continued walking for a while longer before sitting cross legged and faced the ocean. She picked up a handful of sand and let it slide through her fingers. *Life is like this sand. We can hold on to parts of it for a time, but then it slides out of our grasp and we're left with an empty hole.* Callie ignored the tears rolling down her cheeks as she remembered her mother. *When I first think of her, she's in the garden. We're planting foxglove together. Or I see her at the nursing home visiting an old friend. Or holding Kim and looking at her with such adoration. Or later, stretching through yoga poses. Then I remember how daring she was. At eighteen she and her sister caught a bus to Charleston with just a little bit of money they saved. They knew no one in Charleston. And people talk about how I took risks by staying on the island after Joe died. Hmph, that was nothing compared to an eighteen-year old from the hills striking out for Charleston with her sixteen-year old sister in tow.*

Callie sniffled and wiped the tears from her cheeks. Standing up, she saw Luke walking toward her. Waving, she began making her way to him.

"Hi, love." He wrapped his arms around her. "You okay?"

"Yeah, as well as can be expected, you know." Callie buried her head in his chest for a few minutes and then stood back. "I was just thinking how terrified my mother must have been when she stepped off that bus in Charleston. I've got to make sure the grandchildren remember that about her."

"She really had some guts." "

Are you ready to go home?"

"Yeah, need to see if Dad's eaten anything or has been able to look at the arrangements I planned this morning." They slowly walked back towards the house.

"He was reading something on a legal pad when I left." Luke looked out over the ocean. "It's going to be a beautiful day. Do you think Kim will be here today?"

"Probably, although I don't know when. The twins are with Jake today. She told me that he's been going to his AA meetings and has rented an apartment." She let out a deep sigh.

"Well, maybe he's getting himself together. It will be better for Allison and Avery if he does." Luke squeezed her hand gently.

"I'll take my lead from Kim. If she thinks they can do this amicably, so much the better. Only you will hear what I really think about him." Callie exhaled heavily. "Anyway, the twins need to have a relationship with their father that isn't colored by my opinion."

They had left the beach and were walking along the road to the house when Luke pointed to their driveway. "Isn't that Max and Louise's car?"

"It sure is. And dang it, that reminds me, I forgot to set up a way to keep up with who brings what so I can send thank you cards later and get everyone's dishes back to them." Callie blew a breath out between her lips as they turned into the driveway.

Slipping off their shoes in the garage, Callie and Luke went into the kitchen. Max, in a suit, and Louise, wearing a bright blue dress and matching hat, were sitting at the

island with Callie's dad. *They're on their way to church. They could have come by later. No need for them to hurry over. How did they know anyway? Ah, Alma would have called them.*

"Does anyone need something to drink or maybe something to eat?" Luke asked as he started another pot of coffee.

Louise spoke up. "Nothing for us, thank you. We're on our way to church. But I slipped a breakfast casserole in your oven to stay warm and put some orange juice in the refrigerator." She and Max stood up to leave. "Now Bob, you call if you need something. Callie can be a bit stubborn about that." Louise winked at Callie.

Bob nodded. "I will."

She followed her friends through the living room where they paused at the front door as Callie gave each of them a hug. "Thank you for thinking of something for breakfast. You're both so sweet. I don't know when the service will be. I'll keep you posted."

"We'll probably be back later after church. I can't imagine losing your wife after sixty years. Hope it'll help to have someone closer to his age to talk to." Max rubbed his head and then put an arm around Louise's waist.

"Thanks so much. Even in Columbia, Dad never made many friends. He was always looking out for Momma." Callie gave Max another quick hug. "Get going now or you'll be late."

Kim arrived before lunch. Coming in from the garage, she found her mother in the kitchen. "Hey, Momma." Kim hugged her. "That's for Allison and Avery, too. So what have you got going on in here?" Kim hung her bag on a chair before sitting beside her mother.

"I'm trying to figure out the best way to track things the neighbors bring." Callie tossed her pen on the island in frustration. "I don't know. I'm tired. I've been up since four."

"So go take a nap." Kim gathered up the pen and nearby pad. "I'll take care of this and keep an eye on Grandpa. Although I think I saw Luke with him on the porch as I pulled in. Go, before everyone starts stopping by after church." Kim made shooing motions with her hands as her mother stood up.

"Okay, I'll go lay down, but wake me when people start coming." Callie paused in the doorway before she crossed the dining room on the way to her bedroom. *We never did add enough square footage to work a hall in here. Oh well, I don't care. I like having the larger dining room. It looks like we'll need it for a while.* Taking a small blanket from a chair in her bedroom, Callie curled up on the bed and was soon asleep.

"Wake up, honey." Luke kissed her lightly on the forehead as he sat beside her on the bed.

Callie smiled briefly and then frowned. "What time is it?" She sat up and ran her hands through her hair.

"It's twelve o'clock. I thought you might want a shower before people start coming." Luke sat beside her on the bed. "You were sleeping so hard you didn't hear me come in earlier to get a shower."

"No, didn't hear a thing. The nap helped and I'm sure the shower will too," Callie gave him a kiss on the cheek before grabbing her robe on the way to the bathroom. By

the time she was ready, a steady stream of people began making their way to the house, each carrying a platter or casserole. Callie and Kim set food out in the dining room so people could eat as they paid their respects. When Alma arrived, she sent Callie into the living room with everyone else.

A few days later, the corner released Lydia's body to the funeral home. Even though the coroner's office had honored the family's request not to do an autopsy, in the end, Bob decided on a closed casket. "Lydia would want it that way." He told Luke over coffee. "She wouldn't want people gawking at her."

"I can see that. She always was a private person." Luke took a sip of coffee. "Do you want something for breakfast? Callie's still on her walk, but I'd be happy to fix something for you."

"No, I might get something in a while. There's enough food to feed an army in here. The island has really banded together." Bob stood up. "Think I'll go lay back down."

"We're a very close community and always help each other." Luke stood and gathered their coffee cups. "I'm going to the studio now. See you later."

The day of the funeral dawned without a cloud in the sky. Sitting on the front porch with a cup of coffee, Callie was dreading wearing her black dress to the funeral. *It's already hot. Oh well, I guess I should be glad I don't have to wear a suit and tie. Even so, we'll all be sweltering at the grave side. Alma and Louise said they wouldn't go to the cemetery and would come here to set up the food. Those two are the best friends a woman could have. Everything is ready to go. Don't think I've forgotten anything.*

Bobby brought his coffee out to the porch. He and his family had arrived yesterday. "Hey, Sis." He sat next to her on the wicker loveseat. "Funny how you know your parents' health is declining, but when they die, you're still not ready."

"Oh, I know. Just a couple of days before." Callie swallowed hard before continuing. "She was fussing with me because she felt she needed to be doing something productive." Callie brushed at the tears in her eyes. "I know she was really upset to still be using that old-style walker, and needing help if she was doing something in the kitchen. She said the walker didn't really help her get around, just made it harder. But her physical therapist said she couldn't control one of the newer-styled ones."

"Yeah, I know. How's Dad holding up?" Bobby asked as he sat his coffee cup on a side table.

"He seems to be doing all right. To tell the truth, I don't think he knows what to do with himself without Momma to look after." Callie stood and went to the porch railing. Tiptoeing, she could just see the dunes.

"I know. He was always about the family. I'll see if he wants to come and stay with me for a while," Bobby offered. "I know Kim's working through some changes as well. This might give you a break."

Callie turned to face her brother. "Only if he wants to, Bobby. He's no trouble. I just hate thinking about him sitting around with Luke and I so busy all the time."

Bobby nodded. "Where are the twins? Will we see them this week?"

"They're with Jake. Everyone agreed they were too young for a funeral. But I'm sure they'll be here sometime before you go home." Callie glanced at her watch. "I've got to start getting ready." Callie picked up her coffee cup and went inside.

The church was overflowing. The top of her mother's casket held bouquets of roses. Red from her father and white from the rest of the family. Callie felt curiously disembodied, like she was watching herself from the sidelines.

Still, she was able to give her eulogy without breaking down. Bobby spoke too. Pastor Matthews kept his sermon short and then the pall-bearers, Bobby, Luke, Max, and Steve along with Josie's boys, began their slow walk outside. Callie, her dad, and Kim, along with Bobby's family stood near the entrance accepting condolences. Her cousins Claude and Alice, along with Uncle Michael were there as well. *Nice of them to come even though we aren't close.* Callie encouraged everyone to stop by the house for something to eat after the burial.

It was just a short drive to the cemetery from the church. Callie leaned against Luke's shoulder before getting out of the car. *I'm so thankful to have found Luke. Not only did he find a limo big enough to fit us all in, but he seems to know what I need almost as soon as I realize I need something.*

Approaching the graveside on foot, Callie was amazed at how quickly the funeral home had set everything up. The flowers from the church and astroturf to cover all the dirt were in place. Pastor Matthew said even fewer words than he did in church. Family and friends said their final goodbyes to Lydia as they walked by the casket and on to their cars.

"Honey, please get me back to the car. I can't stand looking at her casket sitting there just waiting to be lowered into the ground," Callie told him quietly in one of the few moments when they were alone.

"Okay, love." Deftly Luke led her through the other mourners without being rude or getting caught up in conversation. After helping her into the car and starting it, he told her. "I'll wait out here for everyone else and then we'll go home."

Most people who were at the service came by the house for at least a few minutes. Callie sat with Bobby, and her dad in armchairs brought into the dining room from the bedrooms. There was a chair for Luke, but he hovered behind Callie to make sure Callie and her dad had whatever they might need. Her Uncle Michael, Alice and Claude made a brief appearance.

Alma, Louise, Susan, and Kim kept the food and beverages set out in the dining room fresh. Trey, Monica, and Sally, Bobby's and Susan's children, looked after the community members in their age group. By four o'clock Callie's dad retreated to his bedroom as Luke closed the front door on the last of those wishing to pay their respects.

Everyone else gathered around the dining room table. Women slipped off their heels while men removed their suit coats and ties. Callie wiggled her toes. "I haven't worn heels this long in ages," she said with a small frown. Looking at the other women, she added, "At least I was sitting, I feel for you. You've been standing most of the day. I can't tell you how much I appreciate everything you've done."

Louise waved her hand with a dismissive flutter before resting her arms on the table. "You'd have done the same for any of us."

"That doesn't change how much I appreciate all of you." Callie looked around the table. "I think I'll start putting the food away. I can't sit still anymore. You guys go ahead and take a break." Picking up a couple of platters, she went into the kitchen.

Rummaging in the cabinet for some Tupperware, she was surprised to see Luke and Bobby bringing food into the kitchen.

"Sis, you know I can't sit still either. This afternoon sitting in the dining room was torture on more than one level." Bobby put two platters on the island. "I'll bring them in and you put the food away." He turned around and nearly bumped into Luke. "I didn't see you behind me," he laughed before going back to the dining room.

"How about this?" Luke asked as he opened the dishwasher. "You put the food away and I'll load the dishwasher."

"Honey, I know you're as tired as everyone else. Go sit down and try to relax for a bit." Callie burped the lid of the Tupperware container.

"If Bobby and I help, then we'll finish sooner. Everyone is tired but they're all in there trying to summon the energy to help in here. The quicker this gets done the sooner everyone can call it a day." Luke began loading the dishwasher.

As he started the dishwasher, Alma came into the kitchen. "You organized a lovely service." she hugged her friend. "Your momma would have been proud. I'll see you later."

"Thanks, Alma. You were such an amazing help. Once again, I don't know what I would have done without you." Callie sniffled as tears threatened again. "Here. Let me walk you to the door."

Alma grinned and paused at the back door, "Who do you think you're talking to? I think I can find my way across the back porch."

Callie laughed despite her overall feeling of sorrow. "I guess you can at that. Well, I'll see you tomorrow." She turned and went back to the dining room.

Louise was putting her heels back on as she and Max prepared to leave. "Hey, you two. Thanks again for all your help. You are the most wonderful friends a body could ask for." Callie hugged them each in turn.

With everyone gone, Callie went to change while Bobby and Susan decided to walk on the beach. Afterwards, rather than trying to catch up to them, she took her coffee to the front porch to watch the sunset. Tired as she was, Callie shook her head trying to stay awake. *It's much too early to go to sleep.* Luke joined her on the loveseat. In only moments after he slipped his arm around her, Callie fell asleep feeling comforted and cared for despite the hole in her heart.

16

Callie September 2001

Callie absentmindedly shifted sand through her fingers as she sat watching the white crested waves make their way to shore. The ever-present sandpipers hopped closer to the retreating waves while searching for a midmorning snack. *Somethings never change, even as the world dissolves around us.* In her mind, Callie replayed the images she had watched on the television of the Twin Towers in New York collapsing downward in plumes of smoke. *Things like that don't happen here in the US. All those people gone. All those families will never be the same. Then there was the plane that flew into the Pentagon. What does it mean for us who remain? And how much worse would it have been if those brave people had not crashed the plane heading for a nuclear reactor in Pennsylvania?* Callie took in a few deep breaths filling her lungs with the salty air. *At least we are safe here.* Callie slipped her shoes on and stood up to began the walk home.

Once there she slipped out of her beach shoes and into the sandals she usually wore around the house. "Hey, Luke are you in the kitchen," she called walking up the hall.

"Yeah, I'm here. Are you ready for breakfast?" Luke answered as she came into the room.

"No, I had a bagel before I left." She hugged him tightly. "I'll just have another cup of coffee before I get ready to go into the Emporium. What's your day looking like?" Callie went to the coffee pot and refilled the cup she had left on the counter before her walk.

"I thought I'd go out and do some sketches, in a bit. It seems weird after what we saw on TV yesterday, but I suppose we have to keep doing what we do." Luke stared into his coffee cup.

"I know, but I worry about Trey. He's still young enough to be drafted if we decide to declare war." Callie plopped into the chair next to Luke. "Hell, do we even declare war anymore. I'll be sure to call Bobby and Susan tonight."

Alma had joined Callie and Max at the Emporium even though it wasn't her day to be in the store. Everyone coming into the Emporium had different opinions about what the country's leaders should do about the attacks. Some wanted to send out troops to the Middle East or at least send planes with bombs in retaliation. Most people were worried about their safety because they were so close to the naval base in Charleston.

At lunchtime, the three of them sat in the office with sandwiches and discussed the attacks. "This makes me think of the air raids during WWII. Except now their talking about increasing the powers of Homeland Security." Alma took a bite of her sandwich.

"I know." Max stared out into the store. "I just hope we don't abuse any of these powers. As a people, Americans are used to traveling where we want, when we want." Max looked at Callie across the table.

"Yeah, it would be terrible if we had to carry 'papers' simply to get around the country. I just hope they don't reinstitute the draft. There's nothing wrong with military service, but unless it's compulsory for everyone, I don't think there should be a draft." Callie took a drink of tea.

Alma put her sandwich down abruptly and turned to stare at Callie sitting beside her. "Are you serious? You think the army should draft women?" She asked and continued to stare at her friend.

"Well, yes. Women aren't allowed in combat zones, but there are things women could do." Callie paused for a moment before adding. "There should be provisions for conscientious objectors though, working in the inner cities or something like that. Unless they change the rules about women serving in combat zones women could do that as well."

Alma shook her head as she looked at Callie and smiled. "Well, I never would have guessed you felt that way."

"Come on, you and Max made me very aware of social injustices in this country and then you add my own experiences with the bank." Callie paused to look at her friends before continuing. "What did you expect? I just believe if we're going to be equal, we should be equal in all things." She picked up her sandwich and took another bite.

"Okay, okay," Max chuckled. "I see where you're coming from, but I don't think you'll have many people jumping on your bandwagon."

"You're probably right, but enough of that. Alma, are we still getting together at your place on Friday?" Callie began gathering the remains of her lunch. "Luke got a call from the artists guild before I left this morning. They were looking for a place to do a silent auction to benefit the people in New York. I thought maybe we could help out somehow."

"Yeah, I thought we'd eat about five. We can talk then." Alma wiped her hands on her napkin.

"I like that idea. I know Louise would like to help out, too," Max said. "Several churches are collecting donations, but I think New York is going to need a lot of help." He added as he picked up his lunch remains before leaving for the day. Alma left shortly after.

Friday morning, Callie called Alma before going on her walk. "Alma, would it be okay if Kim and the twins joined us after dinner? We were talking last night and she has an idea about the donations for New York."

"Just tell her to come to supper." Alma insisted. "I haven't seen Allison and Avery in forever and kids grow up so fast. It'll be good to see them. I'll just get out a little more chicken."

"Should I make some rolls or biscuits? Or just tell me what I should bring besides these extra, hungry people," Callie laughed.

"Maybe just the biscuits if you want. I know you're closing the Emporium today."

"I'll do that. Kim and the kids got me a nice bread warmer for Christmas last year. It'll keep the biscuits toasty until we're ready to eat."

Callie and Luke were the first to arrive at Alma's that evening. "Hey, Alma," Callie called from the backdoor. "It's Luke and Callie."

"Come on in." Alma was adding a couple more pieces of chicken to the frying pan. "I'm nearly done here." Alma moved away from the stove as Luke and Callie came through the door.

"I'll just set the rolls here on the counter." Luke stepped around the hugging women.

"So what is this fancy thing you've got here, Callie?" Alma asked as she looked at the spherical container Luke put on the counter.

"It's called a penguin bread warmer," Callie laughed quietly. "Apparently, they were really popular in the early seventies and are making a comeback. Kim said she thought it would go with my Fiesta."

"Oh, with the little winglike black handles, the round black handle on the lid, and stainless outside, it does look something like a penguin." Alma shook her head and smiled.

"I think a bread basket is better on the table, but this does work well if you've got to hold the bread for a while." Callie took Alma's bread basket from the table and put a napkin in it. "I have to confess; I only use it when Kim and the kids eat with us." Callie smiled guiltily.

"I hear a car. I'll see if anyone needs a hand." Luke walked through the kitchen and into the living room to see who had pulled into the driveway. "It's Kim. I'll help her with the children."

No sooner than Kim and the children were inside, Max and Louise arrived. Within a few minutes, everyone took a seat around the dining room table. "Oh, I'm so thankful to have such good friends to share this meal with." Alma began passing the dishes. The talk centered on general topics as everyone turned their attention to the fried chicken, rice, gravy, and collard greens Alma had prepared.

After Allison and Avery excused themselves to go play outside, Kim turned to Luke and asked, "What did the guild think it would send to New York?"

"Actually, all we voted on was helping to sponsor events to raise money to be sent to New York," he said. "Several artists are donating works to raise money."

"Okay, at the clinic we're getting urgent requests for supplies and personnel from some hospitals as the injured have overwhelmed NYC hospitals," Kim said thoughtfully. "Jake is thinking about going to help in the hospitals since there are so many injured. Anyway, I was trying to think of a way we could combine our efforts."

Louise spoke up. "Alma, Callie, Max, and I were talking about holding a silent auction to raise money. She paused before continuing, "What if the Emporium becomes a drop off site and encourages people coming to the silent auction to bring in items as well."

Alma and Callie nodded in agreement. "That sounds like a good idea. I'll get to work with some other artists to get a few posters together. Maybe we could get some coverage from the TV stations," Luke said,

"If we coordinate with the local churches, we might have a little more impact," Alma suggested. "And maybe we can reach our goal more quickly. I know there's an urgent need for somethings."

The group quickly divided up the tasks needed to get the drive underway and helped clean up from supper. As everyone gathered on the porch before leaving, Callie asked about getting the donations to New York. "Let me think about that," Max said rubbing his hand across his forehead. "Some businesses use box trucks, so maybe that would be a way for them to help out. I know someone who might help."

Danny heard about the event and his marketing firm created a campaign to encourage people to donate for the relief effort. Television stations around the area aired it in free spots throughout the week.

Saturday morning, everyone gathered in the Emporium's gallery to put the final touches on the set up for the silent auction. Fabric screens and velvet ropes created a space in the main gallery area while hiding pieces that weren't up for auction. Several local restaurants were providing appetizers and beverages. They would arrive at six tonight for the event at seven.

Callie brushed the hair away from her face as she backed up to see as much of the room as possible. "I think we've got everything ready. What do you think, honey?"

Luke looked down from the ladder he was standing on. "Yeah, this is the last light adjustment." Alex, another artist from the guild, gave him a thumbs up. "I think you've got everything well placed from what I saw earlier." He slipped the screwdriver and pliers into his back pocket and climbed down.

"I can't think of anything else." Callie leaned against a nearby table. "Everyone has been so generous. There are paintings, sculpted pieces, pottery, jewelry and even some really nice textiles."

"I know and so many of them helped me make the screens to create a room that was the right size for them." Luke walked over to Callie. "The full gallery would have dwarfed them."

"Agreed." She stood up. "I'll get my stuff from the office and go home. Max is working today. I might take a nap. Are you ready to go?"

"No, I've got some things to put away first and Alex is still here. I'll see if he needs help." Luke kissed her before she turned to go.

"Do you have your keys?" She paused at the door. "If you do, I'll just walk home."

Luke patted his pockets. "Got 'em."

Sunday afternoon found Callie, Luke, and the others back at the Emporium. A local moving company had provided a large van along with materials to package the donations which had been dropped at the store. Now they had to organize and package everything.

"So how do we want to do this?" Alma asked as she looked at the items stacked in one of the smaller showrooms. "We should probably box up everything first. Some things like the canned goods that came in boxes from the grocery stores can just be put together on pallets and then wrapped with plastic. We should get that stuff together first," she added as she walked among the stacks of food, paper products and cleaning supplies. The hospital will bring their stuff over early Monday morning.

"Yeah, that sounds good." Callie pushed loose strands of hair under her ball cap. "I'll start with paper products and label the box as I fill it."

Everyone chose a category and began packing. After a while Luke, Max and Danny began moving boxes outside so they could see how to load things into the van. Around four, Kim left so she'd be there when Jake brought Allison and Avery home. By five the van was loaded and Louise, Callie and Alma had restored the gallery to its normal set up.

Max blew out a breath and rubbed his hand over his close-cropped hair. "Hmm, I'm ready to eat. How about everyone else?"

Wiping sweat from her forehead with a bandanna, Callie agreed. Louise looked at the wilted group draped across the tables in the lounge area and laughed. "Remember when we worked all day in the store and remodeled the addition? Heck, one of us would have had dinner going in the kitchen." Everyone chuckled, remembering their more youthful, energetic days.

"Well, why don't we just go to the diner on the Isle of Palms. We wouldn't have to change or anything," Alma suggested.

Danny declined, saying he should get home to his children. Everyone else heartily agreed and once they'd taken turns washing their face and hands in the Emporium's bathrooms, they climbed into Callie's SUV and headed to the Isle of Palms.

Over a simple meal, the friends reminisced about their time together on the island. As they finished eating, Luke reminded them that the hospital's donations would be delivered to the Emporium at six in the morning. With the check settled, they went to the Emporium where they split up and returned to their homes eager to get a good night's sleep before returning to load the van before the drivers arrived.

Going into the kitchen from the garage, Callie turned to Luke, "You've got to be tired, honey. Do you want to shower first?" Callie asked as she gave him a hug.

"No, you go ahead. I'll sit on the porch for a while," he said. "I'll get some tea. You just be sure to leave me some hot water."

"When do I ever take a shower long enough to use all the hot water?" She ruffled his hair, laughing as she walked away.

In a short while, Callie joined Luke on the porch. "It's been years since I've worked so hard," she said with a groan as she sat beside Luke on the wicker loveseat.

"I know, I don't think there's a place in my body that isn't sore." He smiled at Callie. "Still, I feel better at having done something. Even though I know it's just a drop in the bucket compared to what they need."

"You're right." Callie smiled back at him. "Go get your shower. It helps."

"I'll do that." He kissed her lightly before slowly getting up.

With Luke inside, Callie stayed on the loveseat a few minutes before moving to her wicker rocking chair. *There's something about rocking that's so calming. I don't know what this world is coming to. All those people whose lives will never be the same. Maybe it's like Momma used to say about visiting people from church. You can't change the world. So, you do an act of kindness for those you can and hope they spread it to others.*

By the time Callie went inside, Luke had gone to bed. She smiled at his sleeping form before she climbed into bed and curled up next to him. Without waking, Luke murmured something and adjusted himself to fit more closely to her.

17

Kim October 2001

I could really go for about a week's vacation. Kim gathered her signed notes into a neat stack. *Everything at the clinic is in a mess since the sale last month. Already they're cutting back on staff. Thank goodness Crystal is still here. Management is expecting me to see three more patients a day. That means twenty minutes per patient unless it's a new patient. That's just not enough time. I'll get my bag ready and leave after dropping off my notes.*

As she walked down the hall, she realized everyone had left for the day. Kim unlocked the mail room and checked her box. Thankful it was empty, she put her folder of patient notes in Crystal's box. Looking at her watch, Kim hurried to the car. She needed to pick Allison and Avery up from their after-school program in the next thirty minutes or pay an outrageous hourly rate in addition to the monthly rate.

Pulling into a parking space, Kim felt relieved. *Ten minutes to spare.* She locked the car door and hurried inside. *Somedays I feel like I'm always on the run, trying to beat the clock.* Children waited for pickup in the small library near the entrance. She waved at the staff member on duty and went to join Allison and Avery. The twins were playing Candyland with another child. "Hey, guys," she said as she sat on one of the small chairs. "Is your game nearly finished?"

"If Thomas doesn't go back, he wins," Allison announced and ran to hug her mother.

"Hey sweetheart. Did you have a good day?" Kim asked as she wrapped her arms around her daughter.

"Yes, Mommy. At school, I wrote my name. Oh, look. Thomas wins."

"Hey, Mommy. We've got to help put this away," Avery told her as Kim gave him a quick hug.

"Okay. I'll grab your bags while you do that."

It was just a short ten-minute drive home. "Here we are. 'Home again, home again'," Kim sang as she helped each child out of their car seats.

The twins finished the line, laughing as they raced to the door. "Jiggety jig."

"Remember to hang up your book bags before you go upstairs." Kim picked up the mail from the floor at the front door. She tossed it onto the counter to look at later. *I need to put a basket under the mail slot. Don't know why I never did it before.* "Dinner will be ready in about thirty minutes," she told the children as they raced up the stairs. "Avery, go to the bathroom and come back down. It's your turn to set the table."

"Yes Mommy," he answered from the top of the stairs.

Kim started the rice, put plates and utensils on the island for Avery and began chopping broccoli. *I'm glad the twins like stir fry. It makes supper so much easier during the week.*

"Mommy, what's for dinner," Avery asked as he set up their places at the kitchen island.

"Chicken and broccoli," Kim answered putting the broccoli in the wok. "It'll be ready in a few minutes. Okay?"

"I'm hungry." Avery hugged her leg.

"Do you want a bite of broccoli? It's a little hot," Kim pulled a broccoli floret out of the wok and put it on Avery's plate.

"Thanks, Mommy." Avery climbed into his seat.

In less than a minute, Allison made her way into the kitchen. "I'm hungry," she said.

Funny how they always seem to know what the other twin is doing even when they aren't together. Or maybe she's just hungry, too. But still, they always seem to know where the other one is. "Here you go, Allison. I put broccoli on your plate."

Kim turned back to the stove. "I'm getting everything ready to put on the table."

After fixing a plate for each of the children, Kim served herself. "Avery, how was your day?" she asked.

"Okay. We had recess. And we wrote our names," he answered and then went back to eating.

Allison told her about the new child in their after-school group. Kim usually tried to have short conversations with them over supper. It was good practice for them and Kim felt it made the meal more enjoyable.

With the twins in bed, Kim started a load of laundry and then went into the living room. *Maybe I can finish the article I started last night. I need a few more continuing education credits for the year. I'd like to go to the convention in Columbia next August, but I don't think I'll be able to unless I can work something out for the twins with Jake. I'm so tired. Wish the laundry was done and I could go to bed.*

Kim woke with a start. *Oh man, I fell asleep.* The washer had completed its cycle so she put the towels in the dryer. *I'll fold these later. I'm going to bed. At least, I don't have to be at work until Monday.*

On Saturday, after parking the car and leaving the twins upstairs, Kim went out to the deck looking for her mother. "What do we need to do out here, Momma?" She leaned over the deck railing and looked down at her mother in the yard.

"Let's get the flowers and citronella candles on the picnic tables." Callie shielded her eyes from the sun with her hand as she looked up at Kim. "I've already got the buffet table set up so we'll be able to put the food out when it's time. There's not much else to do. Where are the twins?" Callie made her way to the deck with bunches of black-eyed susans from her garden.

"Upstairs right now. I'm glad we decided to go ahead and have this. It will be good to see everyone on a happy occasion." Kim winced and then continued, "Sorry, Momma." *The last time we all got together was at Grandma's funeral.* She began setting up the tables.

"It's okay sweetie." Callie stopped arranging the flowers and looked at her daughter. "That's one of the reasons I wanted to keep the traditional October gathering. Besides, everyone's getting older. We should relish every chance we have to get together with our island family."

Josie and her husband, Tom, were among the first to arrive. "Hey, Callie. Where should I put this stuff?" Josie asked as she made her way across the deck, shopping bags hung from her shoulders and she gripped the handles to keep them in place.

"Come over here." Callie pointed to the table she had set up for food as she hurried to help her friend. "Let me carry something."

"I've got it," Josie insisted. "Besides, if I let go of a bag, I'll probably drop everything."

"Okay. I've got serving utensils out and ice so we can keep the potato salad chilled." Callie reached under the table to get ice from a cooler. *It's so cool that everyone on the island when I first came here still get together. Josie has been such a good friend.*

"Great. Where's Luke?" Josie asked looking around the yard.

"He's helping Alma bring her pies over," Callie said. "I'm so glad she's still baking. I make a good cake, but my pie crust is awful."

Max and Louise arrived next. Shortly after that Danny arrived with his mom, Linda, and his two children. Kim offered to help take food to the table so his mother could sit down. The children followed them onto the deck.

"Let's find Avery and Allison. They've got some toys out here, " Kim said once they arranged the food on the table.

After they made introductions, Danny and Kim sat together so they could keep an eye on the children as they ran through the yard. "It's funny, from the time I was five or six, I played out here all the time without Momma being right with me," Kim said shaking her head. "And now we hardly let them out of our sight."

"Yeah, but your two are four. Susie's five and Tommy's seven. So, I don't think we're too over protective." Danny sat back laughing as the children chased a frisbee.

"Got a point there. Looks like everyone's here so maybe we should round up the kids and eat."

Kim and the twins sat at a table with Danny and his family. She found it interesting to learn that his mother was a registered nurse and she kept her license active even though she hadn't worked away from home since her daughter-in-law died in a car accident a few years ago. She moved to Charleston after Danny's dad died. He had been caught in the crossfire of a gang shoot out.

The children finished their food and ran off to play. Linda quietly followed them, leaving Kim and Danny alone at the table.

"Your mother's pretty amazing. I didn't know until tonight that she was one of the home health nurses who cared for Alma after her first heart attack." Kim watched Linda chase after the children.

"Yeah, she's worked as long as I can remember." Danny sipped his tea, wincing with remembered pain. "When my dad was killed, the family wanted her to remarry right away. But she wanted to get us away from the gangs, so she brought me and my sister here. Then when Melissa died, she took off to help me with the children. It was just so hard trying to find someone to care for them while I was at work. Anyway, she wound up moving in with me and the kids,"

"It's awesome that she could do that." Kim turned to watch the children chase fireflies. "I had a nanny come in when I went back to work. She kept working until the twins were in preschool and then she retired. I've got them in an after-school program, but I wish there was a better way." Kim shrugged and then stood up. "Let me take this stuff up to the kitchen. I'll need to get the twins home before long."

"I'll give you a hand." Danny began gathering plates and followed Kim to the kitchen.

The following Monday, Kim was in a meeting with Dr. Abrams and two representatives from the corporate office. They were reviewing her agreement with Dr. Abrams for him to provide the requisite supervision as outlined by the state board of nursing. Unlike the board of nursing which required her to have approval of the state medical board and a collaborative practice agreement with a physician, the corporate office was now requiring she provide documentation of the times she and Dr. Abrams met to discuss patients.

"This is placing an additional documentation burden on both Dr. Abrams and me. Do I understand this correctly, you want us to designate a time to meet and discuss patients?" Kim bit her lower lip as she struggled to stay calm. *They want me to see three more patients a day and now they want a weekly meeting with my supervising physician. What would I do if I had someone besides Dr. Abrams? I thought we were going to discuss ways to improve patient care and maybe getting some updated equipment in.*

"Yes. In recent audits by third party payors, there have been questions surrounding the actual times a nurse practitioner met with her supervising physician. We need to be sure there is no question that both parties are complying with the regulations," Judith, the corporation's Quality Assurance person, insisted.

"But we discuss patients as the need arises. We don't go over every patient on her caseload and another meeting would cut into Kim's time with patients. Particularly, since I no longer see patients here." Dr. Abrams shifted in his chair as if he might get up and leave the meeting. Shaking his head, he crossed his arms over his chest. "Why couldn't a running log work?"

The two lawyers conferred quietly for a moment. "Yes, that could work. You both need to sign off on it weekly though."

Kim smiled at Dr. Abrams. "I can pull something together. I'll fax it to your home office Friday afternoon and you fax it back on Monday. How's that?"

"Okay. But I'm going on the record to say this is unnecessary." Dr. Abrams looked at his watch and stood abruptly. "Now that's settled you don't need me here."

Without Dr. Abrams, the meeting broke up quickly. Kim was disappointed to learn that the proposed budget didn't allow for purchasing any new equipment or hiring another nurse to help Crystal and Rose with their caseload. *I don't know why they don't listen to the people doing the job.* Kim gathered her notes and hurried to see her next patient. *Of course, they danced around the idea of hiring another psychiatric-mental health nurse practitioner since they can't seem to attract another psychiatrist.*

On her way to pick up the twins, Kim thought about her plans for the weekend. *Another exciting weekend of housekeeping.* The nurses at the clinic had tried to talk her into going out for a few drinks on Saturday, but she had begged off even though the twins were with Jake for the weekend. *Just because Jake and I have separated doesn't mean I'm looking for someone else. Of course, going out for a few drinks doesn't mean you're looking for someone, but I just never got into that scene. Oh well, I have loads of time to figure this out.*

At home, Kim helped the twins change and get ready for their dad to pick them up. Tonight's dinner would just be hot dogs and fruit along with macaroni and cheese. Something quick and simple. Earlier, Crystal had questioned why Kim didn't just have Jake pick the children up from daycare. It would be easier, but Kim liked seeing the children before they went off for the weekend. Besides Jake had only been in his apartment for a few months and was still getting things set up for the children.

Once they finished eating, Avery stood looking out the tall kitchen window which faced the street. "Daddy's here," he yelled running to the front door and bolting outside as Jake came up the walk.

Allison was right behind him and clamored for her share of their dad's attention. Jake scooped up both children and continued up the walk. Kim met them at the door.

I've got to be sure and use the deadbolt before one of the twins decides to take a walk. "Hey, Jake. Come in." Kim backed out of the doorway. "How was your day?"

"Not too bad." He sat the children down on the floor. "Hey, guys. How about you play for a few minutes while Mommy and Daddy talk? Then we'll go."

Kim watched both children take off for the play room. "They've had a really good week." She sat down at the kitchen island and showed Jake their folders. "These are the things they're doing in preschool."

"Wow, they're getting pretty good at writing their names." Jake looked through each folder.

"They have. I put some extra clothes in their back packs. You can keep them at your place. They both ate well for dinner, but they might want a snack later. I don't know your routine with them, but we started having an early movie night on Friday's. Generally, it's a Disney tape."

"Oh, well that sounds pretty good. I'll see what they want to do when I get home. I've been picking up some of the tapes I know they like. If the weather is nice tomorrow, I thought I'd take them to the park." Jake pushed back the hair that fell to his forehead. "I've been looking at moving strictly to day shift so I can see the twins more often. If I need to, I'll only pickup extra shifts when they're with you."

Kim took a deep breath and exhaled slowly. "I suppose that makes some sense. We do need to make some sort of formal arrangement. It would be better for them if they know what to expect," She paused a minute before adding. "I want to have a birthday party for them at Chuck E Cheese. What's your schedule like?"

"Just tell me the date and I'll be sure I'm off."

"Okay, I'll schedule it for the afternoon a week from tomorrow." Kim got up and added a note to the calendar. "Let's get the car seats shifted so it won't be so late when you get them to your place." She added as she turned to go down the hall to the garage.

"All right, they'll be in booster seats soon and it'll be easier to make the switch," Jake got up and followed her to the garage. "Oh, I'll grab the back packs, too."

Kim hugged both children tightly before helping buckle them into their car seats. "I'll see you Sunday night. Have fun with Daddy," she told them before going back inside. *Lord, I miss them already. Everything is too quiet without them here.*

The following weekend, Kim loaded the cake, party favors, decorations and presents into the car. Smiling she went inside. *Hope they like everything.*

"Come on kiddos," Kim called from the bottom of the stairs. "We need to get going or you'll be late for your own party."

"Coming, Mommy." Allison started down the stairs. "I wanted to get my baby."

Avery hurried down the stairs, bumping his sister as he passed her. "Watch out, Avery." She plopped down on the stairs. Her lower lip stuck out in a pout.

"Sorry," Avery called up to his sister from the bottom of the stairs.

"Allison, are you okay?" Kim asked. She had seen the incident and felt Allison was okay, but wanted to give her daughter a chance to speak for herself.

"I'm okay." Allison stood up and started down the stairs again.

Kim turned her attention to her son. "Avery, hurrying so fast on the stairs could get you or someone else hurt."

"Yes, ma'am." He turned to look at his mother.

"I know you're just excited, but we have to watch out for others. Let's get your shoes on." Kim bent down to help them put on their shoes.

Once the children were in the car, it was just a short drive to Chuck E Cheese. Seeing Jake's car in the parking lot, she decided to take the twins inside before bringing in the things from her trunk. After setting things up, Kim sat at a table drinking coffee with parents while Jake took the twins off to explore. *I always feel so awkward when there are couples. And besides, today Jake is here. He sometimes tries to act like we might get back together and gets possessive when single men are around.* Looking out the window, she noticed Danny and his children walking across the parking lot.

"Hey Kim, thanks for inviting us." Danny put a present on a nearby table with the other presents and a cake. "I'll get Tommy and Susie settled."

He was back with a drink in a few minutes. "How's everything going?" He asked as he sat down. "Where'd everyone go?"

"Playing with the children. Some of the moms don't quite know what to think about my having a full-time career. as well as my separation from Jake," Kim looked down at her coffee.

"Yeah, it's hard when you first start going out without your spouse." Danny smiled ruefully. "It eventually gets easier."

"I'm sure it will. I think they have a hard time because they can't decide which box to put me in." Kim shook her head. "I don't know why. That's not true. I do know, but what they don't realize is that I still have the same problems they do."

Out of the corner of her eye, Kim caught Jake frowning as he looked at her and Danny. *Isn't that something? That goof. Danny's just a friend. And what's it to him anyway?*

Jake crossed the room and stood by Kim's chair without acknowledging Danny. "When are the kids going to eat?"

"Jake this is Danny, an old family friend. Danny, this is Jake. The twins' dad." Jake frowned. *Don't be so childish.* "Let's get them all to the table here," she said as she stood. "I'm sure they're ready to eat now. Then we can do the presents."

Later that evening, once Avery and Allison were asleep, Kim called her mother as she had promised and gave her a rundown of the party. She was surprised to learn that her mother hadn't taken a walk today even though the weather had been perfect for walking. Before hanging up, Kim promised to bring the twins over in a couple of weeks since they would be with Jake next weekend. *Maybe I should go see her this weekend. Momma didn't seem like herself while we were on the phone.*

18

Callie November 2001

Luke made his way from the studio through the open garage. Seeing Callie's walking shoes by the door so early in the day, he continued into the kitchen. "Callie? Callie, honey? Where are you?"

"I'm in the living room. Reading." Callie marked her place with a finger and closed the book.

"Oh, back from your walk already?" Luke sat down beside her on the couch and kissed her gently.

"No, I just feel off. Don't have much energy." Callie leaned against Luke's shoulder. She set her book aside on the nearby end table.

"Hmm." Luke bent his head against hers. "So what are you up to today?"

"I don't know. I'm not scheduled at the Emporium. Guess I'll straighten up the house. I should work on Mom's and Dad's old room." Callie sighed and leaned on the couch.

Luke put his arm around her and she snuggled in closer. "Do you want me to bring the things in from the garage? I've got time to do that before I leave for my meeting."

"No, don't bother. I'm not really ready for that stuff. I have to pack a few small things to send to Dad. I should have done it months ago, but I can't seem to get going." Callie shifted listlessly in Luke's arm. "Maybe I'll just read here while you're gone."

"Okay then, if you don't need my help, I'll leave now." He eased his arm from around her and stood up.

Callie sat up slowly. "Okay." She tilted her head up for Luke's good-bye kiss. "I'll be here when you get back."

"I'll be gone a couple of hours." He turned to go to the garage.

On his way off the island, Luke stopped at the Emporium. Waving at Alex, who was rearranging a display, he continued to the counter. "Hey, Alma. How's things going today?"

"Pretty good. Made several nice sales as people are starting to buy early Christmas presents." Alma tilted her head to look closely at his face. "Is everything okay?"

"Well, I don't know." Luke hesitated. His lips formed a tight line before he spoke. "I'm just a little worried about Callie."

"Come on to the office and have a cup of coffee." Alma turned toward the front of the store. "Alex, we'll be in the office for a little while."

Seated next to him with coffee, Alma encouraged Luke to continue. "Callie's just not acting like herself. She's not walking. She still hasn't redone the bedroom downstairs where her parents stayed. Usually, she'd have redone that room within a week. Kim's concerned, too." Luke's voice trailed off as he stared into the coffee cup cradled between his hands.

"Luke, she's still grieving." Alma patted his arm. "And everybody does that differently."

"I know, but she doesn't seem to want to talk about her mother or the fact that her dad moved in with Bobby and his family." Luke shrugged and shook his head. "I just don't know how to help her. I can't stand seeing her like this. I don't want to lose her." He brushed at the tears gathering in the corners of his eyes.

"I don't think you have to worry about that. Maybe she's having a hard time talking about Lydia with you because you don't know their history like some of us." Alma took a sip of her coffee before continuing. "I've been trying to give her a bit of space. But maybe it's time for that to change. I'll stop in to see her soon while you're off to Charleston or something."

Luke and Alma stood up from the table. He hugged his dear friend. "I was hoping you'd say that. Thanks. Guess I'd better get going. I might still make my meeting on time."

True to her word, Alma stopped by the house a few days later, when Max was covering the Emporium and Luke had called to say he was out for the day. "Hey, Callie, it's me," Alma said as she walked into the kitchen from the back porch.

"I'm in the living room," Callie called out. "I'll be right there." She wore an old, oversized sweat shirt and jeans. Her hair was tussled as if she'd just got out of bed.

"Thought I'd drop in and see how things are going." Alma walked through the kitchen and into the living room.

Callie put her notebook aside and stood up to hug her friend. "Things are okay. I should be planning Thanksgiving dinner. You know Bobby's family and Dad are joining us this year." She stepped back from her friend's embrace and ran her fingers through her hair. "Would you like something to drink. I've got iced tea or I could put some coffee on."

Alma sat at the kitchen island. "How about starting some coffee. There's a bit of chill in the air today. Should've put on a sweater."

Callie started coffee and took a couple of mugs from the cabinet. By the time the coffee finished brewing, she had placed milk and sugar on the island. Bringing the filled mugs with her, she sat down near her friend. "So, what have you been up to."

"Not too much or rather just the usual." Alma stirred sugar and milk into her coffee. "So when's everyone coming for Thanksgiving?"

"They should get in the Wednesday afternoon before Thanksgiving." Callie shrugged her shoulders.

"Is there something I can do to help out? We've all been really busy since September, but I've got some time now," Alma offered before sipping her coffee. "Where's your notebook?" She looked around the kitchen. "Is it in the living room? I can get it for you"

"No, I'll grab it." Callie got up from the island. "Be right back."

When Callie returned to the kitchen, Alma asked, "Now what's on the list?"

"Oh, I can't seem to even get my list started. The menu's easy. I'll just do everyone's favorites and as it gets closer, I'll plug in the start times since Kim is helping this year." She sat staring at the blank page of her notebook. Tears formed in the corners of her eyes and she puffed out a breath. "I need to get the downstairs bedroom ready. Dad will need it when he comes. Every time I get started; I keep thinking of the Thanksgiving when Momma had her crisis." Callie rubbed at her eyes with her fingers and fought to keep from crying.

Alma put her arms around her friend and patted her back. "There, there sugar. It's going to be okay. These first holidays after someone passes are so hard. I remember."

Callie sniffled. "We had some great holidays afterwards. I don't know why I'm stuck on that one. I wish I could have been a better daughter. That I could have helped her sooner."

"Now, Callie. You know you can't help anyone until they let you. Right? And when Lydia allowed it, you were right there with her." Alma settled back into her chair. "I've always said that we each grieve in our own way, but I'll not let you beat yourself up for things you couldn't control."

"I know you're right. But still, it's hard." Callie got up to blow her nose. After washing her hands, she returned to the island. "Do you need a warm up for your coffee?"

"Yeah, this cup is cold already," Alma answered with a smile.

As she settled at the island again, Alma drew her out about things happening with the twins. After a while Alma asked, "Want to show me what you have planned for the downstairs bedroom?"

With a wane smile, Callie agreed. Grabbing the notebook and a pen, Alma followed her down the hall. As she put her hand on the doorknob, Callie paused for a moment, "I haven't been in here since Dad moved. My dust bunnies have probably had babies."

"So, did you want to paint in here?" Alma asked as she looked around the room. "I don't see any marks on the walls or anything. No need, unless you want a new color."

"No, I don't think it needs to be repainted. I like this pale blue." Callie slowly turned to view the whole room. "I do need new curtains and bed linens. There's a full-size bed in the garage. Dad took theirs to Bobby's along with their other bedroom furniture. He took a lot of their knick-knacks, too, so I have to fill the built-ins. There are a few things I need to send back with Dad."

"Okay, I'm writing curtains, bed linens, knick-knacks and gather up Dad's things on the list." Alma sat at the desk left over from the days when this was Kim's childhood room. "Anything else?"

"No, I don't think so." Callie walked along the built-in cabinets before adding. "I've got pictures and other things around the house I can bring in here. Then there's a great piece at the Emporium. It's blown glass, blues, greens, and a little white twirled in. Even though it's an abstract piece, it makes me think of ocean waves."

Alma made a couple of notes, looked up at her friend and laughed. "Let's go have another cup of coffee before I get back to my own mess of a house."

Callie joined her laughter as they walked along the hall. "Like your house is ever a mess. What does that even mean? Did you leave breakfast dishes in the sink?"

Alma chuckled to herself as Callie began jotting down the Thanksgiving menu while they finished their coffee. Callie looked up from her notebook, "Alma, I don't know..."

"Hush now, my friend. We've been helping each other for a very long time. This just happens to be my turn." Alma made a dismissive motion with her hand. "But I really have to get home now." She got up and picked up her cup.

"I've got that." Callie stood and hugged her friend.

"Promise you'll call when you get stuck again?" Alma turned toward the door.

"It's a promise," Callie said walking her friend to the door before going back the island to finish planning for Thanksgiving.

Several days later, Kim and the twins came to visit. When everyone returned from a seaside walk, Callie said, "I've got some pictures and other things from your grandma. I'll bring the box into the kitchen and you can look at them."

As the women settled at the kitchen island, Callie reached into the box, pulled out several placemats and coaster sets her mother had made over the years and handed

them to Kim. "Not all of these really go with your décor," Callie said somewhat apologetically. "But I thought the lemons might be fun in the summer and there are some specific to holidays."

Kim ran her hands along the fabric. "Oh, Momma. These are beautiful. I remember her lemon-yellow kitchen and all the times we ate there. I'm sure I can use them."

Callie teared up for a moment, blinked a few times and then smiled. "I've still got plenty, but I was hoping you'd like to have some."

"I'm happy to have these, but what about Uncle Bobby?" Kim asked as she watched her mother take a sip of coffee.

"Oh, I have some set aside for him. Here are a few pictures, I didn't have them framed. You can decide how you want to display them."

Kim took the stack of pictures from her mother, smiling as she looked at them. "Oh, these are from the first time we went to the nursing home with Grandma. I remember she made us line up at the entrance."

"She really liked to document our lives with pictures. She was so much better at that than I am." Callie pointed to another snapshot. "Look, here's one of you in your playroom at the Emporium."

"Oh, my. I was so little." Kim continued shifting through the pictures, scowling as she held up an older snapshot. "Who are these people in front of the clerk's office? I feel like I should remember them."

"Those are your great grandparents, Cynthia and Raymond Simmons," Callie said softly.

"Oh, yeah. I remember now. She died tragically and he left Grandma and her sister with family. An aunt, right? Didn't he write Grandma a letter when I was in high school? Whatever happened about that? I don't recall ever hearing about it after you and Luke made that trip to Columbia to show her the letter."

Callie got up to refill her coffee and returned to the island before answering. "Do you remember hearing that he dropped Grandma and her sister, Sally, off when she was four, promising to return? And never did."

"Well, yes. But then..."

"Anyway, just as Grandma was doing so well in therapy and Luke and I were about to get married, he decided he wanted to make amends."

"No, you're not serious." Kim got up, took pimento cheese out of the refrigerator and a pack of crackers from a cabinet. Setting them on the island, she looked intently at her mother. "So, go on."

Callie put some pimento cheese on a cracker. "Momma wrote him a letter basically saying, 'He was a day late and a dollar short'. Still, it's the only picture we have of her mother so I've always displayed it. This is a copy I had made for you."

"Wow, I never knew all that." Kim looked at her mother with sudden understanding. "That's why Grandma was always so anxious about us?"

"Yep, but she eventually conquered those fears." Callie shook her head. "I don't usually tell that part when I talk about her coming to Charleston with Aunt Sally, but I'm glad you asked."

"She always had more spunk than she gave herself credit for."

Alma and Callie had several more conversations about her relationship with her mother before Thanksgiving. She found one conversation particularly comforting. Alma had stopped by for morning coffee on her way to the Emporium and found her friend in the doldrums again.

"Okay, sugar plum. What's got you down this morning?" Alma asked as she settled next to Callie at the kitchen island with a cup of coffee.

"I can't seem to forget all the times Momma and I butted heads." Callie stared down at her cup.

"Honey, all that happened when you were trying to get your own life going and your mother was caught up in all her anxiety." Alma patted her friend's arm. "Even then, I never heard you be disrespectful to your mother. Firm in your decision, but not disrespectful. Take heart in that."

"Maybe you're right, Alma." Callie took a drink of her coffee and scrunched up her face. "This has gotten cold. Do you need a warm-up, too?"

"No, I'd better get going. See you this afternoon," Alma said as she left.

Alma was right. I was a good daughter and things with Momma did get better over the years. I can't worry about things I can't change. I've got to work on remembering the good years we had.

Thanksgiving came and went. Callie and Luke began preparing for their Christmas celebration with Kim and the children. Allison and Avery would be spending Christmas with Jake, but would celebrate with their mother, Callie, and Luke on Christmas Eve. This year Callie planned to incorporate family stories of her mother and a visit to a local nursing home in the celebration.

A few days before Christmas Eve, Callie sat on the front porch in her wicker rocking chair watching the sunrise. The clear sky held promise of a balmy day. Spanish moss wafted in the gentle breeze. Sipping her coffee while thinking about the last few months since her mother died made Callie shake her head slowly. *I really didn't mean to worry anyone. Kim started with Luke and then Luke talked with Alma. They all thought I was depressed, but I was just terribly sad. Dad went to live with Barby and there was no one to talk to about the old days. Hmph, I just missed Momma. We had finally gotten closer. Alma was right when she said we need to talk about those we've lost. Even though she didn't know Momma when they were younger, Alma knew how I struggled in our relationship.* Callie watched the herons fly overhead, taking mighty strokes until they found an air current and began to soar with their wings fully extended. *I could sit here all day. Just watching the birds at the feeders and in the trees, but I need to go into the Emporium early this morning, so I'd better get moving.*

19

Kim August 2003

Curled in the loveseat on her back porch with a cup of coffee, Kim smiled as she looked over the yard and admired the way her mother had helped her transform the townhouse's postage stamp yard into a garden oasis in the middle of Charleston. Over the last couple of years, they had planted two little gem magnolias, crepe myrtle trees as well as daffodils, irises, and many of the other flowers Kim grew up with, like rose campion and coneflowers. She had tried black-eyed susans in remembrance of her grandmother, but they tended to take over. By the time they finished with the plantings, all the grass in the back yard was gone. Now only flowers, short winding paths and a few benches populated the yard. Breathing deeply, she inhaled the magnolias' heavy scent and thought about the upcoming week.

Allison and Avery will be home in time for supper today. Next week, we'll have to go shopping for school clothes. Jake said he'd do some shopping this weekend, but much of that will stay at his house. I don't really like this business of alternating weekly, but it seems to be working out okay for Allison and Avery. That's what's really important.

Once he got back from his stint of volunteering in New York after 9/11, Jake seemed to settle into acceptance and allowed the divorce to go through without any hassle. *Still, I can't believe they're going into the first grade.* She got up to go inside. The phone ringing interrupted her thoughts.

"Oh, hi Mom," Kim said answering the phone. Her mother told her she had picked up a couple of outfits for Allison and Avery while she was shopping in Charleston last week and wanted to come over on the weekend so the children could try them on. "Okay, come over on Saturday around lunchtime. That will give me time to do some shopping Sunday afternoon to pick up a few school supplies and an outfit or two." Kim agreed before hanging up the phone.

After starting a pot of spaghetti sauce, Kim went into the living room to finish the journal article she started reading last night. She frowned as her cell phone rang again. Answering, she recognized Burt's voice, the physician's assistant who recently started at the clinic. He asked her out for next Saturday. "I can't go next Saturday; I've got my twins then." He tried to convince her to get a babysitter for the night and didn't seem to understand her reluctance to do so since she and their father shared custody. Frustrated with his attitude, Kim didn't suggest they go out on the following weekend.

While she tried to refocus on the article, Kim's thoughts kept returning to the phone call. *I'm not sure if I'm not interested in dating or just not interested in Burt.* Not willing to delve into her feelings about dating, she tried again to focus on the article. As her thoughts began to wander again, she tossed the journal aside and decided to clean the kids bathroom upstairs. *I can't stand just sitting around and if I do it now it will be one less thing to do this weekend.* She moved on to her bathroom and was just finishing when she heard the doorbell.

Glancing at the clock in the hall, Kim hurried downstairs. As she opened the door and knelt down, Avery and Allison ran into her arms. "How are my best buddies doing?" She asked as she smothered them with kisses. "Okay now, come on inside so we can close the door."

Both children headed for their playroom. "Hey, hang up your bookbags first." Kim turned to Jake. "Do you want some coffee? It won't take but a minute to brew."

"Sure," he answered as he sat at the kitchen island. "Things were pretty quiet this past week. No bad dreams or anything." For a while, the twins had gone through a period where they were having bad dreams, but thankfully not night terrors. Still, it seemed that when one of them started with bad dreams, then the other twin would start having similar nightmares. Kim didn't know if it was a twin thing or something else. She was just thankful the children were resting better.

Kim started the coffee and leaned against the counter as it brewed. "So you think, they're adjusting to the weekly arrangement?" Kim asked as she took two cups from the cabinet.

"Yeah, at home I have a calendar for them. Together we put a "D" on the days they'll be with me and a "M" on the days they'll be with you." Jake shrugged. "I don't know if it will work, but at different times they each went to the calendar."

Kim poured the coffee and handed a cup to Jake before getting the milk from the refrigerator. "They could find the right day?" She asked as she sat down.

"Well, no, but once I showed them the correct day, they could count the number of days before they came here."

"Okay, okay." Kim nodded. "Maybe I'll make one for them here." She gave him a copy of a calendar that the school emailed her. "When we go to open house, we can ask again for them to email to both of us."

"Sounds good. Like I said everything went smoothly." Jake drained his coffee cup and stood up. "I'm picking up a shift tomorrow and I need to get some laundry done. I keep everything neat, but don't get too involved with other stuff when the twins are with me."

Kim walked him to the door. "Okay, I'm taking them clothes shopping this weekend. Do you have enough of everything for them to start the school year?"

"Yeah, we've been shopping a couple of times." Jake paused with his hand on the doorway leading into the hall. "But I want to get some extra school supplies, so it's not a crisis if they run out of something while doing homework. I'll go say good-bye to Allison and Avery." He went to see the kids in the playroom.

Kim was at the front door when he returned. "See you, later."

"Yeah, see you later." Kim closed the door. Going into the playroom, she sat on the floor near her children. "Did you have fun at Daddy's?"

"Oh, yes." Allison smiled up at her. "We went to the park and I went on the big slide by myself." The six-year old's eyes danced with excitement.

"What a big girl you are, Allison. Kim turned to look at Avery who was intent on "fixing" the wheels of a toy truck.

"And we went to the store and got new clothes for school." Avery puffed out his chest. "I got to pick out my own shirts and some jeans."

"Whoa, you're growing so fast." Kim beamed at him. "I'm making spaghetti for supper tonight. Does that sound okay?" she asked as she stood up.

"Hmm, good." Avery rubbed his tummy.

"I like it." Allison chimed in.

"Okay, I'll cook the pasta and garlic bread. It won't be too long before it's ready."

Saturday, Kim saw her mother's arrival through the kitchen window and met her at the door. "Mom, what have you got there." She laughed as Callie struggled to contain her packages while holding the storm door open.

"Well, I've got outfits for the twins and pimento cheese spread for you." Callie handed one of the bags to Kim and came inside.

Hearing their grandmother, Allison and Avery ran into the kitchen, tackling Callie as she knelt down to give them a hug. "Hey there. You guys give the best hugs ever. Come into the living room and see what I brought you."

Kim put the pimento cheese spread away before joining them. Each child dug into a shopping bag and held up an article of clothing before digging into the bag again.

"More jeans. " Avery dug further into his bag. "And a dinosaur shirt. Dinosaurs are my favorite, " he said with a huge grin.

"What have you got there, Allison?" Kim asked as her daughter held up a tunic dress.

"Look, a purple dress. I love purple. It's my favorite color." Allison grinned as she held the dress up under her chin. "Is it too short,

Momma?" Recently, Kim had put away some of Allison's older dresses because they were "too short".

"No, sweetheart," Callie said as Kim shook her head. "Look in the bag. There's a pair of purple shorts with white polka dots. They're to wear with the dress so you can still climb around."

"Momma, these outfits are so cute. What do you say, kiddos." Kim looked at each of the twins.

"Thank you, Grandma," they said together.

"Can we go play now?" Avery asked.

"Sure, We can try these on later." Kim said as she put the clothes back in the bag as the twins ran off to the playroom. Turning to her mother, she asked, "These look like they'll fit. Sorry, I didn't ask before, would you like some coffee?"

"Sounds great." Her mother followed her into the kitchen. On the way, she stuck her head around the door way to be sure Allison and Avery were still in the playroom. "How are you doing with the twins being with Jake for a week at a time?"

"It still seems weird." Kim filled two mugs with coffee. Giving one to her mother, she sat down. "The twins seem fine, so that's what really matters. I usually spend extra time in the office when they're with him or work on a big project at home."

"Well, yes, that's important, but what are you doing for yourself?" Callie asked as she took the milk out of the refrigerator and joined her daughter. "You need to have a life of your own."

"I don't know. Burt, from work, asked me out for this weekend, but I don't want to leave the children with a sitter when they're with me." Kim sipped her coffee.

"Yeah, I see that, but if it were something you wanted to do, Allison and Avery could spend a night with me."

"He didn't seem to understand working around the kiddos schedule so I don't think anything will come of it."

"Well, just keep my offer in mind. Okay?" Callie finished her coffee and put the mug in the sink. She stopped by her daughter's chair. "Last time I was here, I promised to play Chutes and Ladders on my next visit. I'd better go do that now, but you remember to take care of yourself."

Kim hugged her mother. "I won't forget. Get set up and I'll join you guys in a minute. I've got to throw some things in the dryer."

Avery and Allison had gone to sleep without a hassle. Her cell phone rang as she went through the house straightening up a few things. "Oh, hi Danny. How's the family?" After talking for a while, he asked when the children would next be with Jake.

"He'll pick them up here Friday after school. They'll be with him until the following Friday."

"I've got tickets to a show next Saturday. It's a fundraiser for the women's center here in Charleston." He hesitated a minute. "Would you like to go with me?"

"Well..." She took a deep breath. Letting it out slowly, she continued, "Sure, what time? *Well, at least I know he understands "life with children". I've enjoyed the times we spent together with our kids. Besides this isn't really a date.*

"The show starts at eight. What if we grab a bite to eat beforehand? Say six-thirty?"

"Alright. Are they doing a gala? What should I wear?" Kim went upstairs and began looking through her closet as they talked.

"No, it's not black tie. I'll wear a sport coat, no tie."

"Okay. It sounds like fun." They discussed a few restaurants before hanging up and Kim continued sorting through her dresses. *Wow, everything I own is either 'Mommy and children' or business casual.* Her hand paused over a mid-length black dress with simple red stitching around the slightly scooped neckline. It was still in the dry cleaner's bag. *Oh, I forgot about this. Do I still have those black pumps?* After rummaging through shoe boxes on the closet shelf, she found the shoes she was looking for and slipped them on. *Great, these are still comfortable. Okay, that's settled. My pearls will be perfect with this outfit. It'll be nice to dress up for a change.*

Pulling into the clinic parking lot after dropping Alison and Avery at day care on Monday morning, Kim sighed as she considered the day ahead of her. *Five new patients plus four follow-ups. And I'm supposed to only take forty-five minutes with each of the new patients and spend just twenty minutes with the others, to include dictating my notes. They keep talking about electronic charting, but I don't think that will help. Although, I guess it would cut down on the cost for transcriptionists. I don't like the idea of having computers in the exam room. There are enough barriers in health care as it is.* Taking a deep breath, Kim grabbed her bag, walked across the parking lot, and entered the clinic's back door.

"Hey, Crystal, Rose," Kim said as she paused at the nurses' office. "Did you have a good weekend?"

"Hi," Rose said, nodding and handing Kim her patient list before slipping by her to put patient lists for other providers in their boxes down the hall.

"It was a pretty good one," Crystal said. "Did some shopping. Went out with the girls on Saturday. It was a good time. You should've come with us."

"The kids were home this weekend. Maybe we can get together soon. I'm busy this coming Saturday though." Kim looked at the list Rose had handed her, hoping that maybe someone had canceled. "They aren't going to let up, are they? It seems they just keep insisting I can see more patients all the time."

"I know. They're fussing about some of the wellness classes Rose and I do, too." Crystal shook her head. "I know they can't bill for services provided by a Registered Nurse. And we still do everything else in the office." Crystal grimaced. "The days when we run the classes are rough because the other nurse has to cover all the providers by herself."

"I try to help out by being sure to enter the vital signs for all my patients. Is there something else I can do to help out?" Kim shifted her bag on her shoulder. *She's the best nurse we have. I don't want her to leave.*

"No, you're great. Some of the others can't seem to find their way without Rose or me leading them by the hand. 'Call this doctor for me' like I'm a secretary. That's why we have people at the front desk. All because they don't want to wait for the person to get on the line." She smiled briefly. "Hey, thanks for listening. Sorry about all that. Guess I'd better get to it if I'm going to leave on time." Crystal turned back to her computer.

"It's okay. We all need to get stuff off our chest sometime. Call when you're ready for lunch. I'm buying today."

"Okay. " Crystal answered without looking up from her computer.

Kim hurried to her office and opened the door. *I'm already behind even though I don't see my first patient until nine.* Dropping her bag behind her desk, she turned to put today's list on a small chart rack and went to the medical records room. *If we all just get our own charts that would be a big task off the nurses' list. I think Burt would get on board, but I'm not sure about the docs.* Within a few minutes, Kim had gathered her charts for the day, grabbed a cup of coffee from the break room and was back in her office. Parking the chart rack so it was in reach from her desk, she pulled her first patient's chart. She had just finished reviewing their notes when the front desk called to let her know a nurse had taken her first patient to an exam room.

20

Callie September 2003

Callie took a drink of her coffee after settling into her rocker on the front porch. A slight motion of her foot kept her chair rocking gently. *Life is good. Sea breezes, warm sun, birds, and family.* A Carolina wren perched on the railing warbling his morning song. As he began each measure, the small, russet brown bird puffed up momentarily before stretching upward and releasing his notes. She smiled at his antics. "Good morning to you," she whispered. Although the wrens thought nothing of darting around the porch in Callie's presence, the sound of her voice would scatter them back to the nearby shrubs. As the last notes ended, there was an answering trill from across the yard. The small bird looked toward the sound and with a final nod to Callie took flight. *Goodbye friend. See you later.*

Luke came into the kitchen as Callie poured another cup of coffee. "Hey, sweetheart. Did you sleep well?" He wrapped his arms around her and pulled her close.

"I did. And the birds have given me my morning serenade so I'm nearly ready to start the day. Just need to eat something." She grasped his arms to pull him closer for a minute before stepping away. "What are you up to today?" Callie took note of his dress slacks and polo shirt.

"Just a guild meeting this morning." His eyes crinkled as he smiled. "What are you doing?"

"Working in the garden for a while. Don't forget that Alma, Max, and Louise are coming over for supper." She popped a bagel into the toaster.

Luke nodded. "That's right. I won't be gone but a few hours. Do we have everything for supper? I could stop by the store and pick it up for you."

She tilted her head as she thought. "No. I've got everything." After a kiss, Luke headed to the garage.

Callie slowly straightened up. *Dang, my back and knees sure are stiff.* The afternoon sun cast long shadows across the yard, as she began pushing the wheel barrow toward the compost pit. *At least I got all the roses pruned. They'll probably bloom again and I'll leave those blossoms for the birds. They really like the rose hips.* After adding her day's work to the decaying matter in the pit, Callie gathered her tools in the wheel barrow and put them away. *It felt so good to be outside in the flowerbeds. Hard to get out here as much as I'd like.*

Inside, she glanced at the clock on the microwave as she washed her hands. *Great! I'll get the seafood boil started and get a quick shower. Luke should be finishing up in the studio soon.*

She and Luke had just finished setting the table when they heard Max and Louise come in through the kitchen door. Callie met them in the hall while Louise was hanging up her purse. After giving Max a hug, she turned to Louise. "It's good to see you. Haven't seen much of you lately." *Max seems really tired. His eyes are bloodshot.*

"I've been kinda busy at the shelter helping those young people figure out their hair." Louise gave Callie a hug and turned to greet Luke. "How's the painting going? Did I see you over on the western side of the island the other day?"

"Yeah, I was there. Things are going good. I'm working on having some pieces turned into notecards, maybe postcards, too. But we're not sure there's really a market for postcards anymore."

Max grinned. "That's pretty cool. But yeah, don't think people send postcards much anymore." As he handed Callie the cheese straws Louise made, Alma came in from the back porch.

"Let me take that pie, Alma." Luke put the pie on the counter and turned back to the group. "Can I get anyone something to drink?"

"Nothing right now," Louise paused as her brow furrowed. "But I'd like a glass of that hmm, white bubbly wine that Callie likes with dinner."

"Uh, the Prosecco?" Luke asked.

Louise's face relaxed into her usual jovial expression. "Yeah, that's the one."

Max shook his head as he put his arm around his wife's waist. "Just water with dinner for me."

"I'll just grab a glass of iced tea," Alma said as she made her way to the drinks set out on the kitchen island.

"The cornbread should be ready soon. I've got to have one of the cheese straws," Callie said while putting them on a plate. "How were things at the Emporium today, Alma?"

"It was a pretty good day." Alma sat perched on a stool at the kitchen island. Even at eighty-three, she almost never leaned back in a chair. "Expect things will be slowing down now that the kids are all back in school."

The timer dinged and Callie turned to get the cornbread out of the oven. She had put the seafood boil into the large Fiesta tureen just a few minutes before. "Everybody head into the dining room. Luke, will you take the soup in? I'll be right there with the cornbread."

Luke tagged along behind their friends and went to the dining room. Placing the dish in front of Alma, he encouraged her to serve herself and pass it along before taking his place at the table. Callie brought in the cornbread and settled into her seat.

Louise was uncharacteristically quiet throughout the meal. She kept looking around the table uncertainly. There was a bit of awkwardness when Louise didn't serve herself, but kept staring at the soup tureen. Max quietly served her. Alma smoothed things over with a story about Francine. She added that Francine and her children would come to the gathering in October.

After supper was over, everyone had a small piece of Alma's peach pie and coffee.

With her pie finished, Louise began fidgeting with things on the table rearranging salt and pepper shakers, gathering dishes and putting them at the unused end of the table. She stood up and then sat back down a few times. Her pursed lips and small frown as her eyes darted around the room, let everyone know something wasn't right. Max ran his hand over his head and took a deep breath. "Let me help get things into the kitchen. Then I think Louise and I will call it a night."

Callie waved a hand dismissively. "Don't worry about any of that. You both seem a bit tired tonight. Luke and I can get this."

"It's just been a rather long day with doctors' appointments in Charleston. A good night's sleep and I'll be right as rain. I'll just get our dessert plates and coffee cups into

the kitchen." As he gathered their dishes, Louise looked up at Max hesitantly. He looked down at her and smiled softly. "Get your purse, by the door to the garage, sweetheart. I'll be right there with you." Louise stood and trailed behind Max.

Taking a few dishes with them, everyone followed Max and Louise into the kitchen to say goodbye. After they left, Callie and Alma began loading the dishwasher while Luke finished clearing the table.

Callie paused as Alma handed her a plate. "Did Louise seem okay to you tonight? She was so fidgety and after we ate, she was looking around like she didn't recognize where she was."

"She's probably just tired after all the appointments Max said they had today. Besides she's just getting over that flu." Alma shrugged as Luke walked up to the sink.

"Here, Alma. I'll help Callie finish up. You take a break." He winked at Alma as he sidled in beside her at the sink moving her away from the work area.

Shaking her head, Alma grinned. "If you insist." Stepping back from the sink she dried her hands and added. "It has been a long day for me, too. Think I'll head home now. You guys keep the last of that pie. Callie, I'll see you tomorrow."

A few days later, Callie breezed into the Emporium's office after pausing briefly to talk with Sheila about the new display she was working on. Seeing the circles under Max's eyes and his stooped shoulders stifled her cheery mood. She immediately sat beside him. "Max, what's wrong?"

Max scrubbed his hand across his head a few times before answering. "It's Louise. All those appointments last week." His eyes glittered as he blinked several times. "The doctor says she's got dementia. I couldn't sleep last night worrying about how to take care of her, to keep her safe."

"What can I do?" Callie squeezed her friend's shoulder.

"I'm not really sure. Last week she got lost coming back from the shelter in Charleston. They finished that new bypass, you know." Max sighed heavily.

"She really likes her volunteer work. Has she had any problems there?" Callie's brow furrowed as she tried to think of ways to help her friends.

"I don't think so. At least, no one's mentioned anything to me." Max put his elbows on the worktable, rested his head on his hands and stared down at the table. "The doctors say its best to keep her doing things she's used to, that changing her routine would be hard for her and make matters worse. Apparently, she's in the early stages. Whatever that means." Without looking up, he rubbed his hands over his head again.

"If she wants, maybe I could drive her to the shelter and bring her home sometimes. That would give you a break, too." She paused, trying to come up with a plausible excuse for Louise. "I'll just have things to do in Charleston that day. She knows I'm usually in Charleston once a week anyway."

Max sat up straighter and looked at his friend. "That might work. She seemed nervous about getting lost again, but didn't want to burden me with driving her all the time."

"Okay, she usually goes on Wednesday, right?" Max nodded. "I'll call her Tuesday night and suggest we go together. Maybe have lunch or get a coffee after." Callie hugged

her friend. "I know we were going to overlap today so I could go to the bank. But you go home and rest. I'll make the deposit after I close today or ask Sheila to stay a little longer."

"If you're sure. I could use some sleep." Max stood and reached for the windbreaker on the back of his chair.

"Of course, I'm sure." Callie punched him lightly on the arm. "You've always helped me when I needed it. Time I returned the favor."

Max's smile didn't have its usual flash, but Callie was happy to see it. "Okay," he said. "I'll go home."

Callie locked the Emporium's door and put her bag in the car. She had made the bank run while Sheila was still in the store. *I really need a walk today.* Undulating sea oats bordered the path across the dunes. Callie found herself inhaling deeply as if bringing the salty air into her lungs would buoy her heavy heart. *I really can't believe that Louise has dementia. Otherwise, she's healthy as a horse. They should be able to enjoy their last years together.* After a short while, Callie realized the sun was low on the horizon, Its rays painted the ocean red and gold. *Hmph, guess I'd better turn back. Nothing I can really do to change this. Just have to be the best friend I can be.*

21

Kim July 2004

Kim settled on the loveseat, sipping her morning coffee while she surveyed the plantings in her yard. *I could almost forget I'm in the city. The little gem magnolias smell so good. It's makes me think of Momma's house on the island. So peaceful. Tonight, Danny and I are going out again. I really enjoy spending time with him. Such a relief not to have to consider someone's ego all the time. All the kids seem to get on well. Maybe there's something to this.*

A Carolina wren perched on the back of a rocking chair and began his morning trills. Kim laughed as the wren cocked his head, and trilled even louder. *Good morning to you.* She watched the bird go through its morning song several times before he flitted over to the feeder next to a crepe myrtle. *Okay, you're right my feathered friend. It's time to get on with this day. I've got a few things to do here at the house.*

Over the past year, Kim had developed a routine for maintaining the house which kept her from feeling so overwhelmed. It helped that the twins were older and better about putting toys away when they finished playing. Then too, she did much of her heavier housework when they were with their dad. In just a few hours, the townhouse sparkled.

By the time Danny picked her up at six, she was ready to relax and enjoy some adult conversation. "Hey. Come inside while I grab my purse," Kim said as she opened the front door.

"All right." Danny waited near the door.

Returning to his side, she asked, "Where are we going tonight? You said it was a surprise."

"It is. There's a new place I heard about. Rue 13." Danny held the storm door open as Kim locked the door. "It's just beyond the houses on the battery."

"That's a great location," Kim said stepping onto the sidewalk. Danny lightly held her elbow as they walked to the car.

"I've heard the food is good. We'll see." He backed out smoothly and, in a few minutes, they were at the restaurant.

"Good thing we've got reservations." Kim stared at the line forming in front of the restaurant.

"I'm going to let you off up front and then park. It's always so hard to find a spot along the Battery." Danny made a U-turn so he could let Kim out on the right side of the street. "I'll be right back."

Kim rested her hand on his arm briefly before getting out of the car. "I'll be fine."

Over an excellent dinner, Danny told Kim about some of his troubles during high school. "Mom had just finished her nursing degree when my dad was killed. My grandparents, in New Jersey, were pushing her to get a job locally, find a nice doctor to marry and stay home to take care of us kids. They didn't really support her decision to become an RN. Anyway, like I said before, she had a job offer as an RN in Charleston. So we moved." Danny sighed and sipped his wine.

"That had to have been hard. Losing your dad and then moving to such a different part of the country." Kim looked at him with concern.

Danny's lips tightened. "When we got here, she found out that she had to wait while her license was transferred to South Carolina. But there were bills to pay, so she

took a job as a certified nursing assistant working the night shift. Mom was doing the best she could. We were living in a crummy apartment. My friends were giving me a hard time about watching my younger sister. Linda was seven. I didn't handle it very well. When I was seventeen, I got in with the wrong crowd and was arrested for driving a getaway car in a robbery that I didn't even know was going to happen."

Kim reached across the table to squeeze his hand. "But all that's be-hind you now."

"True, but I felt you should know. With Steve's help, me and my family got back on the right track." He looked off as he saw the waiter walk towards their table. "Would you like dessert ?"

Kim shook her head. "No. I'm fine."

They declined the waiter's offer of dessert or more wine. With the check paid, the couple walked out into the light breeze coming from the ocean. "I can go get the car," Danny offered as they moved away from the restaurant's entrance.

"No, let's walk on the Battery for a little while. It's so pretty with the houses lit up and the lights on the monuments."

As they walked, he continued. "I was trying to figure out how to be a man and didn't realize that all I needed to do is figure out how to be a decent human being."

They sat on a bench near a display of cannons and stacks of can-nonballs welded together. "As teenagers, we all think crazy things some-times. For some reason, I picked out my path and stuck to it. But also, I grew up here so I didn't have to put up with not knowing the cul-ture and then too, I chose a traditional woman's field so there wasn't any conflict there. And although I was raised by a single woman, everyone on the island protected me so I never felt too out of place."

They sat quietly watching the waves in the harbor. Kim shivered. "Maybe we should get the car now."

Danny chuckled. "Yeah, it's cooler than when we left. Here's my jacket." He slipped out of his sports coat and put it around her shoul-ders.

They both laughed when the jacket began sliding off as they walked toward the car. "Hold on a minute. I'll put my arms in the sleeves."

Danny pulled into Kim's driveway. "Tonight was great. Thanks for a wonderful dinner. Maybe next Saturday you can bring Tommy and Suzie over. I'll cook and we can hang out for a while."

"Sounds like an idea. I'll see what Mom's got going on. She might enjoy a quiet night for a change."

"Let me know what you guys figure out. Your mom's welcome to come along if she wants." Kim gave him a quick kiss before getting out of the car.

Getting ready for bed, Kim sighed deeply. *Danny's a great guy. I'm glad he told me about his past. Not that it matters to me. It's just hard to get to know anyone as an adult.*

Sometimes we're so careful protecting ourselves. And when you have kids it's even harder. Guess we just need more time to get to know each other. She let out another loud sigh. *I thought I knew Jake and how well did that turn out. And maybe Danny's not over Melinda.* With these thoughts churning in her head, Kim eventually fell into a fitful sleep

22

Kim August 2004

Kim waited in the interior doorway of the nurse's office, knowing she couldn't be seen by anyone coming up to the window between the nurses' office and the waiting room. She frowned slightly as she ran her hands through her hair, untangling her auburn curls. *I really should break this habit of tugging at my hair. It's a wonder I have any left.* She smoothed her expression as she saw her last patient turn away from the counter.

"Hey, Crystal. Would you come down to my office when you get a minute?" Crystal nodded and Kim returned to her office, leaving the door open.

In a few minutes, Crystal paused in the doorway. "What's up?"

Kim gave her a small smile. "Close the door and have a seat. I want to talk about my last patient. "I'm going to refer her to another service. But please do call in the scripts for her." Kim ran her pen through her fingers. "Do you know who's accepting Medicaid patients?"

"I think the clinic on Hawthorne is taking new patients. Is there a problem?" She looked at Kim closely.

"She's Danny's sister." Kim's eyes flickered down to her notes. "Mary says she's been out of touch for a few years and doesn't know his phone number. Anyway, she knew his address and gave us permission to contact her family and talk to them about her situation."

Crystal's eyes popped open in surprise. "Wow. What are the odds of that happening? I'll work to get her transferred quickly. Where is she staying?"

"She's in the shelter next door. We'll have to arrange transportation to the Hawthorne clinic as well." Kim looked toward the ceiling thoughtfully. "I'll tell Danny that she's in town and let him take it from here."

"Surely he'd want to know about his sister." Crystal shrugged before standing up to leave.

"Knowing Danny, I'm sure he does. But you know the behaviors exhibited by many people with uncontrolled bipolar disorder. The manic phase when they feel they can do anything when they often act irrationally. Then comes the depression where they can barely get out of bed and see no reason to continue. It can take quite a toll on families."

Nodding, Crystal paused at the door. "Open or closed?"

Kim looked up from her notes. "Closed, please. I need to make that phone call."

While she put plates and silverware on the island for a casual supper, Kim thought about her earlier phone conversation with Danny. He had definitely been concerned about his sister, but was hesitant to talk on the phone for very long. *Of course, I did call him at work and he would want to talk to his mother, as well. Still, he offered to pick up Chinese food so we could talk more here since the twins are with Jake this weekend.* A knock at the front door broke into her thoughts.

She opened the door with a smile. "Hey, Danny." She stepped back to let him inside. "How did the rest of your day go? Have you talked to your mom?"

Pausing to give her a quick kiss, Danny went into the kitchen while Kim trailed behind him. He put the bag on the counter and began passing Kim the containers. "No, I haven't talked to her about Mary yet. I wanted to hear a little more about what's she's like right now first."

"Okay. Let's get started with the food. I'm starving. You can ask me whatever you want as we eat. She listed you as an emergency contact and said I could discuss her case with you."

"We haven't heard from her in about five years, since she went back to New York. Her old phone number isn't in service and mom's cards were returned. None of the family in New York wants to deal with her." Danny paused to take a couple of bites of crab rangoon. "Did she tell you anything about where's she's been for the last few years?"

"Not a lot. Apparently, she worked for a while as a messenger, but lost her job. Then things got vague. She had a hospitalization a few weeks ago and at discharge they sent her back to Charleston." Kim began putting some of the chicken and broccoli on her plate.

Danny frowned. "How did she seem? Is she taking meds again?" He rested his forearms on the island and stared at his plate.

"Well, she's not manic right now. Seems to be in a depressive stage, but not suicidal. Mary told me she's been off meds for about a month since leaving New York. According to her hospital paperwork, she was supposed to be in a group home here in Charleston. At least until she could get on her feet." Kim shook her head and pursed her lips. "I'm not sure what happened or how that mix-up occurred, but she wound up in our shelter. One of the nurses called her scripts in to the pharmacy. So she should have meds tonight. But you see, given our relationship, I can't ethically treat her." Kim rested her hand on his arm. "This has to be hard for you and your mother."

"Of course, I see why you transferred her to someone else. I'm glad she's safe and getting treatment. Just hope she sticks with it. We've been through this so many times since she was in college. Maxing out her credit cards on some scheme to get rich. Then she'd be so depressed. Wouldn't get out of bed. Once she even tried to kill herself. That's the first time she was admitted to the hospital." Danny covered her hand with his and gave it a squeeze, before letting it go to pick up his fork. "Hopefully, she's not using again. Did she mention that?"

"She denied using currently, but admitted to a history of drug abuse. She didn't seem under the influence to me. I ordered labs and a tox screen like I usually do." Kim paused to take a bite of her food. "It's not unusual for patients to deny drug use. They've got a whole host of reasons, shame, fear or denial that it's even a problem."

Danny shook his head. "She was always so smart, so talented. She was always sketching and designing clothes. Mary used to say she was born in the wrong time." He laughed softly. "She always said she felt she should have been living in New York in the late forties. Why did the New York hospital send Mary here, to Charleston?"

"Hard to say. She listed you as family contact. So maybe they thought she'd have support here. Sometimes they ship people away because the resources in their area are overburdened. It depends on where they can find a bed." Kim shook her head sadly.

"I see. What's the plan for her now? I hate to think of her in a shelter." Danny stared at his plate.

"The clinic I referred her to will help her find a place to live. Maybe a group home. Hopefully, if she responds well to treatment, they'll help her get into a supported, independent living situation." Kim patted Danny's arm. "There are a few complexes like that in Charleston. But all that depends on her and how invested she is in her treatment plan."

"Thanks for looking out for her and letting me know she's back in town." Danny paused, looking at the ceiling. "Lord, I hope she can stick to it this time."

Quietly, they finished their food. And after putting the dishes in the sink, the couple settled on the couch in the living room. Resting his head on her shoulder, Danny soon fell asleep. Kim slipped her arm around him trying to find a comfortable position. *He probably needs the rest. He'll be up with his mom for quite a while tonight.*

After a while Kim's arm grew numb. As she tried to slip it from under Danny's side, he sat up. "Man, I'm sorry about that." He ran his hands through his hair and blinked several times.

"I figured you were worn out. It's all right. Not like we planned a night on the town or anything." Kim rubbed her arm trying to restore its circulation.

"Still, I feel pretty bad. Conking out like that." He grinned sheepishly and then frowned. "I do have to let my mom know about Mary being back in town."

Kim stood and stretched. "Guess there's no time like the present, huh."

"You know I'd rather stay here." Danny stood and gathered her into his arms.

"I know. I wish you could stay, too, but I understand you need to let your mother know about your sister." She leaned into his embrace for a moment. Stepping back, she grinned. "Call me tomorrow and let me know how things go or just to get together later."

Upstairs, Kim decided to get a shower before calling it an early night. The bathroom filled with steam, almost a sauna. She let the hot water soothe her tense muscles. *Guess I was more worried about Danny's reaction than I thought. He seemed to understand that my continuing to treat Mary would be unethical. Through the office I'll make sure she gets picked up by the new service quickly.*

23

Callie November 2008

Callie wrapped a small blanket around herself as she settled into the porch swing with her morning coffee. Rain pattered on the porch roof. *We've been really lucky with hurricanes the last few years. Of course, all the modern hurricane proofing stuff makes a big difference. I hope the rain stops soon. Rain always keeps people from coming out to vote.* A Carolina wren perched on the porch railing and began his morning calls unbothered by her presence less than three feet away. The wind shifted to bring the rain onto the porch. Shaking her head, Callie retreated to the kitchen.

Luke came through the garage, wiping his feet before entering the kitchen. "I don't know why we didn't connect the studio to the back porch." He ran his hands through his damp, dark hair before going to the counter and pouring himself a cup of coffee. Callie smiled seeing how the dampness had accentuated his hair's waviness. "What time to you want to go vote?"

"I'd like to go early. Just need to get a quick shower." Callie took a bite of her bagel as Luke joined her at the kitchen island. "We're opening late today in case the lines at the polls are really long. What's your day like?"

"I had hoped to get out to that old church on Sullivan's Island, but unless the weather breaks that'll be a wash out." Luke took a few sips of coffee.

Pushing her plate aside, she opened her planner before continuing. "Aren't we supposed to go to your parents' at the end of the month?"

Frowning slightly Luke agreed. "The weekend after Thanksgiving, right?"

"That's it. Dad, Bobby, Susan, and their kids will be here Thanksgiving Day and then go to Susan's parents in Columbia on Saturday." Standing up, she picked up her plate and cup, putting them in the dishwasher, she continued. "Allison and Avery will be with Jake for Thanksgiving; Kim of course will be here and I think Danny and his family will be here. Alma too. Steve and his family are at Max's and Louise's. So, we won't see them at dinner."

"Are Kim and Danny becoming a thing?" Luke got up and managed to get his cup in the dishwasher before Callie closed it.

"I know they go out and take the kids places together, but I don't know how serious it is or whether or not they're more than good friends." Callie hugged him. "I'll get my shower and be ready to go in a few minutes."

The Board of Elections moved their usual polling place to a mall in Charleston County since there were expectations of a larger than usual voter turnout. Callie had voted since she was eighteen. *I always felt voting was a way of trying to find a solution to the country's problems. But with the lobbying that goes on in Washington, I don't know how anything gets done. Still, I'll do my part.*

Even though it was only nine o'clock, there were long lines of people waiting to vote. After dodging the last-minute campaigners at the mall's entrance, Callie and Luke joined the slow-moving line.

"Glad I thought to bring a water bottle." She opened the plastic bottle and took a drink. "It looks like we'll be here a while."

Luke nodded as he looked at the orderly line of people snaking its way to the desk to check their voter registration. "Look at all the young people here. I bet this is the first time a lot of them have voted."

"Yeah, there are a lot of them here. That's a good thing. For a while I thought a lot of younger people were apathetic. Glad something got their attention."

They left their voting booths and walked back into the mall area where people continued to wait. Sunlight poured through the atrium at the mall's center. A hum of voices reached their ears. Luke remarked that the lines seemed even longer and some people were sitting cross-legged on the floor. "I know," Callie said. "Oh my, look a woman with her kids in the stroller. That's a way to get them started young."

"It looks like the rain has passed." Luke held the door open as they left the mall.

Her hopeful mood continued as Luke drove back to the island. "Now we'll just have to wait and see. I haven't been this excited about an election in a long time." Callie took another sip of water and replaced the bottle's cap.

"I know, honey. We'll have to sit up and watch these returns." Luke pulled into the Emporium's parking lot. "Are you working alone to-day?"

"No, Alma will be in this afternoon." Callie leaned over to give him a kiss. "I'll walk home when I'm through."

The next day the three partners sat around the work table in the Em-porium's office. "Here Alma, have one of these cinnamon rolls I made with Allison and Avery while they were here last weekend. I need you to help me eat them." Callie laughed.

Alma joined in her laughter. "I can't let good home baking go to waste. Pass me that platter." After taking a roll, Alma set the platter in front of Max. "So tell me Max, did you get any sleep after hearing the election results?"

"Have to admit it took me a while to settle down. A Black man as president of the United States. I've often prayed for this day." Max took a bite from his cinnamon bun and washed it down with a sip of coffee. "Still, he's only one man."

Callie grimaced. "I just hope nobody gets any fool notions and starts making trouble between Blacks and whites."

"Honey, haven't you learned anything yet? There will always be someone looking for that kind of trouble," Alma stood up and gathered her things from the table. "Well, I'll go ahead and run my errands. See you later."

A few days later, Callie and Luke were both stretched out on the couch reading. "Hey, honey. Have you heard from Kim lately?" Luke asked as he peered over his book.

"Not since the election." Callie returned to her novel.

"That's strange, isn't it? With Thanksgiving coming up." Luke set his open book down across his chest. A groove formed along the book's spine.

She frowned. "Don't do that. You'll break the spine." Laughing, she shook her head. "You did that on purpose."

Luke grinned guiltily. "Well, I didn't think you were listening. Isn't it odd she hasn't called? You guys are usually on the phone every other day, at least."

Shaking her head, Callie smiled back at him. "No, she's busy, work, the twins, figuring out her relationship with Danny and his children." Her voice trailed off. *I do miss*

talking with her though. But it's as it should be. She's living her life and Danny seems to be good for her.

Callie breathed deeply, inhaling the salty air as she made her way to the shore. The early morning sun broke through the few clouds hovering above the horizon. Blue gray herons took wing as she passed tidal pools on her way to the dunes where sea oats danced in the light breeze. *Just a short walk today. Everyone will be waking up soon. The turkey's already in the oven so there's not much to be done right now, but people will be hungry. So I'll need to get some of the pastries out.*

The smell of roasting turkey greeted her as she stepped into the hallway leading to the kitchen. Passing the closed door of the bedroom where her dad was sleeping, Callie took care to tread lightly. Her dad had sat up late reminiscing about the family's early days in Columbia. *It's good to see him engaging with everyone. Seems like the move to Spartanburg has been good for him.*

In the kitchen, Kim was peeling potatoes at the island. "Hi, Momma. I put the eggs on to boil." Kim stopped peeling and hugged her mother as she walked up beside her.

"I see you found my list. Thought you might have taken the opportunity to sleep in today." Callie turned to the counter and poured a cup of coffee. Opening a bakery box she began putting apple turnovers, cinnamon buns, and scones on a platter. "One day I should learn to make a breakfast casserole."

"I guess you could, but casseroles never were your thing, Momma. Seriously though, when did you start making a timetable for holiday meal prep." Kim brushed a strand of hair from her forehead. She still kept it short and her curls swirled around her head, a warm auburn aura.

"Oh, Susan and I started doing it the Thanksgiving we had to jump in and take over for your grandma." Callie sat down at the island and looked at the list. "Your Grandma always made a list of what she was serving because one year she forgot to put out the cranberry sauce. I just continued it when people started gathering here."

Kim laughed. "Well, cool. It certainly makes jumping in to help easier." Kim took the potatoes to the sink to rinse them and then set the pot on a back burner. "Aren't Max and Louise joining us today?"

"No, Steve and his family are in town and they wanted to do something at home. Steve's trying to spend as much time with his parents as possible." Callie smiled. "I think Tina is trying to get down all of Louise's family recipes. Tina has a few from her family, but even she says they don't cook like Louise." No one mentioned that the recipes needed to be gathered before Louise forgot them completely.

"I know how I feel about family recipes. I'm glad Avery and Allison like cooking. It's important to keep family traditions alive and it's easier if they just grow up helping in the kitchen, kinda like I did."

"It does make it easier if you learn as you go. When are Danny and his family getting here?" Callie asked, looking over her shoulder as she crumbled up cornbread for the dressing.

"They should be here any time now." Kim glanced at her watch. "Danny and Linda wanted to be here in time to help with the prep work. How much celery and onion do you need chopped?"

Callie chuckled. "One day I'll measure this stuff. Let me see, one medium onion and three stalks of celery should do it."

Several minutes later, Callie was blending the ingredients for the cornbread stuffing in a large bowl. "I think I hear a car in the driveway."

"I'll go give them a hand. I think Linda is bringing a pumpkin pie and peas with pearl onions. Apparently, the peas are a family favorite." Kim walked to the garage to welcome Danny and his family.

Callie had just pressed the last of the cornmeal mixture into a Pyrex baking dish when everyone entered the kitchen. After politely acknowledging Callie, Tommy and Suzie went upstairs to the game room.

"Come on in. There are plenty of hooks next to the garage door. Let me wash my hands," Callie said turning to the sink. "Kim, how about putting the peas in the warming oven." Drying her hands, Callie joined everyone around the kitchen island.

"Can I get you something to drink? We've got coffee, sweet tea and some Cokes." Kim offered as Linda sat down at the kitchen island.

"Coffee would be good," Linda said.

Danny paused to give Kim a hug as he went to the coffee pot. "If I remember right the cups are in the cabinet above the pot." He turned to see Kim nod. "Mom C, do you need a refill?"

"Yes, thanks, Danny." Callie smiled at his thoughtfulness.

"The turkey smells so good. All the cooking smells are making me hungry. And thanks, son," Linda said as she took a cup of coffee from Danny.

"Thanks, Linda. I'm getting hungry, too," Callie said grinning. "We've got a fresh vegetable tray and some other appetizers. I should probably get them out of the refrigerator so everybody can get to them." Callie started to get up.

"Sip on your coffee a little longer, Momma. Danny and I can set up the appetizers. You want to use the l folding table again?"

"Yes, it's in the laundry room along with the table cloth I want to use," Callie said before giving Linda her attention. "How do you keep up with preteens? My hat's off to you. I know I couldn't do it."

Linda smiled. "Hmph. From what I've heard you could do just about anything you set your mind to. Besides they're really good kids. Everybody pitches in. It's not like I have to do everything myself. But tell me, what else needs to be done for dinner?"

"Excuse my reach," Callie said, as she stretched to pick up her notebook and looked at her list. "The cornbread stuffing is in the oven, along with the candied yams. The turkey is in the roaster. That just leaves the green beans, deviled eggs, and mashed potatoes. Kim's peeled the potatoes already. The boiled eggs have been cooling next to the sink."

"Well, I'll get started peeling the eggs and you can tell me how you like to make them." Bringing her coffee cup with her, Linda went to the counter and began peeling the eggs.

"Thanks." Callie tilted her head toward the door leading to the deck. "That sounds like Luke and Alma."

She was reaching for the door as Alma and Luke entered the kitchen. "Let me take one of these pies." Callie gave Alma a quick hug. "Come on in you two. Luke," Callie

paused before continuing. "Oh, I should have known you'd help Alma with her jacket. Let me take the other pie." With both pies in hand, Callie started toward the dining room.

On his way to hang up Alma's jacket, Luke paused behind Callie and gave her a quick hug. "Be right back to join this prep party."

Kim joined Linda on deviled egg duty while Danny went up to tell the children about the appetizers. "How much longer until dinner?" Alma asked as she began to bring serving bowls from the dining room.

"About forty-five minutes or so," Callie answered over her shoulder as she turned on the burner under the potatoes that Luke had rinsed and put in fresh water. "Luke, when the kids are finished eating would you get them started setting the table?"

"You got it." Luke went to join the kids in the living room.

Bobby and his family came in from a walk on the beach. Within a few minutes after the introductions, Bobby and Susan joined in the meal preparation and the kids joined their Tommy and Suzie upstairs. Callie's dad, Bob, came in from the downstairs guest room. "Hey, did I sleep long enough to skip all the work?"

Susan laughed while everyone else grinned or rolled their eyes. "Well, yes. But we could use more coffee."

Glad someone appreciated his humor; he made his way to the coffee pot. "Looks like I need to make some more. Callie-girl, everything still in the same places?" He looked to Callie on his left.

Callie gave him a kiss on the cheek. "Yes, Dad. Thanks for keeping us going."

"We'll decorate the tree after dinner, won't we? You guys found a beautiful one this year."

"We sure will, Bob." Luke answered as he gathered dirty prep dishes. "That's one of my favorite Thanksgiving traditions, putting the tree up as a family."

Linda smiled and nodded. "We do a similar thing, but on the Saturday after Thanksgiving."

A short time later, everyone stood behind their chairs as they gathered at the table. Luke said a brief prayer of thanks and encouraged people to help themselves to the food in front of them and then pass it along the table.

"Callie your dinnerware is so pretty," Linda said as she passed a turkey-filled tray to Alma who was seated on her left.

"Thank you, Linda. I inherited most of it from my aunt." Callie beamed. "I've added a few pieces over the years, mainly plates and some larger platters to accommodate a growing family."

"I've seen the pattern before. It's Fiesta, right?" Linda rubbed her fingers lightly over the concentric rings along the outside of the serving bowl before setting it next to Alma.

Passing her a gravy boat that looked like it could have been Allacin's lamp, minus the lid, its graceful, curved handle sat perfectly on the oval dish with its curved spout, Callie nodded. "It is. They stopped making it quite a while back. Although I heard Homer Laughlin is coming out with some new colors."

Danny chuckled. "Guess it's true then. Everything comes and goes in cycles. Pass me the rolls, please, Avery." With his roll secured, he began applying a liberal helping of butter.

"In the 50s and for a long time afterward, pediatricians told mothers that making formula was the best way to feed a child. You should see some of those recipes. Now, it's all about breastfeeding." Kim shook her head. "Momma, this turkey so tasty and juicy."

"Of course, corduroy has come back along with platform shoes and bell bottoms." Linda added. "I sure loved my platforms and bell bottoms."

"This dressing is delicious," Callie's dad said as he got ready to take another bite.

The talk turned to plans for the Christmas holidays. Luke and Callie would have a dinner with Kim and the twins before traveling to Spartanburg to spend Christmas with her dad and Bobby's family.

"Do you guys usually do a big Christmas Day dinner?" Danny asked, looking at Kim.

"When I was a kid, we did. Momma and I would open presents at home early Christmas morning and then we'd go to my grandparent's in Columbia. Uncle Bobby and his family would be there." Nodding Kim smiled remembering her grandmother's holiday tablecloths and Christmas china. "Now at Christmas, the kids and I usually have a simple dinner with Momma and Luke on Christmas Eve, usually vegetable beef soup and cornbread. The rest depends on what Jake and his family is doing. Since they're with him today, we'll come over later for Allison and Avery to put their special ornaments on the tree."

"It can get complicated, but you just have to remember that it's all about the kids anyway and be willing to share," Luke said as he squeezed Callie's hand.

Callie nodded as she smiled down the table where her family and friends had gathered. Turning her attention to Trey, Bobby and Susan's oldest, she asked, "Are you guys getting restless? Have you had enough to eat?"

"Yes, ma'am," He nodded enthusiastically.

"Please help clear the table before going upstairs again. We'll call you when the desserts are out and when we're ready to decorate the tree." Callie turned to the adults. "Would anyone like something more to drink or dessert?" Everyone shook their heads and some looked down to their stomachs. "Okay, let's move to the living room for a while and let our food settle. Then we can get started with the tree."

24

Callie January 2009

Callie locked the Emporium's front door. After dropping her bag into her SUV, she went along the side of the building for a brief communion with the ocean before going home. White topped waves crashed against the shoreline. Branches of the palmetto trees along the boardwalk leaned in the brisk wind. Most of the birds had taken shelter from the brewing storm.

I even like storms on the island. This is only supposed to be a tropical storm. No real threat. She continued a short distance before turning back toward home. *I should get home. Something's troubling Luke. He's not sleeping. Not sure what though. I don't think it's an 'us' thing. Still, it's odd; he's usually so unflappable.*

Having changed shoes in the car, Callie made her way into the kitchen and was surprised to see Luke at the island with his laptop open. *He usually works in his office in the studio.* A frown creased his forehead and he jumped when she called his name. "Oh, hi love. Is it that late already?" Luke tapped a couple of keys, closed his laptop, and turned to greet her.

"Yeah, it is." She wrapped her arms around him. "Is everything all right? You seem especially tense." Callie rested her head on his shoulder and tried to pull him even closer. *Last time I saw him like this Momma was in the hospital.*

"Well, yeah." He hesitated, gave her a tight squeeze, and patted the chair next to him. "Sit down. I'll explain." Seeing her troubled look, he continued. "Everybody's okay. It's nothing like that. Just some stock market stuff."

After an hour of explaining, Luke summed up the problem. "I've lost a good deal of money recently. I managed to get out of some investments just in time, but it will be a while before the portfolio gets back to where it was." Luke rested his hand on the counter. "Day-to-day we won't really notice the difference. We're lucky."

"I remember you talking about the dot com bubble breaking and there being trouble with banks and the housing market, but I didn't realize it would affect us so much." Callie closed her hand around his. "But we're going to be okay, right? The Emporium is doing as well as ever. Should I turn some profit into CD's or something? We've got time to straighten out our retirement accounts, don't we?"

Luke nodded. "We do. I'm having some second thoughts about how we're investing." He ran his hands through his still thick wavy hair. "But I'll figure it out. Maybe talk to my dad. Don't make any decisions right now."

"You want to drive up to Charlotte next weekend? I'm not scheduled in the Emporium." Callie stood up and went to the refrigerator. "We haven't been to see your parents in a while."

"Sure, I'll give them a call." He slapped his forehead. "I totally forgot to take anything out for supper."

Callie laughed. "Oh, well. We've got some leftovers. I'll pull something out while you call your parents."

Luke's parents' home in Charlotte was deceptive as you pulled into the driveway. Architecturally, it could not compete with their former home in Charleston. That was such a grand home, purchased and furnished for a successful stock broker with partners and clients to entertain. This home was a little more sedate, but still designed for a more

discerning client, one with money to spend, with amenities designed to appeal to individuals downsizing, smaller yards, wide walkways and screened in porches. Plantings in the common areas lent a feeling of privacy to the smaller lots in the development.

However, once you walked through the front door of the house, it was clear that Melony had decorated their home with the same flair she had used in Charleston. They had an open floor plan. Only the bedrooms, bathrooms and storage areas had doors. The large screened-in porch was decorated with her favorite filigreed wrought iron pieces.

On their first visit, Callie had recognized most of the furnishings as having come from Charleston. *Melony likes nice things, but isn't a spendthrift.* Over the years, she became more comfortable with Melony and Tony and had little trepidation as they walked to the front door and rang the doorbell.

"Hi son, Callie." Luke's dad gave them both a big hug as they came in. "Come on into the great room. Would you like a drink?"

"Maybe later, Dad," Luke said as they followed his father through the short entryway to the great room. "But if there's coffee on, that would be great."

His mother joined them. Luke hugged her before she turned to Callie for a hug. With greetings out of the way, Melony went into the kitchen. "I'll start the coffee. So, how was the drive?"

"Not too bad," Luke said as he and Callie sat at the kitchen island. "A little traffic around Lancaster but, otherwise, smooth sailing."

His dad came into the kitchen and began taking mugs and small plates from a cabinet. Melony pulled a cream pitcher and a crystal dish containing a spread from the refrigerator and put them on the island in front of Callie and Luke. Turning to a counter behind her, she uncovered a basket containing a variety of crackers and placed them near the spread. "Help yourself," she encouraged as she turned to pour coffee.

"Ah, those look really good," Callie said, putting some of the spread on a couple of crackers and resting them on her plate before taking a bite. "That's a nice spread."

Melony smiled. "I knew you liked seafood; it's crab and cream cheese with a bit of salsa on top."

"These are great, Mom," Luke said after eating a cracker.

They chatted for a while over coffee before Tony looked at his son. "Have you decided how to adjust your portfolio?"

"I've thought of a few things. But after my initial changes to stop the bleeding, I decided to wait until we could talk through it. I wanted to know what you thought. After all, you've been watching the market much longer than I have." Luke looked at his father with affection and admiration.

"Well, refill your coffee and bring a plate of those crackers to my study. We can talk there while Callie and your mom catch up." He gave his wife a kiss and went down the hall. Luke picked up his plate and mug to follow his father.

Melony refilled Callie's coffee mug and sat beside her. "So how are things going with your family?"

"Kim and the twins are doing well." Callie took a sip of coffee. "You know my dad moved to Spartanburg after Momma died. He's doing well with my brother's family."

"My grands are growing like weeds. Tony and I like to go to their games or recitals." Melony got up to refill their coffee cups. "They visit every now and then."

Callie looked around the room, uncertain how young children would ever be comfortable here. *Of course, Melony's grandchildren are older.* "I really enjoy spending time with Allison and Avery. They keep me feeling young."

Melony's eyebrows shot up. "Really..."

Before she could finish the thought, Tony and Luke rejoined them. "Stacey called and asked us over for dinner. She really wanted to see her brother and Callie. I told her sure."

There were murmurs of agreement from everyone else. *I've gotten used to Melony and think the world of her, but talking with her one-on-one can be difficult We've just led such dissimilar lives and our way of mothering is vastly different. It will be good to see Stacey. She's more down to earth than their mother.*

Tony nodded as he saw a consensus within the group. Looking at Melony, he added. "Be a dear and cancel our reservations. Stacey said to come by in an hour. Leo's going to grill steaks." He and Luke sat down in the great room.

Melony went to the kitchen and carried out her instructions. With that accomplished, she turned her attention back to Callie. "I'm sure you'd like to freshen up before we go. The guest bathroom is set up like before. Make yourself at home."

Getting a few items from her suitcase. Callie was once again struck by the fact that the house's architect had put a Jack-and-Jill bathroom between the two guest bedrooms. *How convenient. Wish we had thought about this when we were remodeling.*

As Callie came into the bedroom from the bathroom, Luke came in. "I thought you might be finished. I'll grab a quick shower while you get dressed. You know how Dad hates to be late."

She grinned. "Yeah, I won't be long. I'm just going to braid my hair."

"Okay, love." He gave her a quick kiss before going in the bathroom.

Dinner at Stacey's and Leo's was much more relaxing than hanging out with Luke's parents or going to their favorite restaurant. Leo was in banking and Stacey was a teacher. While eating at the Amber House was always enjoyable, it tended to be crowded in the evening. It had a long history of serving celebrities like Dick Smothers and James Gardner. According to Melony, the restaurant might close soon. Callie thought her in-laws liked to eat there because of its reputation as a meeting place for prominent business men. *It just seems old and tacky to me. It might have been the place in the sixties, but they've certainly fallen behind the times.* Stacey and Leo promised to visit on the island at the end of the school year.

Everyone had a nightcap when they returned to Melony's and Tony's home. Although nothing specific was discussed, Callie understood Tony had been able to reassure Luke about his current plan for investing. She chatted a while longer before going to bed.

For a moment, Callie wasn't sure where she was when she woke up. It was just too quiet. Luke was already up. After pulling on her clothes, she repacked the suitcase and joined everyone in the kitchen. There were pastries, along with coffee to fortify them for the drive ahead.

Their drive home was leisurely. Luke reassured Callie about their investments and that their retirement account would recover over time. With a stop in Columbia, they were able to enjoy a late lunch with Brenda, Callie's dear friend. She was doing well. Having gotten her Bachelor of Arts degree following her divorce and move to Columbia several years ago, Brenda taught at the community college and loved it. Brenda hoped to attend the October gathering this year since she couldn't attend last year because of her class schedule.

It was nearly nine o'clock when Luke and Callie pulled into their garage. Luke grabbed their suitcase from the trunk while Callie opened the door into the kitchen and headed straight to their bedroom. She was already changing into night clothes as Luke entered the room.

"Are you calling it a night already?" Luke asked as he put the suitcase next to the armchair.

"No, just want to be comfortable. Thought I'd get some tea and sit on the front porch for a while. I've missed the ocean, but I'm too tired for a walk. Smelling it from the porch will have to do for now." She ran a brush through her shoulder length dark hair as she looked in the mirror hanging over the dresser. *A few strands of gray are showing up.*

"I'll join you in a minute." Luke looked over his shoulder on the way to the bathroom.

"Okay, I'll see you then." Callie made her way to the porch after getting a glass of tea. Settling on the porch swing, she inhaled deeply. *That's the smell of home. Even at night it's never quiet here. I don't like the sounds of traffic, but I do miss the croaking frogs and night birds when we travel. Ah, that was a screech owl. We're so lucky, some people lost everything in this crash. It will take them years to recoup their retirement savings, if they ever do.* Focusing on her surroundings, she took another deep breath and let it out slowly as she heard Luke step across the porch.

"Have you realigned yourself?" Luke sat beside her and put an arm around her shoulders.

"Close enough. Tomorrow's walk will truly set everything right." Callie leaned her head against his chest letting the swing's gentle motion lull her into calmness.

25

Callie April 2009

The afternoon sunlight shimmered across the ocean. Callie settled her sunglasses on her nose and looked back toward the island. Her eyes skimmed over the sea oats dancing in the soft breeze drifting from the water and the sandpipers dancing alongside her. *Where are you, Louise? This is the third time you've wandered off from the house.* Ignoring the rowdy, squawking seagulls, Callie continued to scan the area as she made her way toward the rocky prominence at the south end of the island. *What's that bit of red up there?* She drifted down to the packed sand and broke into a trot. *It's the long, narrow scarf from Louise's hat.* Picking it up, she scanned the area again. Seeing no further sign of Louise, she called Max to let him know she found the scarf and told him she would call the others to let them know where to focus their efforts. Since they had only been looking for a short time, Max had asked her not to call the Sheriff's Department for help.

She walked another ten minutes before she saw a lone figure leaning against a palmetto tree, partially hidden by the top of a dune. As she watched, the person sat down and leaned against the tree. Callie stretched to her tiptoes, craning her neck to see the person at the base of the tree. *Looks like Louise. That'd be quite a hike for her—from their place to here. I'll get closer before calling Max.*

As Callie approached, Louise continued staring at the water. "Hey, Louise. You sure took a long walk today."

Louise jerked her head around to stare at Callie and frowned. "What are you doing out here?"

Knowing something was off, Callie pushed her sunglasses up on her head so Louise could see all of her face. She kept her expression bland and her voice light and friendly. "I was looking for you. I thought we might walk together for a while. Are you thirsty? I've got some water." She held out a water bottle.

Louise squinted as she peered at Callie from under a wrinkled brow. "I'm too tired to walk anymore, but I am thirsty." After taking a long drink, she continued. "Shouldn't you be in the Emporium?"

"Yeah, but I'm taking a break. Let me call Max." She sat down beside Louise and punched Max's number into her cell phone. He answered quickly. "Hey, I'm with Louise. If you come down to the access at Caines Road, you'll see us under a palmetto tree."

"Was that Max?" Louise took another long drink of water. "Oh, you've got my scarf. I wondered what happened to it."

"It must have worked its way loose." Callie held out the scarf. "Want to put it back on your hat? Max'll be here in a few minutes. He's bringing the car."

By the time Max arrived, Louise had re-threaded the scarf onto her hat and had it securely tied under her chin. "Momma always told us not to go bareheaded out in the sun. Make us all dark."

Callie stepped away to make a couple of discreet phone calls to let everyone know Louise was safe. Seeing Max at the beach access, Callie waved and called out. "Here we are."

He tried to run, but the shifting sand dragged at his feet, forcing him to slow down. Max sank to his knees beside Louise and cradled her head against his chest. "Sugar baby, what you doing way down here?" He slowly rocked her. "Come on, my sugar baby, let's go home. Here I'll help you up."

"Okay, honey bun. I was just walking and got tired." Louise began brushing sand from her clothes as she stood up.

"Hey, Callie." Max turned to his friend with a tight smile. "Thanks. I'll give you a ride back to the store."

"Sounds good. I've passed the word that Louise is with us." Callie frowned and then shook her head. *Louise hasn't called me by name the whole time I've been here.* "Look, I can open up tomorrow if you want."

"I'll give you a call a little later and we can talk about tomorrow, okay?" As Louise moved ahead of them across the beach, Max added softly. "I'm worried, but don't want to talk about it in front of her."

"Of course, I understand. We can talk later."

When Callie returned home after closing the Emporium, she found Luke in the kitchen. "What are you doing sweetheart?" She asked as he met her part way across the kitchen and hugged her. "I was going to broil some flounder for supper."

"I'm just getting the salads together." He nuzzled her hair as she leaned closer into the hug. "Figured you be tired after everything today. Would you like a glass of wine while you fill me in?"

"Sounds good." Callie moved away and sat down at the kitchen island. "You know I found Louise about two miles away from the pavilion."

Luke nodded as he gave her a glass of Prosecco and sat beside her.

"Except for being thirsty, she seemed okay. Funny thing though." Callie pursed her lips as she remembered. "I had the feeling she didn't know who I was at first."

Luke raised his eyebrows. "Are you sure, honey?"

"Yeah, I'm sure. She knew I was from the Emporium, but never called me by name. I think her dementia is getting worse. She's ninety and Max is ninety-two, I think." Callie squinted before taking another sip of wine. "Anyway, I offered to open tomorrow, but I'm not sure Max'll take me up on it."

Luke gave her shoulders a squeeze. "We'll have to wait and see. Maybe she just got over tired or dehydrated."

She shrugged and stood up. "Max'll let us know what he needs. He's supposed to call tonight about the store. I'd better get supper started so we can watch the ballgame later."

With supper out of the way, they curled up on the couch to watch a game between the Mets and the Braves. The Braves were always a tough opponent for the Mets, but tonight things seemed to be going the Mets way. Callie and Luke always joked about being on opposite sides of this baseball rivalry. The game was in the fourth inning when Max called.

"Hang on just a minute." Muting her cell phone, she told Luke. "It's Max, honey. I'll go out on the front porch." Settling into a rocking chair, Callie unmuted the phone . "Okay, I'm back. How did things go once you got home?"

Max let her know that when he pulled into their garage, Louise began acting like herself, except she was fussing about being late starting supper even though it was still early afternoon. But after dinner she began to get anxious, asking about Steve and wondering where he was. Asking why he wasn't home yet. They talked a while longer and Max finally agreed Callie should open in the morning. Before going inside, she called Alma and asked if she could come in later tomorrow and close up. Alma agreed to the change in plans.

Luke muted the television when Callie rejoined him on the couch. "How's Louise?"

"Max said she seemed better when they first got home, but after supper she started worrying about Steve. Didn't seem to remember he was grown and had a family of his own. He's going to try and get her into the doctor tomorrow. I'll go in early and Alma will come in later so she can close." She curled up closer to Luke, nestling her head against his chest.

"Honey, I'm so sorry they're going through this." He rubbed her arm gently. "Is there anything I can do right now?"

"No, not really. We just have to wait and see what her doctor says." She flashed him a smile. "Turn the sound back on. The Mets are winning."

Alma and Callie were both at the Emporium when Max stopped by the store on his way back from the doctor's office. He joined them at the counter while Louise went to get coffee. "Dr. Jones feels certain Louise's dementia has progressed."

"Oh, Max." Callie's eyes glistened. "I'm so sorry."

He ran a hand across his graying hair. "He ran some tests and it doesn't look like she has an infection or anything else that would cause confusion. The office is arranging a consult with a neurologist. Dr. Jones told me there are some promising drugs on the market that may slow the progression somewhat." Max blinked rapidly and squeezed the bridge of his nose. "We'll just have to see how things go."

Alma came out from behind the counter and put an arm around his shoulder. "You know you're not alone in this. We'll all walk with you through this journey."

Max reached into his pocket for a handkerchief. Dabbing at his eyes, he said, "I know. I need to get her home. Not supposed to let her get overtired." Max squeezed the bridge of his nose again. "She's always been so strong." Sighing, he went to get his wife from the office.

Later Callie and Alma talked about ways to support them. "Maybe a group of us can start visiting with Louise while Max is at the store. Doesn't have to be a big thing. Just pop in." Alma began making a list. "Of course, we'd have to be careful of Louise's feelings. Not to mention Max's."

"That's a great idea. We could start up our weekly potluck dinners again. They kinda fell off. Since we do it at our houses, it shouldn't stress Louise too much. I'll take the first one. How about Saturday?"

"Sounds good to me." Alma made shooing motions toward her friend. "Go on home now. I've got everything here."

A few weeks later, Alma and Callie were enjoying a morning coffee on Alma's front porch. Alma pursed her lips and spoke slowly. "I'm not sure we're really helping Max and Louise with all this visiting."

Setting her coffee aside on a nearby table, Callie nodded her head in agreement. "I think we're probably aggravating Louise more than anything." She rubbed her forehead as she thought a moment. "She's got it together enough to know what's happening and to feel like we're babysitting her'."

"That has to hurt her pride. I still think the potlucks are okay, especially when all the kids and grands come." Alma chewed her lower lip as she thought.

"Problem is, I don't think Louise has any hobbies. She stopped going to the shelter." Callie picked up her coffee mug and took a sip.

Shrugging, Alma agreed. "She did hair and visited sick or shut in members from church. She and I used to can together a lot. Maybe I can talk to Marvin, at church, about the sick list. He used to go with her on sick calls."

"I like it. It would give her a reason to get out of bed. To be giving, rather than receiving."

"Yeah, I get it. We're all rather prideful." Callie chuckled. "We've all worked hard for what we have and it's hard not to be busy. To have time on our hands and not feel needed."

" Maybe Louise could partner up with someone. I know she's stopped driving. What time is supper tomorrow?"

"About five-thirty. We're going to do a fish fry. Louise is making some slaw. I've got fresh corn, too." Callie stretched before standing up. "Guess I should get moving. Steve and Tina will be here with their brood, grandchildren and all. He's been trying to get Louise to record more of their family history. Danny and Kim are each bringing their kids."

As she picked up their cups, Alma placed a hand on her arm. "I've got this. I'll bring a couple of peach pies tonight."

Callie leaned over to hug her friend. "Okay, call if you need help with anything. See you later."

Following dinner the next night, while everyone else was roasting marshmallows, Callie and Alma told Louise of their idea about visiting church members.

"I know about visiting the sick and shut-ins. Marvin's a good man." Louise leaned forward in her chair.

Steve and Tina's youngest, Lou, hurried up the stairs from the yard to the deck. "Grandma, are you ready to tell more stories?"

Louise smiled at her granddaughter. "Does that mean your dad wants to go home?"

Lou hesitated a moment. "Well, he does want to go home, but I want to hear more stories."

Enveloping her namesake in a hug, Louise said, "Come on girl-child, let's get everyone rounded up and we'll go home." She grinned as she stood up. "I'll get my dish while you let everyone know I'm heading for the car."

Lou took off like an arrow on her mission of rounding up her family. "She sure is fast," Callie said as the women entered the kitchen. "She's such a bright young woman as well."

"Yeah, she's a straight A student." Louise grinned with noticeable pride.

Callie looked at the display on the dishwasher. "It hasn't finished yet. I'll get your dish back to you tomorrow."

Max and Louise's family leaving seemed to be a signal for everyone else. Danny and Kim left next. Alma departed soon after. Callie settled in a rocking chair on the front porch watching the sunset as the Carolina wrens began their evening serenade.

We are so fortunate to have such caring family and friends. I've always been afraid of losing Max, Louise, and Alma. Losing Momma created a big hole, but these three have been part of my daily life here on Caines Island. I can't believe that the time is coming when I'll start losing them.

The Aricept Louise's doctor prescribed can't cure her, but they say it will slow down her memory loss. Maybe it'll give her and Max a few more years. I've just got to remember to cherish all the time with my loved ones and not brood about tomorrow.

Callie inhaled deeply, letting the sweet scent of the magnolias soothe her as Luke joined her on the porch. After settling into the nearby rocker, he took her hand and kissed it before they sat back to watch the fading sunlight.

26

Kim March 2010

Kim pushed back from her desk and began shoving things into her bag. *I'll have to dictate these notes at home. Another call from school. Allison left school after first period. I don't know what's gotten into her lately.* When she called home, Avery swore he hadn't seen her since they parted to go to their homerooms. She tried calling Jake, but the call went straight to voicemail. Her tote bouncing on her shoulder, Kim made her way to the nurse's office. Stopping in the doorway, Kim let Crystal know she was leaving for the day and asked her to reschedule her last patients.

Not wanting to upset her mother with news of another one of Allison's escapades, Kim's hands shook as she entered Danny's phone number in her cell. *This car is so stuffy.* She rolled down the window.

Danny answered quickly. "What's up? Is everything…"

Kim rushed on. "Hey, know you're probably still in the office so I won't be long. Could you check with your kids to see if they've heard from Allison? She's skipped classes again." Kim pressed a hand to her forehead and leaned against the steering wheel. He agreed to talk to his kids and call her right back.

For once uncertain as to the best course of action, Kim waited a couple of minutes before reversing her car out of the parking space. Her cell rang. *Should have known he'd get right back to me.* Putting the car in park, she answered. "Hey, there." Danny told her his kids hadn't talked to Allison since last weekend. "Well, it was a long shot. Thanks. Look, I gotta run. I'm going to drive around to see if I can find her at the mall or something." After talking a few minutes longer, Danny convinced her to pick him up at the office. They would look for Allison together.

Kim pulled up in front of his office building as Danny came through the double glass doors. His suit jacket was draped across his arm and he was removing his tie while making his way to her. "Is Avery at your house or Jake's?" He asked as he quickly settled in the passenger seat and fastened his seatbelt.

"He's at my place." Kim shook her head.

"Call him and let him know my mom will pick him up. That way he'll have supper and you won't worry about him." He opened his cell phone as Kim dialed the house.

"Avery, Danny and I are looking for Allison. His mother is coming to pick you up for supper. I'll get you after I find Allison." She listened a minute. "No, I had to leave a message for your dad. Okay, love you, son."

Danny turned to look at Kim's distraught face. "Look, why don't you let me drive. I can focus on the road while you focus on the sidewalks."

Kim's shoulders sagged. *I feel so inadequate. My teenage daughter is acting out and I can't help her.* "Okay, let's change cars," Kim said as she turned to grab her bag from the backseat. "This makes a lot of sense. I can't seem to think straight."

On the way to Danny's car, they agreed to check areas around the school before widening the search to area malls and other places teenagers might hang out. Pausing after he unlocked the door and held it open for her, Danny hugged Kim tightly. "It's going to be okay. We'll find her."

"I just want to find her soon. It's not safe for young girls on the street." Kim squeezed his shoulder before settling into her seat. As they were pulling into the school parking lot, Kim's cell phone rang. It was Jake and after listening to Kim, he told her he had no idea where Allison might be. He did say he would check areas near his apartment and get back with her.

Danny and Kim parked and began walking across the campus. "She's so smart and talented. I don't understand what's gotten into her lately." Kim scanned the nearby playing fields while holding her hand up to shield her eyes from the glare of the afternoon sun.

Kim headed along the right sidewalk while Danny took off to the left to talk with a group of kids who looked to be about Allison's age. One of the kids knew her slightly from art class, but hadn't seen her today or noticed her hanging out with any new kids.

Kim and Danny quickly completed their search of the campus. All the school buildings were locked. Although they checked, there were few places to hide between the buildings. For whatever reason, the schools landscaping was low and spread out.

Walking back to the car, they talked about Kim's favorite mall and the arcade she liked there. After a short drive, Danny parked near the mall's entrance. Unsurprisingly, the parking lot was pretty empty since it was Wednesday afternoon. Danny said the kids at school told him Thursday through Saturday was the time to hang out at the mall.

I still have to look. I couldn't live with it if something happened here and I didn't check. By the time they entered the mall, Kim had taken several deep breaths to help her focus. Inside, they split up, with Danny going to the right and Kim taking the left.

It took a couple of hours to check each store. Meeting up near the food court at the center of the mall, they were both disheartened not to have found Allison.

"I don't know what to think." Kim sank onto a bench. Her hands were shaking as she dialed her mother's number.

Danny plopped beside her. "When you're through talking to you mom, we should get a burger to go and head for the next mall. I know eating is the last thing on your mind, but you're looking kinda pale."

Kim nodded as she updated her mother on Allison's disappearance. "I don't know how she would get to you, but please call if you hear from her." Her mother assured her she would call and even offered to help look. Kim said it was best if she stayed by the phone.

As she hung up, Danny was walking toward her with a paper bag and two sodas. "I just got each of us a cheeseburger and fries." He handed her a drink. "I figure we could eat in the car."

Jake called as they were getting settled in the car and Kim let him know he was on speaker. "Hey, none of my neighbors have seen Allison. But I was finally able to track down the super for my complex." Jake's voice broke. "He told me he had seen Allison around three this afternoon. She told him she was waiting for me to get off work." Tears made their way down Kim's cheeks. Danny put an arm around her shoulder.

Jake gave her a moment before continuing. "He offered to let her in but, she said she was fine. I've got my mom on the lookout, too."

Kim struggled to talk through her tears. "Did you and Allison have plans?" she asked. *I know they didn't. Jake would have told me if they were going somewhere since this is their week with me.*

"Kim. Swear to god we didn't. You know I would have told you." Kim squeezed her eyes shut and opened them slowly.

"I know. I just had to ask. I'm going to the police department and file a missing person report. I won't stop looking, but damn it, she's only thirteen." Kim stared wide-eyed out the windshield.

"Okay, I'll meet you there. Is Danny still with you?"

"Yeah. We'll see you there." Kim closed her phone and sipped on her Coke. She tried to take a couple of bites of her burger. But her stomach lurched, trying to reject solid food so she shoved it back into the bag. *It's beginning to get dark. Come on Allison. Where are you?*

After filing the police report, Kim felt she needed to see Avery. *He must be as scared as I am.* Danny drove back to his office to get Kim's car while Jake continued to drive around and check out teenage hangouts. When they reached Danny's house, Kim bounded out of the car as soon as she cut off the engine, nearly running to the front door.

"Here, let me unlock the door for you." Danny stood beside her on the small porch.

Kim nodded, tapping her foot so rapidly she nearly vibrated. "I know he's fine, but I need to hug him right now."

Danny went through the door first, calling out as was his family's habit. "Hello the house. I'm home." He and Kim went into the living room.

Footsteps pounded on the stairs from the basement rec room. "Mom, have you got her? Is she all right?" Seeing her sad expression, Avery hurried to his mother, burying himself in her hug. Danny's family stood around them in a protective circle.

"No, honey. We haven't been able to find her yet." Kim held her son tightly, willing herself not to fall apart. "Your dad is still looking. I just had to see you for a few minutes."

Linda came in from the kitchen. "Kim, should I put on coffee? Although you look like you could use some food." Danny's mother looked at Kim's pale face. "I've got some soup in the fridge. Come sit a minute. I'll warm some up while you figure out what you're doing next."

"Coffee sounds good, Linda." Kim nodded. "I tried to eat a burger earlier and that didn't work out so well. Maybe I can sip on the soup."

Everyone gathered around the large kitchen table. The teenagers were anxious to be helpful, once more going over their last interactions with Allison. Avery's usually cheerful face was drawn down with his sorrow. "Mom, I didn't know she was going to skip today." His eyes pleaded for his mother to believe him. "She hasn't been talking to me as much since Dad started talking about getting married and moving, you know."

Kim ruffled his hair before remembering that he didn't like that affectionate gesture as much lately. "I know baby. We'll find her."

Linda slid a cup of rich vegetable beef soup in front of Kim. "Here you go."

Tentatively, she took a sip. "This is really good, thank you." Kim drank deeply from the mug.

"Now what are your plans for the rest of the night?" Linda asked as Danny brought
coffee for Kim and himself to the table.

"I feel like I should be out there looking. I don't know any specific place. At this point, I'd just be driving through Charleston." Kim covered her face with her hands. *She's so young.*

Her cell phone rang. *That's Momma's number. Why is she calling?* "Hey, Momma. She's with you? How did she? Let me talk to her." Kim nodded as Avery mouthed, "She's at Grandma's?" The leaden atmosphere in the kitchen lifted as if infused with helium. Tears flowed down Kim's face as she walked to the living room to talk to her daughter.

After hanging up with Allison, Kim called Jake to let him know their daughter was at the island house and reassure him she was unharmed. She and Avery would be leaving in a few minutes to pick her up. Kim agreed to call him when they were on their way home.

While Avery gathered his belongings, Danny and Kim had a few minutes to themselves in the living room. "You were amazing today. I'm usually in better control of myself." Kim leaned into his hug.

"Your daughter was missing. How could you be objective at a time like that?" He nuzzled her hair and then let her go. "Look, I'm just glad you called me. Are you going to stay at your parents tonight?"

Kim began gathering her bag and keys. "No, I told Jake I'd let him know when we were headed back to the townhouse. He'll probably be there for a little while."

The skin around Danny's eyes tightened as he turned his head away for a minute. When he looked back at her, Danny wore a lopsided grin. "I can understand he'd want to see her tonight. I'll talk to you tomorrow." He gave her a quick kiss before everyone returned to the living room.

Linda brushed off Kim's thanks with a wave. "Nothing you wouldn't do if the tables were turned."

On the drive to her parents, Avery was quiet. Kim tried to draw him out, but he

seemed too tired to talk about anything. *This whole thing has been exhausting. I'm torn between just being thankful to know where she is and wanting to strangle her for scaring me to death. But I've got to stay calm through this. I don't want to push her further away.* At her parents, Avery jumped out of the car and ran through the garage to find Allison sitting at the kitchen island with their grandparents.

"Allison, what were you thinking?" he yelled as he gave his sister a bear hug. Both of them were crying.

Kim took in her parents astonished faces as she too entered the kitchen. "What's going on in here?" Kim hadn't heard what Avery said as much as the tone of his voice and he was definitely angry.

Allison pulled away from her brother and ran to her mother. "I'm sorry, Mom. I was so scared. I'll never do anything like this again."

Kim resisted the urge to shake her daughter as she sobbed against her chest and squeezed her tightly while murmuring "I love you, Allie. Always. No matter what, I always love you." Taking her daughter's hand, Kim led her to the living room while everyone else gathered at the kitchen island. "Tell me all about what happened today." Kim sat beside her daughter and put an arm around her shoulders, forcing herself to relax the tension gripping her body. *I could just—oh, I don't know. I've never hit one of the kids, but it sure is tempting tonight.*

She knew Allie first started skipping class so she could go sketch the houses on the Battery, ignoring Kim's offer to drive her there on the weekends. "The sun was perfect this morning," she said. "I had really intended to come home when school would have been over. I shouldn't have skipped. I went by Dad's. Thought I'd see him for a little while.

He wasn't there. But Marion came by with her brother and boyfriend as I was leaving. They were going to Folly Beach." Allison looked down at her hands.

"Sweetie, did anything happen today, drinking..." Kim asked softly, letting her thoughts of possible sexual activity hang in the air between them. She had been forthright in her discussions about sexuality with both of her children and at least until this point neither child had expressed an interest in sex.

Allison scrunched up her nose and shook her head vigorously. *Oh thank God.* Kim let out the breath she had been holding as her daughter continued. "No, Momma. We went to the beach and hung out. They wanted to go get some beer and I wanted to go home. Anyway, they got beer and were drinking in the car." She began clenching and unclenching her fists.

Kim rubbed small circles between her daughter's shoulder blades. "They were so stupid driving around like that. Marion started talking about going to her boyfriend's place in Mount Pleasant and her brother started looking at me all weird like. Grinning and grabbing his privates. After a while, I jumped out of the car at a red light. I had my book bag and sketch book, but no money. So I just kept walking. Sometimes people honked their horns or yelled crazy stuff out of their car windows, offering me a ride, but I just kept walking. It took a long time, but I made it to Caines Island and Grandma."

Kim held her daughter close. "We'll talk more later. Are you hungry?" she asked as Allison leaned against her.

"No, Grandma fed me as soon as I got here. Am I going to be grounded again?" Allison sat up to look her mother in the eye.

"Yes, but we'll talk more later. Let's go tell Grandma and Luke goodbye. I need to let your dad know we're headed home. He might come by to see you tonight. He's been pretty worried, too."

Jake was waiting in his car when Kim and the twins returned home. He grabbed Allison, gave her a hug and then shook her briefly. "Don't ever scare me like that again." He hugged her once more before they entered the house.

Everyone grabbed a drink and gathered in the living room. Within a few minutes, Avery said good night and went up to his bedroom. Kim and Allison sat closely on the couch and Jake slumped in an armchair. It gave Jake and Kim some time to talk with Allison about what led to her recent behavior.

Kim hid a yawn behind her hand. "I think we need to call this a night." She

hugged Allison before continuing. "I'll write you and Avery a note for school tomorrow."

Allison got up to hug her dad. "Look, I'm off tomorrow," Jake said, looking up at

Kim for her approval. She nodded. "I'll pick you and Avery up tomorrow for the afternoon."

After locking the front door when Jake left, Kim crept up the stairs. She gently opened the door to Allison's room. Her daughter was cocooned in her comforter, holding the worn stuffed bear of her childhood. Smiling as she pulled the door closed, Kim made her way to Avery's room. She almost laughed out loud as she opened the door to find him sprawled across his bed with the covers nearly on the floor. Yawning, she pulled the door closed. *You'd think I'd be exhausted but I'm really too wired to sleep. Maybe a cup of tea will help.*

With a cup of tea in hand, Kim settled into a chair on the patio, rotating her shoulders to dispel tension-induced soreness. Soft lights illuminated the little gem magnolia and crepe myrtles in her yard. The night was still, no sound of traffic. *I'm so thankful that things worked out the way they did. Allison was scared, but no real harm was done. I really don't know how I would have handled things otherwise. I just feel bad that I didn't realize how upset she was about Jake getting married and moving.* Sipping the tea, Kim was able to reconcile the day's events and begin to find a way forward as a family.

27

Callie July 2010

A strong breeze blew Callie's hat off her head and left it hanging by the chinstrap. Laughing to herself she flipped her hair from under the hat. *Don't know why I try to wear a hat out here. They usually fly off just like that.* Tall grasses swayed in the breeze. Herons stretched their blue-gray necks toward the water, seeking their next meal. Reaching packed sand, Callie took off her shoes and set them aside. *They should be fine there. It will be good to see Brenda and Josie again. Everyone is so busy. It's been forever since the three of us got together.* The sandpipers dancing along the water's foamy edge caught her eye and made her think of Kim chasing sandpipers when she was a child. *Lord, I hope things stay settled with Allie. She's always been such a good kid. I'd hate for this to lead her down the wrong path. For her. And for Kim.* With a sigh, she pushed her daughter and granddaughter out of her thoughts as she turned toward home.

Callie's classic seafood boil simmered on the back burner when Luke came in from the studio. "Hmm. Sure smells good in here." Callie stopped stirring when he stepped up behind her, nuzzling the back of her neck as he wrapped his arms around her waist. "Dinner smells good too."

She chuckled as she turned into his embrace. "How's your day been? Supper will be ready in about half an hour. Do you want some coffee?"

"I'll get it. Do you need a refill?"

"Sure. I left my cup on the island." Callie covered the pot and joined Luke at the kitchen island where he settled after getting their coffee.

"When are Brenda and Josie getting here?" Luke sipped his coffee.

"Hmm. I don't think they'll be here much before supper. Around five I suspect. And probably stay just a few hours afterwards."

"That'll work out. I have the Guild meeting at seven." He looked thoughtfully over his coffee. "I might meet up with Dante for a couple of drinks after that. Hey, why isn't Tom coming tonight?"

"He's out of town on a business trip. He's trying to win a major contract with a company in Atlanta." She took another drink of coffee. "I made a blackberry cobbler for dessert tonight."

"Oh, that'll be real good." Luke put his arm around her waist and kissed her lightly. "I'm going to close up the studio, but I'll be back in to get the dining room ready."

She was just putting the cornbread in the oven when she heard Josie's car in the driveway. Callie hurried to the front porch to greet them. "Hey, you two. Come on inside where it's cool."

Meeting halfway along the walk, the women hugged each other and chatted happily about how glad they were to finally be together again. Laughing, the three women went inside.

Brenda smiled with amazement. "Callie, I can never get over how you and Luke remodeled this place after the '87 hurricane. Somehow you managed to keep that sweet cottage feeling with all the additions."

"Thanks, Brenda." Callie beamed.

Luke joined the women in the kitchen. "Brenda, how was the drive from Columbia?"

"It was a good trip. Never really ran into any traffic," she said and settled onto a stool at the kitchen island.

"That's good." Luke turned to Josie. "Would you like me to open that bottle of Prosecco for a drink before dinner?"

Josie nodded and joined Brenda at the kitchen island. "That'd be great. Thanks, Luke."

There was a pop, as Luke eased the cork from the bottle. "At a time when I wasn't so smooth, I let the cork go." His eyes crinkled as he laughed. "I never did find that cork. Even when I moved out of the apartment." Everyone laughed.

With a toast to friendship, they sipped their wine. Brenda announced she was working on her master's degree. "Brenda, that's fantastic," Callie said as she sat down beside her friend. "Will you stay at the community college?"

"Probably. Not everyone can start out at a four-year college." Brenda tilted her head. "I loved writing in high school and studying the classics."

"Yeah," Josie put in. "I'd never have passed any of the lit classes if you didn't explain the books to me. I knew what happened in the story, but then the teacher would start talking about similes and metaphors it might as well have been a foreign language."

"You've always been a numbers person, that's for sure, Josie. I'm so proud of you Brenda," Callie said glancing at her wristwatch to check the time. "The cornbread will be ready in about ten minutes. I'll get the seafood boil in a serving dish."

Luke left once the kitchen was cleaned. The three friends went out onto the deck. "So, Callie. How's Allie doing?" Josie asked as she held up the Prosecco bottle and refilled glasses when the other women nodded.

"Much better now. She didn't handle Jake's upcoming marriage and his plans to move to Conway well. And she was really frustrated with school. She's spent some time talking with her school counselor. Kim is looking into some enrichment classes or maybe a charter school next year. The whole incident seems to have scared her." Callie shook her head. "Scared me too when she showed up here while everyone was looking for her."

Brenda lowered her eyebrows. "Man, I remember when Matt was putting me through this." Her face relaxed. "But he came through it and is doing well now."

"At least, she trusted you enough to come here. That's saying something, Callie." Josie sipped her wine.

"We've always been close. Just glad our relationship seems to be surviving these teenage years," Callie said. "Kim got the twins cell phones so they can call in an emergency. And once Allie got off restriction, Luke has let her work in his studio a couple of days a week."

"He's always been so good with them. Surprising really, since he never got to be a dad." Josie's eyes stretched wide as her hand flew to cover her mouth when Callie's lips turned downward. "Sorry. I wouldn't have said it if he were here." Brenda leaned forward in her chair to pat Callie's arm.

Shaking her head, Callie replied. "It's okay. He is a great dad to Kim. They just got a later start. So Brenda, how long are you in town?"

"I've got to go back Sunday. I'm still working part time in the admin office at Richland. Can't really stop working there, although I'm looking at some grants for school."

Callie grinned. "I'll keep my fingers crossed."

"Thanks." Brenda settled back in her chair. "How's business at the Emporium?"

"We're doing well. The store has sure come a long way from when you two helped me build that stand years ago. Alma and Max are cutting back on their hours so I stay pretty busy." Callie set her wine glass on the table beside her. "Josie, how do you like working for the firm in Charleston? As exciting as you thought?"

"It's not too bad. The workload isn't a problem. I can do that in my sleep. It's the office politics and being the only female CPA that gets my goat. We go into a meeting and people assume I'm going to take their coffee orders." Josie scowled. "Then too, I just got permission from the corporate office to wear pants with my suits instead of having to wear a skirt all the time."

"This isn't the 1970s. There are plenty of professional suits with a pants option." Callie shook her head. "Bet you have to wear heels, too."

Josie tilted her head to scowl at Callie. "You know I do. At least they're more comfortable than they used to be. Easy Spirit has a real good line." Josie's eyes brightened. "Why don't we all go out to eat to-

morrow. Tom should be getting in around noon. I know he always enjoys seeing everyone."

Brenda nodded. "Hey, I'm staying with you. Where you go. I go."

"Dinner out sounds like fun. Luke will enjoy it, too," Callie said, trying to hide a yawn behind her hand.

Josie stood up and stretched. "It has been a long day. I'll make reservations and give you a call tomorrow."

Gathering wine glasses, Callie followed her friends inside. Leaving
the glasses in the kitchen, Callie walked with them out onto the front
porch. After hugging her friends and watching them leave, she settled
into a wicker rocking chair.

An owl dipped low, nearly touching the ground before it flapped
its wings with a loud whooshing noise and landed in a nearby oak tree.
Did you get your supper? Shaking her head, Callie's thoughts returned to
Josie's comments about Luke being a dad. *Josie's such a hot mess. Sometimes I wonder at her success in business. But I guess no one hires a CPA
for their tact. Luke adores Kim and the twins. No one would guess they
weren't his biological offspring.* She inhaled deeply. *That magnolia tree
smells so good. There's nothing that smells sweeter.* Stretching out her arm,
she pulled the blanket from the rocker beside her. Within moments of
snuggling deep in its folds, she drifted off to sleep.

Kim August 2010

Kim noticed her heartrate slowing as she crossed the bridge onto Caines Island and rolled down her window. *Funny, I've done that as long as I can remember. Do I feel better because of the ocean air or because I'm going to Momma's? I know she's disappointed not to see the twins, but I'm glad I have some time alone with her before Luke's family gets into town. So much is happening these days.*

Getting out of her car in her mother's driveway, Kim heard voices drifting her way from the deck. Once there she found her mother and Alma enjoying the warm summer sun and glasses of iced tea. "Hey ladies." She gave each one a hug and settled into a chair.

Callie stood up. "Would you like a glass of tea? Or should I start coffee?"

"Tea's fine, Momma. Thanks." Smiling, she watched her mother walk away before turning to Alma. "How have you been?"

Alma waggled her fingers. "Pretty good. Don't get around as quickly as I used to, but I can't really complain. How about yourself and that family of yours." The afternoon sun glinted on the silver strands scattered through her long, slate-gray braid.

"Things have settled down. Thanks, Momma." Kim paused as her mother handed her a glass of tea before she settled back in her chair. "Allison and Avery have a better understanding of how they'll see Jake and seem to realize that the move doesn't have anything to do with them. It didn't help that he told them he was getting married and moving at the same time. They didn't have much time to get to know Beth while she and Jake were dating."

Her mother and Alma nodded. "Well, I'm glad to hear it. I couldn't see Allie bent on a rebellious path, but it's hard to tell about teens," her mother said.

Kim cocked her head. "Still there are some things coming up that may upset the kids. But I don't think so. They seemed genuinely happy when we talked about it."

"So out with it." Alma turned to face Kim directly.

"Danny and I are getting married." She paused and looked at her mother from the corner of her eye.

Callie's smile lit up her eyes. "Oh, I wondered when you guys were going to make it official."

"You two haven't been fooling anybody, you know." Alma's nearly black eyes danced as she laughed softly.

Kim's cheeks turned a rosy pink. *Why do I feel like a teenager confessing a first love or something?* "We weren't trying to fool anyone. Just trying to be discreet around the kids."

"Okay, honey." Callie's shoulders shook with suppressed laughter. "What brought this change on?"

"Momma. Be serious." Kim shook her head while grinning at the two other women. "I admit, we both seemed to be dragging our feet at making any changes in our relationship. Always waiting for the right time. Anyway, during everything with Allie, Danny was right there, helping me."

"Go on." Alma leaned forward in her chair.

"I realized I was wasting so many of the years with Danny. And the twins are close to him as well." Kim paused to sip her tea. "Anyway, I was nearly ready to propose myself, but he asked me first."

Luke came out on the deck. "Did I hear something about a wedding?" He leaned over to hug Kim. "I'm so happy for you. Have you set a date yet?"

"Thanks, Luke. No, the logistics are a little complicated. Neither of our homes are large enough to give the kids the privacy they're used to. And being jammed in together won't make things any easier. The kids get along well, but blending a family can present challenges."

"So what about Danny's mother?" Alma asked.

"Oh, the house will have to have a mother-in-law suite with easy entrance to the main house or something like that. I know he's talked with her about this." Kim fluttered her fingers indicating there was much to be worked out before they could even set a date. "I couldn't ask Linda to move out after she helped Danny raise Tommy and Suzie."

Luke smiled as he shook his head. "You guys are going to have to make a lot of adjustments. I don't envy you."

"I know. Linda's talked about returning to nursing recently. This may make it easier for her." Kim tossed her head which set her auburn curls bouncing. "Right now, everyone gets along well. The twins and I have known Danny for a long time. We'll just have to work through the bits about having different roles and relationships." Kim looked down at her lap.

"Honey, we're all happy for you." Callie reached out to squeeze Kim's hand. "And we're ready to help out anyway we can. But you guys seem to have talked through a lot of stuff."

Kim's shoulders relaxed as she smiled and squeezed her mother's hand. "I know, Momma. And thanks. Mostly I'm concerned that the kids may have trouble seeing Danny and myself in different roles. They know Danny and I are dating so maybe I'm worrying about nothing. Jake kinda sprung his marriage and move on them at the same time."

"I think you and Danny are smart enough not to force the relationships. I mean the kids have to be respectful to both of you." Luke held his hands up. "Like you were with me. They're going to be fine."

Kim stood up and gave her mother a hug. "Well, I know you've got company coming so I'll get out of your hair."

"You're welcome to stay for supper, if you want," Callie said as Luke and Alma stood to hug Kim and give her their best wishes.

"Thanks, but I have a few things to do. Allison and Avery are coming back early from Jake's this week. And we're going to look at houses on Saturday."

She left her window down as she made her way across the small island. *Okay, glad that's done. I knew they'd be happy for me. But they're right. There will be a lot of adjustments for all of us. And how will Linda and I share the household? I don't want her to be stuck with all the house-work or feel that I'm pushing her aside . At least all the kids are used to having household responsibilities.* Kim inhaled deeply before she rolled up her window as she left the bridge on her way to Charleston.

Kim knocked on Allie's door. "Morning sweetheart. I know it's Saturday, but we're going to look at houses so you need to get ready."

Kim heard a groan from the other side of the door. "Okay, Mom. I'll be down in a minute."

Avery opened his door as Kim started toward his room. "I'm up, Mom. Do we have time to eat before we go?"

"Of course. I can scramble some eggs and make toast or a bagel." *Typical teenaged boy, always hungry.*

Kim grinned as Allie stuck her head out of her bedroom door. "I showered last night so I'll be ready soon. Was just trying to finish my book. I'd like two eggs and toast, please."

"Okay, Allie. I'll get started now." Kim bounced down the stairs. *Thank the Lord, I have good kids. Hopefully, we'll be able to find a house that will fit all of us that's still affordable. Danny's been smart with money too, but I don't want to get in over our heads. I wonder if we should rent one of our places rather than sell it outright. I'll talk it over with him later today.*

With breakfast over, Kim and the twins met Danny and his family, along with a real estate agent, at the first house. It was a two-story brick home. The yard was large, pretty much a blank canvas for Kim and her mother to create another group of flower beds. Danny liked Kim's back-yard at the townhouse and his mother wasn't really into gardening unless it was vegetables. The kids were ecstatic over its swimming pool, but none of the adults wanted to take on all that maintenance.

Walking towards the car, Tommy looked back at Danny. "Dad, having a pool would be so much fun. We could hang out at home more."

Danny shook his head. "Keeping up with a pool takes a lot of time. Besides, you're involved in baseball all summer."

Allie looked at Kim hopefully. "Come on, Mom. We'd be the coolest family on the block."

"No, I agree with Danny. If I'd known there was a pool, I wouldn't have even looked at it. Come on we've got other houses to look at." Pausing for the teenagers to pass her, she made shooing motions with her arms.

There was a chorus of groans as they loaded up and moved on to the next house on the list. After looking at several houses, there were two strong candidates, but in both, the space for Linda's area was near the rec room. Although she seemed a little distracted, Linda found them acceptable, but Kim thought the kids might disturb her when they hung out with their friends.

After looking at the last house, everyone went back to Danny's. The kids darted off to the rec room while the adults convened in the kitchen. Danny started coffee while Linda checked a roast she had put in the crock pot earlier this morning.

Kim got the coffee mugs out. "Linda, what else do we need for dinner?"

"I thought we'd just have this roast, potatoes and some of those green beans your mother gave us," Linda answered as she added milk to her coffee and took a seat at the kitchen table. "I didn't make a dessert."

"That sounds good. We don't usually have dessert, so I'm fine with that." Kim joined her at the table as Danny sat down.

They savored their coffee in silence for a few minutes when Linda held out her hands, palms up. "I want you two to listen to me for a few minutes." Kim's brow furrowed and Danny's mouth opened as if he was going to interrupt. "No, just listen for now."

"Danny, I never really planned to live with you forever. I'd like to have my own space. I've already signed up for some refresher courses and plan to go back to nursing."

Kim's eyes teared up. "Linda, the last thing I want is to push you out."

"Honey, nobody's pushing me anywhere. I've had enough of that in my life. You know me well enough to know that." She reached over to pat Kim's hand. "This is what I want. Do you realize I've never lived alone except for a couple of years? I lived with my parents until I got married at nineteen. Then there were children."

Danny stared into his mother's deep blue eyes for a minute and with a resigned sigh, he asked. "So, Mom, where do you want to live?"

"I'm not sure. Here in Charleston. I don't want to be far from the kids. I definitely want to stay involved in your lives." She winked at her son as she brushed her blonde hair away from her face. "I'll look for an apartment. I definitely don't want a yard to take care of."

Kim's eyes sparkled as she looked at her future mother-in-law. "We haven't decided what to do with my townhouse. What would you think about living there?"

Linda shook her head. "It's a lovely place and in a great neighborhood, but I can't afford to rent it."

Danny and Kim shared a quick look, remembering their earlier conversation, before she said, "Who said anything about renting it. You just maintain the place, protect our investment."

"Well, let me think about it." Linda pushed her chair away from the table.

"Just remember, you'll always have a place in our home." As the two women stood up, Kim hugged her.

"Oh, Kim. I'm so happy you two found each other." Linda stepped back and dabbed at her eyes. "Will you make the gravy tonight?"

"Of course." Kim turned to get a saucepan from the cabinet.

Danny squeezed her hand. "I'll round up the kids and get the table ready."

Later that night while Kim sat on her patio, she and Danny talked on the phone as they did most nights. They decided to have another look at the two houses that were strong possibilities tomorrow. He helped her realize they would have to let his mother at least pay some nominal rent. "Like you, she's a very proud, strong woman. We have to let her do what she can." Reluctantly, she agreed.

On her way to bed, Kim stopped by the game room to say good night to Allie and Avery. "Hey, kiddos. Danny and I decided to look at the last two houses again tomorrow. Do you want to go to Danny's or stay here?"

"I've some homework so I'll stay here," Allie said, looking up from the book she was reading.

Avery looked over from his video game. "Yeah, me too. Do you think they'll come over after?"

"I'll ask and let you know. See you in the morning. Love you both." Kim said, as she ruffled Allie's hair.

"Good night, Mom. Love you, too," the twins chorused.

Kim and the twins were still at the kitchen island when Danny arrived. She kissed him lightly as he stepped inside. "We're just finishing lunch. Come in for a minute."

Allie greeted Danny enthusiastically. "Hey, if you guys come over for supper can we all play Monopoly?"

Danny smirked. "Are you prepared to lose?"

Laughing, Allie smirked back. "Remember, you lost the last three games we've played."

Nodding, Danny joined in the laughter. "Okay, we'll have a rematch. I'll beat you yet." He turned to look at Kim. "Mom wanted to know if she could bring something for supper."

"Not tonight. Allie and Avery are making a salad to go with the pizza I'll order." Kim dried her hands on a towel. "It was either that or burgers and hotdogs. Frankly, I don't feel like cooking anything tonight."

"Sounds good to me." Danny kissed her cheek lightly. "I'll call Mom to let her know. Are you about ready to go?"

"Yes. I'll just grab my purse." Turning to the twins who were headed to the game room, she added. "Allie, be sure your homework's done first. No games until it's done."

Allie stifled a sigh and headed upstairs. "Yes, ma'am. See you later. Love you."

"Love you, Allie." Kim called after her before turning her attention to Avery. "Is all your homework done?"

"Yes, ma'am. I'll just watch TV until Allie's finished." Kim smiled as she hugged her son. "We'll be back in a couple of hours. Love you."

After looking at both houses carefully, they stopped for coffee. "Well, what do you think, love?" Danny asked as they sat down.

Kim smiled before answering. "I think the second one. It's rooms are larger. I love the kitchen, so much room in there. And it's move-in ready. I don't really like all the beige though." She took a sip of her iced mocha.

"Yeah, I like the kitchen, too. Especially the way it's open to the family room. There's the large dining room, too. You know eventually, we'll be hosting family get togethers. Painting wouldn't be that big of a deal."

"I'm so glad you like the idea of getting our families together. It's one of the things I love about you." Kim sent him an air kiss across the table.

"Are you sure you like the bathroom off our bedroom in this house? Seems a little small to me." Danny looked at her questioningly.

Kim tilted her head. "That would be the one thing I would change besides the paint. But there's probably a way to enlarge it using part of the big walk-in closet."

Danny nodded. "Hmm. You're probably right. Okay, if, you're sure, I'll call and put in an offer." Kim nodded vigorously. In a few minutes, Danny was off the phone. "Belle will put in our offer and call us."

They sat for a while longer making plans for their future together while waiting for Belle's phone call. Kim held her breath when Danny's phone rang. Grinning, he answered while holding Kim's hand tightly. His vigorous nodding and even wider grin let her know the offer was accepted. When he hung up, Kim leaned over and hugged him tightly. "This is fantastic. I can't believe we found a house so soon."

"I know. I was afraid it would take a few months to find the right house. Are you ready to go and tell the kids? Belle will call us about closing and all that." Danny stood up.

"Of course. Let's get home. With this out of the way, we can finally work out a date for the wedding." Kim picked up her purse and followed Danny out of the coffee shop.

Allie and Avery went upstairs after Danny and his family left, since tomorrow was a school night. All four teenagers had handled cleanup after their simple meal of salad and pizza, so there was little to do as Kim surveyed the downstairs. *Hmm, nothing left for me to do, but start the dishwasher.* She stopped by each of their rooms to say goodnight, Kim felt good about finding a home everyone would enjoy.

Curling up in bed, Kim found she couldn't concentrate on her book. Her mind kept wandering. *I have to admit that part of the reason I've hesitated to take this last, big step—marriage---was I was afraid. Afraid of failing again. Afraid of getting hurt. Afraid of waking up one morning and wondering who I married. But with Danny, I don't have to be afraid.* Presently, she drifted off to sleep dreaming of the future.

29

Callie September 2010

Callie walked slowly across the dune. She licked her lips, savoring the salty breeze wafting inland from the ocean. Sea oats swayed with the wind as she made her way to firmer, moister sand, leaving a trail of footprints in her wake. The ever-present seagulls made their disappointment over her lack of food known by squawking noisily overhead. Sandpipers went about their ceaseless dance with the water's foamy edge as they looked for tidbits buried in the sand. Nearing the new lifeguard station the county had put up at the beginning of the summer, Callie moved to the dry loose sand, sat down and lifted her face to the sun's warmth.

With a contented sigh, she dropped her head and opened her eyes to gaze at the white-crested waves moving toward the shore. *Imagine Kim wanting to be married under the old magnolia. That tree has to be seventy years old, maybe older; I remember it being big when I came back to the island in the 60s. She just gave me some broad strokes about the ceremony on the phone last night. I know they found a house. I'm sure I'll hear more about everything at dinner tonight.*

I was surprised when they first began dating. Shouldn't have been. They've known each other since Kim was in high school. Like Kim, Danny's devoted to his family and obviously adores her. She's less edgy around him. Seems she's found someone who doesn't take the softness in her as a weakness. I'm happy for her. I hated thinking of her being alone for the rest of her life, especially since one day I won't be here. I know some people are happy living alone, but I don't think Kim wanted that. Dang it, where did those thoughts come from? I've got a lot of time left. Better get on with this day. Standing, Callie brushed thoughts of getting older from her mind like the sand she brushed from her clothes.

Today she would be alone in the store since Max was taking Louise to a doctor's appointment and Alma wasn't due to come in. Once Mike set up the seafood counter, cleaned up and delivered the day's restaurant seafood orders, he generally went home. It turned out to be a good day with just enough customers to keep her busy.

The sun dipped below the horizon. She balanced a travel cup filled with coffee as she locked the Emporium's front door. Business had been brisk both in the gallery and the store itself. Opening the door to her SUV, she placed her bag on the seat and stretched trying to ease the kink in her back. *Man, too bad Luke won't be back until tomorrow. I could use a back rub.* Inside the car, she rotated her shoulders once more before starting it.

Pulling into Danny's driveway, Callie gathered her bag along with her travel cup and walked to the front door. As she reached for the doorbell, Allie stepped onto the porch. "Grandma, you're here." She hugged her grandmother. "Come on inside. Supper's nearly ready." Allie led her to the family room where they found Danny, Kim, Linda, and the other teenagers. Her arrival led to a round of hugs.

It's nice that Tommy and Suzie hug me so naturally. It's great having more grandchildren. They certainly help keep you young. And all the kids are so smart. Callie settled in an armchair.

"Mom C, can I get you something to drink?" Danny asked as the rest of the family settled comfortably around the room.

"Do you have fresh coffee? This stuff was old when I filled the cup." Callie waggled her travel mug gently.

"Of course. With you in the house we couldn't not have coffee." Laughing, Danny took her travel cup. "I'll just rinse this out for you and be right back."

Seeing two groups of paint chips on the coffee table, Callie raised her eyebrows. "What's going on here?"

Kim smiled at her mother and pointed at a group of paint chips. "These are colors for the new house. You know me, I tend to like blues, greens and yellows." Pointing to the second group she added. "These more earth-toned ones are for the townhouse."

"Did you decide to sell the townhouse?" Callie turned in her seat to look more directly at her daughter.

Kim shook her head as Linda explained. "I've decided to get a place of my own." She held up a hand at Callie's surprised expression. "My choice. Kim and Danny have agreed to rent the townhouse to me. I never thought I would live with Danny and the kids as long as I have."

Danny returned with coffee and talk turned to the different colors and where they would be used in each house. As Kim, Danny and the teenagers left the room to get supper on the table, Linda shared her desire to return to nursing. "I won't go back to hospital nursing. I know the agency I used to work for is looking for RNs."

Callie nodded. "From what Kim tells me everybody's looking for nurses. What made you decide to go back?"

"Tommy and Suzie are older now. I'm getting tired of being around the house most of the time. Kim and Danny getting married just makes it easier." Linda shrugged.

"Oh, I get that," Callie said. "I don't know what I would do if I didn't have the store. Since I hit sixty, I don't have quite as much energy, but I can still do what I want. Maybe just a bit slower for some things." Callie laughed.

"Oh don't I know. That's why I'll go back to home health. No twelve-hour shifts. Make my own schedule."

Suzie came into the family room. "Excuse me, grandmas." She grinned at her joke. "Supper's on the table."

A group effort quickly had the dining room and kitchen cleaned up when supper was over. The kids drifted off while the adults reconvened around the kitchen table with more coffee, their planners and a couple of legal pads. "Okay, so you want to get married under the old magnolia?" Callie said as she flipped open her planner. "What date are you thinking of?"

Kim and Danny looked at each other and grinned before she answered. "The second or third weekend of October."

"Definitely not Halloween." Danny chuckled and added. "It's still warm in October."

Callie raised her eyebrows. "Good, 'cause Halloween weekend is our October get-together. What kind of ceremony are we talking about?"

"Simple," Kim said as Danny nodded in agreement. "We're thinking family and close friends. Danny's sister, Mary, Alma, Max, Louise and family, Grandpa, Bobby and family, Linda, you, and Luke. We each might invite a friend or two from work."

Linda looked up from her notebook. "Thirty to forty people max, then? Better get that list nailed down. That's not much of a turnaround time for invitations." She shook her head.

Kim looked around the table with a half grin. "I know. I know. I thought we'd call the out-of-town people first to help solidify the date. Then we'll get a rush order on the invitations."

"I think most people we're inviting will already know and the invitation is just a formality." Danny put an arm around Kim's shoulder.

"Okay." Callie nodded. "So what about a reception? Food?"

"Hmm. I'd like the ceremony to be at two with heavy hors d'oeuvres following." Kim looked at her mother. "What do you think, Momma?"

"Sweetheart, I'm ready to help you do whatever you want. Who do you want to cater?" Callie flipped her pen through her fingers. "Dante at the Inn in Mount Pleasant caters for outside events now."

After spending a few minutes reviewing their individual lists, Callie went to the rec room to say goodbye to the teenagers. Back upstairs, she gave Kim another hug before heading home. At home, Callie got a glass of water and went out onto the front porch. *Ah, this old rocker sure is comfortable. Only the bats are moving tonight, hopefully they'll eat all these mosquitos.* She puffed out her cheeks before exhaling a long, slow breath. *I'm glad Luke will be home tomorrow. Things aren't quite right without him here.* She sighed deeply as her eyelids grew heavy. *Better go inside and get ready for bed. It's going to be real busy around here, if we pull this wedding off in just six weeks.*

30

Kim October 2010

Kim rolled over. Cocooned in the bedcovers, she thought about going back to sleep. It had been hectic for several weeks now as everyone prepared for joining the two families and all of their possessions. Noises drifting up the stairs let her know Allie and Avery were already awake. The bathroom remodel was finished and last week the painters had completed their work on the new house on Seaview. She and the twins had packed most of their belongings over the last few weeks. *Living out of our suitcases is a pain. By Thursday, we should have everything unpacked at the new house.* Thoughts of what still needed to be done ricocheted through her mind. *Not only for the wedding next Saturday, but the move too. Ugh. I might as well get up.* Kim threw off her covers and went into the bathroom.

Downstairs Allie and Avery were in the kitchen having just finished eating cereal for breakfast. School was closed for a teacher workday. "Morning, Mom," the twins said. Kim smiled. Sometimes they still spoke in near unison.

Kim paused on her way to the coffee pot to hug each of them. "Hey, thanks for letting me sleep in and starting the coffee."

"You're welcome." Avery nodded and pointed to his sister. "Allie did the coffee."

Allie blushed slightly. "Figured it would help get things going. Besides, I'm starting to like it. What do we have to do today?"

"Unpacking what's at the house already." Kim rubbed at the creases in her forehead. "I know Danny's had most of their things moved last week."

"So everybody will be there today?" Avery stood up from the island and made his way over to the dishwasher as his mother sat down.

"Yeah, I'd like to finish getting things unpacked so it's at least functional." She took a drink of coffee before continuing. "They're delivering the furniture for Danny's and my bedroom after lunch."

Allie raised her eyebrows and sighed. "Mom, are we going to be busy all weekend?" Avery propped against the counter waiting to hear the outcome of this discussion

"What's up sweetie?" Kim put an arm around her daughter.

"I'd like to go to the arcade with the gang this afternoon." Allie looked down at her plate.

"Hey, that shouldn't be a problem. Who are you going with? And who will be driving?" Kim took another drink of coffee. Allie had been toeing the line since the skipping school and going to the beach. *Please don't say you and Marion are friends again.*

She looked up at her mother before answering. "Leah, Lionel, and Tyler. They're all in my art class. Lionel's mother is driving. She'll pick us up at three. Everybody has to be home by eight."

Kim nodded and grinned. "Sure, honey. You can go. Mostly I want you guys to get your bedrooms arranged today. The décor stuff can wait. You know after Saturday we'll be in the new house. Linda will want to start working to make this place her own."

"That's going to be weird." Avery's mouth turned down as he frowned. "What do you mean?" Kim tilted her head to look closer at him. *Hope he's not having second thoughts about Danny and me getting married.*

Avery gave a nonchalant shrug. "We've lived here all my life and now someone else will live here. It'll be different. That's all."

Kim looked at her children's muddled expressions. "Hey, are you guys, okay? Tell me what's on your mind?"

Avery left the counter to hug his mother. "Of course. It's just going to be different, our becoming a bigger family."

"I'm happy you found someone, Mom." Allie said as Kim brought her into the hug. "And I like Danny and his family a lot. It'll be good. Just different, like Avery said."

"I know. I promise I'll still make time to have our time together. Everything doesn't always have to be done as one big family, you know." Kim squeezed them tightly. "Some things will be the same. Like family dinners, hanging out with your friends, visiting grandparents, and seeing your dad." Kim hugged the two of them again. "You two are the best. Anything else?" The twins shook their heads. "I'm so lucky. All right. Let's get moving."

Danny, Suzy, and Tommy came out to help unload the SUV as Kim parked in the driveway of the Seaview house. She stepped around to the back of the vehicle. "Everything is labeled so we won't have to move it later," Kim said as she leaned into the back of the SUV.

Danny pulled her back and gave her a hug. "Let the younger ones take the first load. "I've missed you," he said before releasing her.

Kim smiled up at him. "Missed you, too. Let's get this stuff inside so we can move my car before the delivery truck gets here. They're due any minute."

It didn't take long for the men to empty the moving van. While setting up the kitchen, Danny and Kim reviewed the family's schedule for the upcoming week. "We're going to have to get a desk calendar and put it on the wall to keep up with everything." Kim chuckled while she began unpacking and putting dishes in the dishwasher.

Danny unloaded food into the refrigerator and sorted which frozen foods to put in the larger freezer in the garage. "I know. By the way, Suzy's going to the arcade with friends this afternoon. We don't have to drive today, though."

"Funny thing. So is Allison. Lionel's mother is driving them." Kim stretched as she straightened up. "Are you sure you've got enough beds at the old house?"

"Yeah, Tommy's got the guest room and Suzy will bunk with Mom for a couple of nights." Danny closed the cooler. "I don't know who's the most excited about this move, me or Mom."

By three o'clock, the kids had their bedrooms ready. Suzie and Allie left with their friends. Tommy and Avery were playing corn hole in the back yard. Kim and Danny began setting up their bedroom.

"You know one of the things I like about our room is that the sitting room alcove is the first thing you see, not the bed."

Danny looked at her quizzically. "You know, usually the first thing you see going into a bedroom is the bed. I never liked that." She laughed and tossed him a pillow. "Come on. Let's get this bed made. Then we can unpack our clothes."

Kim sank onto the couch after Danny left to help his mother, not even bothering to open the journal she picked up on her way into the den. Avery was in the game room setting up the PlayStation. *Just a few more days until the wedding. Glad I took this week off. I'm exhausted. It's worth it though. We'll be functional from the get go.*

Lionel's mother dropped Allie off promptly at eight. They chatted about the arcade for a while before she joined her brother in the game room. After turning on the dishwasher, Kim stopped in to check on the twins.

"Hey, kiddos." Kim leaned against the doorway. "Thanks for getting all your stuff done today."

"You're welcome, Mom," Avery said without taking his eyes from the screen.

Allie nodded enthusiastically while remaining glued to the screen as she watched her brother's progress in the game.

Kim chuckled. "Okay. Don't be up too late. I'll have to take you to school until we sort out the bus schedules. I'm going to get a shower and go to bed. Love you both."

"Yes, ma'am. Love you, Mom." Allie said looking over her shoulder.

"Love you, Mom. I'll be up on time," Avery said as he paused the game.

Saturday dawned sunny and warm. The weather forecast promised pleasant temperatures for the outdoor ceremony. *So glad the hurricane season has been uneventful this year.* A slight breeze ruffled Kim's auburn curls as she opened the back of her SUV. "Hey kids, grab the suitcases for me. I want to check out the awnings." Her mother waved as she approached.

"Hi, sweetie." Callie hugged her daughter closely. "Everything is nearly ready. Eddie will be here with the flowers anytime now and Dante has touched base. He'll be here just before the ceremony starts to set all the food up on the deck. "

Kim stood at the edge of the outdoor space created by large sail-like canvas triangles which were suspended high enough that the blossoms from the lower limbs of the magnolia tree were visible. Large ferns provided a backdrop to the altar while ferns placed around the perimeter lent a summer-like feel to the space. Outdoor rugs placed over temporary flooring completed the look. "Momma, you've done such a fantastic job. This looks and feels like a room." Kim beamed as she pivoted to take it all in.

"Luke was a big help. There's a service that actually rents the live plants. And once the canvas was up, they arranged them." Callie looked up at the deep rose canvas overhead. "He was right about using the rose canvas, too. It'll keep the light from being too harsh."

Kim nodded enthusiastically. "I'll be sure to tell him how much I appreciate his help. Adding the temporary walk from the drive was so smart. I always get frustrated trying to keep my heels from sinking into the dirt."

Callie looped an arm around her daughter's waist. "Come on, let's go inside I need a little something to hold me over until the reception."

In the kitchen, the two women found the twins hovering around the trays of food covering the island as they filled a small plate with samples of pimento cheese on

crackers, wedding sandwiches filled with ham salad, tiny bite-size peach pies, deviled eggs and cheese straws.

Kim raised an eyebrow and looked at her mother. "What's all this? You said Dante wasn't coming until later."

"I knew you, Linda, and all the kids would be here early. As you can see, Louise and Alma helped out." Callie grinned. "Everybody will be starved if they wait for the reception."

"Okay, Momma. I'll eat before I shower." Kim began filling her own plate. As she joined the twins in the dining room, Kim heard a car pull into the driveway. "That's probably Linda and the kids. I'll go help them."

Luke stopped in the dining room on his way from the bedroom. "I've got it. You eat while you can. Callie, don't you forget to eat, either."

Callie lifted her plate so Luke could see it and sat by Kim in the dining room.

In a few minutes, Linda, Tommy and Suzie joined them in the dining room with plates of their own.

"Hey, there." Linda paused to set her plate down and hugged Kim. "Looks like everyone's ready for the big day." She took a bite of a wedding sandwich. "Hmm, these are so good. Why are they called wedding sandwiches?"

Kim laugh quietly. "Well, first off, depending upon when they're given, these little gems are known as wedding or funeral sandwiches."

"You don't say?" Linda frowned slightly. "Wedding or funeral?"

"Every Southern family has their favorite recipe, often handed down through generations. Many people use small Parker-House rolls, but biscuits or other bread will do," Callie said. "The idea is for them to be small and to keep well."

Linda smiled and nodded. "I can see the appeal." She turned to the children sitting at the opposite end of the table. "Do you guys know what you're doing today?"

"Avery and I are ushers. We walk people to their seats. And I get to hold the rings," Tommy said with a smile. "We're supposed to walk you and Grandma Barnes in first."

Avery sat up taller in his seat. "Then we help the other ladies."

"And what are you doing, Suzie and Allie?" Kim looked at the two girls and winked.

Suzie tilted her head as she looked at Kim. "We're to stand just inside and give people a program. When all of us have done our jobs, we go stand near the altar and wait for Luke to walk you down the aisle."

"You got it." Kim stood up and picked up her plate. "I'm going to get a quick shower. After that I'll be in the downstairs guest room, if you need me."

Wrapped in a terry cloth robe, Kim looked at her wedding dress. *This is just the perfect shade of pale yellow. The chiffon layered over the sheath under-dress gives it a light feel.* A knock at the door and her mother's voice disrupted her thoughts.

"Sweetie, it's me."

Kim pulled the towel from her hair. "Come on in, Momma."

Opening the door just wide enough to slip inside, Callie came into the room. She held out a velvet box. "Here are the pearl combs I wore when Luke and I got married."

"Thanks so much for letting me use these." Kim opened the box and placed it on her childhood desk that her mother had transformed into a makeshift dressing table by adding a large mirror brought in from another room.

"I'm glad you want to use them." Callie walked to the wedding dress hanging on the back of the closet door. "You did such a nice job picking out your dress. And the girls' dresses too. The slightly darker yellow satin empire waist bodice with the chiffon around the skirt compliments your dress well. But still, the dresses are special without making the girls look too grown up.”

"Linda was a big help with that. She poured over catalogs, bringing me different pictures. When we finally found one, I took it to Pat's shop in Mount Pleasant. Pat had to order the one for Allie.”

"When is the hairdresser coming? Sorry, I've forgotten her name.” Callie frowned slightly.

Kim grinned as she began getting into her underclothes. "Marcie. I still can't believe the nurses at the office. You know, Marcie doing my hair and makeup is my wedding gift from them.” She shook her head as she straightened up. "They couldn't believe I was going to do my own thing.”

Callie patted her daughter's arm. "Even I went to the salon before I got married.”

"Okay, Momma. It just seems a little silly to me. She should be here in about twenty minutes.” Kim sat down, pulling her pantyhose out of the package. "I need to walk around in these heels for a while. Oh, will you ask Suzie and Allie to come in here for a minute?”

"Sure, I'll send them in. When Marcie gets here, I'll bring you gals some food and a couple of drinks.”

Giggles and a soft knock alerted Kim to the girls' presence. "Come on in.”

"Hey, Mom. What's up?” Kim patted the bed and the girls took a seat on the bed next to Kim, one on each side.

Kim reached into the bag near her feet and pulled out two packages. "I have a little something for each of you. When Grandma married Luke, she gave me this strand of pearls I'm wearing today. So, I thought we'd start a tradition.”

Each girl carefully opened her package.

Suzie's eyes brimmed with tears as she saw the necklace, a single strand of pearls. "Oh, thank you. These are beautiful.” She threw her arms around Kim and squeezed her tightly before looking at Allie.

Allie nodded with excitement as she opened her package. "Mom, these are fabulous. How cool that Grandma and you had the same idea."

Kim dabbed at her eyes. "I'm glad you both like them. I was a little older than you two when Grandma started buying me nice jewelry, but I thought this was a good time to start."

Callie stuck her head inside the door. "Kim, Marcie's here and I've got a tray for you."

"Okay, Momma. Come on in." She gave both girls a hug before they got up to leave.Kim slowly paced the length of the bedroom. *Everyone's out of the house and I haven't heard a car in a while. Is that Luke I hear in the kitchen? The other voices must be Dante and his staff.*

"Kim." Luke's voice was soft as he knocked on the door.

"Come on in Luke." She picked up her bouquet of Calla lilies.

He stood in the door for a moment and smiled. "You're especially beautiful today." Luke crossed the room and hugged her.

Blinking quickly, she smiled. "You'll make me cry if you keep that up. But thank you and not just for today, but for everything."

"Do you need my handkerchief?" He reached into his jacket's inside pocket.

Kim gave him a small smile. "Think I've got it under control."

"You're so much like your mother." He crooked his arm. "Come on. It's time for you to take center stage."

31

Callie September 2011

Callie strolled along the wet sand. White foamy water swirled around her feet as she paused to look out over the ocean. The early morning sun glittered across the sea. She squinted against its brightness. Sandpipers danced a few feet ahead of her, always pausing in search of food before running from the incoming tide. Usually, this scene stirred up happy memories for Callie, memories of Kim as an infant, Joe, and her early days on the island. But today her mind was in a turmoil. *Why does everything have to change?*

It seems things never slow down or stay the same. There's always something new going on and it's not always for the best. Louise is drifting away from us. Alma's in the hospital again. The doctors aren't so positive this time. Her heart has gotten weaker and can't circulate her blood right.

Then there's everything with Danny, Kim, the kids and Mary. It's amazing that his sister walked into the clinic where Kim works seven years ago. I hope she and Danny aren't taking on more than they can handle. I remember Momma's ups and downs with anxiety and depression. I think someone with bipolar disorder would face even more challenges. Callie let out a deep sigh and ran her fingers through her hair in a vain effort to keep it out of her face. Retracing her steps, she returned home.

She was pouring a cup of coffee when Luke came in through the back door. He stepped behind Callie and held her close. "Have you heard from Francine?"

Callie turned to rest her head on his chest, trying to draw on his strength as she had done more times than she could remember. "Yes, she and William will be getting into Charleston Tuesday." Squeezing her eyes closed against tears, she stepped out of Luke's embrace to pick up her coffee cup. *If I don't get busy doing something, I'll break down completely.* Picking up her planner, she sat down at the kitchen island.

"Do they need a ride from the airport?" Luke sat beside her.

"No, they want to rent a car. But they will stay at Alma's." Callie set her cup down. "William was insistent that he didn't want to impose on anyone. "I did invite them to eat with us."

Luke gently covered her hand with his. "Sure, we'll do whatever is needed. But, honey, Alma's had…"

Tears filled her eyes and her nostrils flared as she pulled her hand away and cut him off. "Don't say it. I don't want to hear about her 'long and full life'. It makes it sound like this is the end." She wiped a hand across her eyes.

"Love, I didn't mean…" He put his arm around her shoulder.

She buried her face in her hands. "I know. I just don't want thoughts like that out in the universe." Callie squared her shoulders and ran her fingers over her eyes again. "Anyway, I'm supposed to meet Kim and Mary for lunch. Almost cancelled."

"It's good that you didn't. Probably do you good to get off the island for a bit." Luke chuckled softly. "Don't think I've ever said that to you before."

Callie's sniffle turned into a snort. "Only person who ever said that was Momma." Her smile quivered as she stood. "This might be the one time it's true."

Later that morning, Callie opened Kim's front door. "Hey, sweetie. I'm here." Taking off her light sweater, she sat down at the kitchen table after putting the pimento cheese spread in the refrigerator.

Kim called from the top of the stairs. "Momma, I'll be down in a minute. Mary and I were going through some things."

Once downstairs, Kim leaned over to hug her mother tightly. "I was afraid you'd change your mind." Mary hung back in the doorway.

A smile played across Callie's lips. "Can't say I didn't think about it. I put some pimento cheese in the refrigerator. I thought you might like it later." Looking over her daughter's shoulder at Danny's sister, she added. "Hey, Mary. Good to see you. I'd like to hear more about your apartment."

"Hi, Callie," Mary said and leaned against a counter.

Going to the stove, Kim uncovered a pan of rolls. "Thanks, Momma. I've been doing a lot of cooking on the weekend and freezing things like you used to. These won't take but a few minutes and then we can eat." She put the rolls into the preheated oven.

"It sure saves time during the busy week." Callie got up and went to the refrigerator. "Anybody else want iced tea?" she asked.

Kim and Mary nodded, so she took three glasses from the cabinet and poured the iced tea. Taking the glasses to the kitchen table, Callie sat down, pulling out a chair beside her.

"So, you're getting an apartment?" Callie asked before she sipped her tea.

Putting her glass on a lemon shaped coaster, Mary nodded as she sat beside Callie. "Yes. It's in Mount Pleasant. I move in next week."

"That's fantastic." Callie's smile actually reached her eyes momentarily.

"It is. The Hawthorne Clinic helped me get this apartment in a small complex for people with disabilities." Mary grinned. "They're helping me get basic furniture from a local church, but Kim and Danny are giving me some décor items they aren't using anymore."

Kim joined them at the table. "It's a really good program." She turned to look at Mary.

"There are several homes nearby. Nice neighborhood. No stores though." Mary tilted her head. "But there's a bus stop at the entrance."

"Well, that's good. At least you'll be able to get around. The transit system is pretty good from what I remember and I hear they expanded it to include Mount Pleasant," Callie said.

Kim got up to take the rolls out of the oven. "That's right. Momma, sometimes I forget you lived in Charleston when you and Dad left Columbia. Mary, would you get the salads out of the refrigerator while I get the rolls on the table?"

"Glad to." Mary put the chef salads on the table and then went back for salad dressings. "I wasn't sure what everyone would like, so I brought several."

As they ate, Mary went on to tell them that she had enrolled in classes at the community college. She wanted to get back into design. "I was always really good at designing clothing. I'd like to do that again one day. I have a place with good light to draw in, but it will be a while before I save enough money to buy a decent sewing machine."

Callie nodded. "I used to design beachwear, sun dresses, coverups and shirts. Haven't done any of that for a while. I have a sewing room you're welcome to use."

Mary's eyes lit up. "Really." She paused and exhaled deeply. "That's wonderful. I don't know when I'll get back to designing. I've a lot going on right now. But Mom's helping me get a computer and some design software. It seems to be what people are using these days."

"I understand. But when you get your software, I'd like to see it. I worked from sketches. It's always good to learn something new." Callie smiled as she nodded. "The offer is there when you're ready."

Talk turned to more general topics as the women finished lunch. Callie sat back in her chair. "Kim, thanks for lunch. Luke was right. I needed to be off the island for a little while." She stood up and began gathering dishes. "I do have to go see Alma before I go home though."

Kim shook her head. "You're welcome. We've got these dishes, Momma. Give Alma my love when you see her."

The sun was an orange slice on the horizon as Callie parked at the pavilion after her visit with Alma. She missed seeing the herons any time she drove to the beach. *But it doesn't make sense to park at the house and then come back. Don't have that much time before dark.* The ocean was streaked with shimmering bands of red, rose and gold. The ever-present sandpipers continued their oscillating dance along the water's foamy edge. Shoulders slumped; Callie walked aimlessly. She stopped, closing her eyes. *Seems Mary is doing well. I hope she'll be able to get back into design. Alma looked so frail in the hospital. It may be a matter of time before she goes, but I'm going to enjoy what time we have. And who knows, she may get better, sometimes the doctors are wrong.* Tears gathered on her closed eyelashes. *Breathe in, breathe out. Come on Callie, get a hold of yourself.* Blinking rapidly and straightening her shoulders, Callie walked back to her car to go home...where Luke waited for her.

32

Kim October 2011

Rubbing sleep from her eyes, Kim entered the kitchen and was surprised not to see her mother or Danny. She started the morning coffee. *This last week has been terrible. It's going to take buckets of this to keep us all going today.* Waiting for the coffee to brew, she began emptying the dishwasher. *Another thing that will do double duty.* She focused her thoughts on the things that needed doing rather than the hole in her heart. *When are people coming? Where did Momma put the pad, she always makes a list on?* Kim went to the message board her mother still kept near the kitchen phone. *Ah, there it is.* Pouring her coffee, Kim set up milk and sugar on the island. *No sense having to open and close the refrigerator so much. Now let me see how things are supposed to go today.*

She had just begun reviewing the list when her mother came into the kitchen. "Hey, Momma. I've got milk on the table.

"Morning." Callie made her way to the coffee pot. "Thanks, sweetie. I see you found the small thermos creamer I got a while back. Somewhere I have a thermos server for the coffee. Callie continued as she sat down beside Kim. "Has Grandpa gotten up yet?""

"I haven't seen him. Bobby and Susan's crew was beginning to wake up as I came downstairs. So everybody should be here by eleven?" Kim asked looking down at the list.

"Yes." Saying 'everybody' makes it seem like there'll be a crowd, but some time ago Alma laid out directions for her memorial. "Besides Max, Louise, Danny, Jodie, and Brenda, along with their families she asked that we notify Francine, William and Macy. Do you remember Macy?"

Callie looked into her coffee cup and sighed before continuing. "She's Deborah's daughter. Deborah taught Alma how to weave seagrass."

"Oh, yeah. I remember seeing them at Alma's." Kim got up and began looking through the kitchen cabinets, intent on finding the coffee server.

"People who want to speak can. Then we're supposed to make our way down to the shore and release her ashes." Callie paused, blinking away the tears in her eyes.

"Ah, I found it," Kim stood up, triumphantly holding the coffee server. Seeing her mother's distress, Kim walked over and hugged her. "Momma, I'm so sorry. I miss her, too."

"I know baby. It will get better, this hurt, but right now it's like an open sore someone keeps poking at." Callie reached for a tissue. Blotting her eyes, she continued. "Anyway, once the ceremony at the shore is done. Luke, Max, you, Danny, and I are supposed to read her will together. She asked Luke to be her executor quite a while back. Sorry to run on so, but it took me a while to work up the nerve to get it out. I still have a hard time accepting that she's not next door."

Kim filled the coffee server with hot water, started another pot of coffee and looked at the platters of food in the refrigerator before closing the door and sitting by her mother again. "Well, so much food has been dropped off, I'll just put it out and keep refreshing it as the day goes on. Avery and Allie will be here all day."

Noises from upstairs alerted the two women that the children were awake and would be down soon. Shortly after they first heard the children, Luke made his way to the kitchen. "Hey, love. Did you sleep at all?" He held Callie close as she turned towards him.

"I fell asleep eventually. Sorry I was so restless. I hate that I disturbed you," Callie said as Luke sat on her other side. Kim filled the server with coffee and put it on the island.

"I slept fine. Don't worry about it. Morning, Kim," Luke looked sideways at the list and continued. "I see you've got today's agenda." He started to get up when Callie sat back in her chair.

"Morning. Yeah, Momma brought me up to date. Here's a cup. There's coffee in the server," Kim said. She told him she and Danny would manage the day and added, "I don't want Momma to worry about anything and I want you to be able to look after her today."

Luke smiled faintly, "It sure was a wonderful day that brought you two into my life. I couldn't have asked for a better daughter. Thank you."

The twins and their cousins came bounding down the stairs and into the kitchen. Seeing the sad adults around the kitchen island, they apologized for being rowdy. Luke chuckled and told them not to worry about it. "Are you hungry? What about scrambled eggs and toast?" He asked. As the children agreed, Callie slipped away to get ready for the day.

The memorial's participants assembled on the deck promptly at eleven. Tina and Steve accompanied his parents. Brenda, Josie, and their boys were there as well. The brisk wind carried a chill even with the bright sunlight so the group decided to remain indoors. In hushed voices they shared stories of Alma's legendary personality. How she had helped them. Stories of her stubborn independence. Louise even managed to talk about the first time she met Alma and Nate before sinking to her chair, her brow wrinkled in confusion. All expressed their certainty that she had finally been reunited with her babies and Nate. Luke managed to stay close to Callie's elbow.

As the mourners fell silent, clouds covered the sun and rain began falling, just hard enough to alter the plan to walk to the ocean. Kim and Danny gathered their brood and handed out extra umbrellas as the sorrowful group assembled in their cars for the drive to the shore.

"Look Avery, Allie," Kim said as Danny pulled into the pavilion's parking lot, "All the artists, waiting to say good bye to Alma."

"They're trying not to bother us," Avery said as he turned to stare out the window while Danny parked near the group. "See? They're moving away."

"Come down to the water's edge and join us," Kim said as she rolled down the car window. "We're just going to release Alma's ashes and then go back to the house."

"Are you sure?" Sheila asked. Kim nodded 'yes' emphatically. "Okay," Sheila replied.

Kim gave each person a small portion of Alma's ashes to send out to the ocean. They had to reuse some of the small cups since there were now more people than they originally planned for, but no one seemed to mind.

After speaking briefly to those who needed to be present for the reading of the will, Kim invited the artists to join them back at the house. *I'm glad everyone agreed with me, even though it's not exactly what Alma said, it would have been wrong to exclude these people who loved and worked with her for so many years.*

Kim parked in her parents driveway. She and Danny hurried in to set out fresh platters of food. Danny corralled the children and their food upstairs before returning to Kim's side. No one stayed long, just long enough to express their condolences and get rid of the chill they all acquired while standing in the rain.

As Kim walked the last person to the door, Callie encouraged those remaining to gather in the living room, "At least Luke's got a fire going in there."

Everyone regrouped as suggested and Luke returned from their bedroom carrying a large manila envelope. Sitting in an armchair near Callie, he cleared his throat as he ran a hand across his eyes and said, "I'm not sure why Alma made me her executor. Anyway, here goes." He read the will.

Without all the legal terminology, Alma had left her home to Kim because "I know Francine or none of her brood will ever move back down South", her share of the Emporium partnership to Danny and the residuals from her book on basket weaving and all her basket weaving materials to Macy. She gave the picture of her house Luke painted and her family Bible to her niece, Francine. She asked Callie to keep many of her photographs because "you understand what a family is".

Now the house was quiet except for the low swishing sound of the dishwasher as it was cleaning yet another load of dishes. *It seems this would have been the time to use some type of disposable plates. But then Momma loves her dishes and there is the environment to consider.* Kim made her way to the front porch. Wrapping herself in a blanket she curled up in one of the wicker rocking chairs. *I miss Grandma but not like I miss Alma. Alma was in my life nearly every day for as long as I can remember. Never in my wildest dreams would I have thought she would leave me her house or Danny her partnership in the Emporium. The house has to stay with family.* Kim pulled the blanket closer and let her thoughts wander aimlessly. *Danny and I have a lot to be thankful for. I'm so glad we're together.* Kim's head began to nod. *Maybe I should go to bed. Hopefully, I can sleep. Tomorrow, we have to get on with this business of living.* Having made her way to the upstairs bedroom, Kim quietly slipped into bed. As she curled up against Danny's back, he moved slightly so they fit closer together.

33

Callie October 2011

Around three in the morning, Callie managed to slip out of bed without waking Luke. When she realized sleep would continue to be elusive, she started the coffee. Several minutes later, Callie sipped at her coffee while sitting on the porch, cocooned in a blanket, staring at Alma's house. She listened to the sounds of the island's awakening. Herons were launching themselves skyward, their wings whooshing through the air as they sought a higher air current. From further away, the seagull's squawks drifted into the periphery of her hearing. *The magnolias still smell sweet. We've got one of those rare seasons with a second bloom.*

Funny, the house doesn't look different on the outside and yet it seems empty. Before, I felt Alma there. Her quiet determination. Her ability to help me sort things out. But now, there's nothing. What will I do without her? Callie let the tears slide down her face. Tears she had been unable to shed when she had gone to check when Alma didn't come for coffee as expected, couldn't wake her and found her body had grown cold. Tears she had held back at the memorial service with just family and close friends in attendance. *If Alma could stand the loss of her babies and Nate, I'll just have to keep going. Maybe if I act like I'm okay, then maybe eventually I will be.*

The low creak of the screen door heralded the arrival of Allie, the oldest of Kim's twins. Callie smiled as she wiped away her tears, "Come here, sweetie. Do you need some of my blanket?"

Callie and Allie had forged a bond with each other, the porch, and early morning when Kim and Jake first separated. During those difficult times, Allie often woke during the night. To allow her daughter some rest, Callie would bring the little girl to the porch where they would sit slowly rocking as Callie talked softly about the different things they heard and smelled.

"No, Grandma. I'm fine in this rocker," Allie drew her feet under herself in the mate to Callie's wicker rocking chair. "What's going on today?"

"Well, I've got to go into the Emporium around ten. Uncle Max and I want to meet with Danny and see what he wants to do since Aunt Alma left him her share of the partnership. I'll be home after that. Do you know if your Momma is going into work today? I can't remember what she told me."

"I think she's doing some stuff at Aunt Alma's, but I don't know what." She sniffled and then continued. "It's weird without Aunt Alma; she was teaching me to weave baskets."

"You know a lot already. It's good you want to keep the old skills going. Macy said she would be happy to help you." Callie reached over to pat her granddaughter's hand. "Are you hungry? I'm going to start breakfast. Maybe some bacon, eggs, and biscuits?"

"Yummy. I'll go back upstairs and play games until it's ready. If that's okay?" Allison looked at Callie for approval of the plan.

"Sure, it's early still, so keep the volume down. We'll let everyone wake up on their own today." Callie stood and draped her blanket over the loveseat near the rocking chairs.

Taking her grandmother's hand, Allie led the way inside. Parting with a hug in the kitchen, she went upstairs as her grandmother found her largest cast iron skillet and started frying bacon. With the bacon started, Callie pulled out the Bisquick and milk for biscuits. *Oh, Lord. I remember when Momma told me she had started using Bisquick instead of making biscuits from scratch. We pretended to be scandalized at the thought of "good" Southern women using a package mix.* Covering the biscuits with a dish towel so they had some extra time to rise, Callie started another pot of coffee as she heard small noises from upstairs, letting her know others would be downstairs soon.

Stretching and yawning, Luke gathered Callie into an embrace as he walked up behind her, "Morning, love. How long have you been up?"

Callie leaned into the embrace. "I finally got up for good around three. Hope I didn't bother you too much."

"Nah, I was dead to the world. Is anyone else up?" He moved away to pour himself some coffee. "Do you need a refill?"

"Please. That cup is beyond cold. Allie's upstairs playing video games. I think I heard Avery and maybe Kim or Danny upstairs. Not sure about Dad or Bobby's crew." Callie handed him her cup.

After fixing the coffee, Luke sat Callie's cup within her reach near the stove. "Your dad's more habitual than any of us. I expect he'll be along soon, though. Bobby and Susan might take a while longer." Luke chuckled as he sat at the kitchen island.

Before long everyone was in the kitchen waiting for breakfast. Kim had taken the day off and would be going through some of Alma's things at the house and make other arrangements about the property. Kim and Luke took over the cleanup when Callie went to get ready for her meeting with Max and Danny. Bobby and Susan agreed they would keep an eye on the children.

Max had the seafood orders ready before Callie reached the Emporium. Other than a quick greeting, Callie didn't feel much like talking and to her it seemed Max didn't either. She pulled the register's drawer from the safe and began getting everything ready before Sheila came in to cover the store and gallery. Shortly after she arrived Callie joined a somber Max in the office.

"I'm still in a daze." Callie plopped into a chair. "It's like I'm stuck somewhere between now and yesterday or somewhere else. I don't know where really."

Max rubbed his hands over his head and down his neck. "Did you know about Alma's will before yesterday?" He took a drink of coffee.

"I had no idea." Callie sat up in her chair. These days if she slumped too long her shoulders and back began to ache. *This day will be bad enough without any of that.* "You know how private she could be about some things. Still, if Danny wants to maintain the partnership and not sell out, it could be a good thing. Having a younger person as a partner, I mean. Guess we just have to see what he wants to do."

"Agreed. I'm fine with her choice. Everything has just taken the wind out of my sails and then Louise had a rough night last night. She's getting smarter about the extra locks I put on the doors." Max stared into his coffee cup.

"I was afraid this would be extra upsetting for her. It was nice that she was able to say a few words about Alma." Callie began twirling a pen through her fingers. She felt she should be doing something, but was unsure about what the something should be.

"I'll get the coffee set up back here. I'm sure Danny is as tired as we are." Max slowly stood and turned to the office door.

"Yeah, I brought a small tray of pastries. I'll get them out of the kitchen. Everyone has been so kind. We've got more food in that house than we'll ever be able to eat. I'm going to send the kids over with some of it once you're home." Callie followed Max into the kitchen.

As they returned to the office, the door chimes sounded and Danny walked across the store, pausing briefly to chat with Sheila before joining Max and Callie. Everyone had tears in their eyes when they hugged briefly.

"Would you like some coffee, Danny?" Callie asked as she poured for Max and herself. "Help yourself to a sweet roll or something." She couldn't help noticing the dark circles under Danny's eyes. *What a fine trio we make this morning.*

"Sure, Mom C. That sounds good. I can't seem to get with it this morning." Danny shook his head slowly.

"Don't worry we're all in the same boat, here," Max said with a shadow of a grin. "Not to rush you into a decision, but do you have any idea what you want to do with your share?"

"Just so you know, I had no idea Alma would leave me her partnership. Kim and I discussed it for a while last night, but even so I hardly slept thinking about it." Danny shrugged tiredly. "I'd like to come into the business as an active partner. Are you okay with that?" Kim and Max nodded. "Alma talked to me about your idea for building a website and I certainly have abilities in that area."

"I think it will help if we update a little." Callie looked down at her coffee cup. *We're doing what she wanted, but this feels so weird.*

"I agree." Danny smiled "You guys and the Emporium have always had a special place in my heart. I'd like to be part of its future. Besides, I think I'll enjoy the flexibility of working here. Kim's pretty locked into her schedule. This will be better for our family. Still, it will take me a couple of months to wrap up things with my current firm."

"Certainly understand. That's great," Callie and Max said nearly in unison.

The three of them talked for a while longer until exhaustion forced a halt to any meaningful discussion. Before Max and Danny left, they decided to get together again after Danny gave notice to his present firm. On her way out, Kim stopped at the counter to let Sheila know she'd be back to lock up.

The evening sun hung low over the horizon when Callie slipped off her shoes as she reached the water's edge. *So much has happened. Losing Momma and Alma is nearly too much to bear.* The foamy water was cool as it pulled sand across her feet, making Callie feel that the whole earth was moving beneath her, not just the sands. *Everything is moving too fast these days.* It was low tide. The only sound came from the waves' gentle movement as they ran outward toward the vastness of the open sea. *Nearly lost myself for a while after Momma died, but everyone rallied around and pulled me back, refusing to let me fall over the edge of that black cliff. I miss Alma so much. Because of all she taught me I'll have to hang on here. I'm awful lucky to have known her and have such caring people around me.* Callie lifted her chin and turned toward home anxious to see Luke, Kim, Danny and her grandchildren.

Acknowledgements

Even for the indie author, who wears so many different hats, there are so many people who play an integral part in getting a book published. As always, I have to thank my husband, Keith, for his unflagging support and his willingness to help haul my stuff to author events. Thanks also to my children, James, David, Kenny and Sarah. Kenny and Sarah our conversations keep my neurons from getting in a rut. My sister Terry and my brother, Benny, provide unwavering support through phone chats or liking and sharing all my social media posts.

Then there's my Thursday night critique group. This talented group of writers never seem to tire of reading about Callie and Kim. I've learned so much about the craft of writing from these women. Our discussions keep me motivated.

Mary Turner, a great writer, was the beta reader not only for *Riptides,* but also for *Low Tide,* Mary is more than generous with her wealth of writing knowledge.

Finally, there's Shawna Gentert at Persnickety Books. She took a chance and allowed a novice author to place her first novel in her bookstore. Along with Burlington Writers Club, she sponsored the Writers Cafe which meets weekly in the store. Giving me and other Burlington writers a great place to gather and work.

To all of you, I give my heartfelt gratitude.

Chapter 1 Callie May 2016

Sunbeams streaked earthward between thunder clouds making their way across the ocean toward the island. Callie left the Emporium through the back door. She hoped a short walk would help her calm down before visiting Louise. In just a few minutes, she was walking along the foamy water's edge; sandpipers scattered before her in their ceaseless search for a tasty morsel buried in the shifting sands. A brisk wind blew her hair out like spidery tentacles and then whipped it back across her face. In exasperation, she fished into a pocket for a hair tie. Between one step and the next, her hair was more or less confined in a ponytail. She looked out toward the horizon. *Everything is just out of sorts today. I've got to get into town the see Louise. Funny thing, Louise's ability to pick up on someone's mood has intensified over the last few years. I really need to get a grip on myself.*

A child's laughter drew her attention back to the beach. A dark haired young woman, in denim capris, tie-dyed tank top and chambray over-shirt, chased a little girl darting after another group of sandpipers. *They must have bought Brenda's old place.* A smile came to Callie's face as she walked toward them.

"Hi, I'm Callie Barnes. It's a little blustery, but still a good day for a walk," she said stopping near the young woman.

"Hey, I'm Stella and this is my daughter, Trinity. We just moved in over the weekend and she's been begging to 'go see the water' since we got here." Stella's eyes danced as she smiled.

"How old is Trinity? She reminds of my daughter. Always chasing the sandpipers."Callie shrugged. "Of course, she's grown now with children of her own."

The young girl paused, smiled, waved and them continued her pursuit of the sandpipers.

"She's four. I'll have to take her in soon. Hopefully, we'll make it home before the rain starts."

The two women chatted while they followed along behind Trinity. Stella painted, mostly watercolors, and wove textiles. She had been in the Emporium to visit the gallery and hoped to get her work displayed there. Callie let Trinity know she was happy to see a new family on the island.

Looking out to sea, Callie stood still a moment. "We'd better turn back. The rain is moving in." Taking turns carrying Trinity, they made it under the Emporium's awning just ahead of the rain and fell laughing into the deck chairs.

"So how long have you lived on the island?" Stella reached into her bag and handed Trinity a couple of toys.

"My first husband and I moved here in 1969." A smile flickered across Callie's face. "Raised my daughter here and met my second husband tight here in this store."

Stella's eyes grew wide. "This is your place? And Luke Barnes, the artist, is your husband? I've always admired his work."

Nodding, Callie grinned and briefly described the process for getting her work in the Emporium. "You'll have to stop by the house sometime. We're over on Kiawah Trail, just a short walk from your place. They look, the rain has stopped. I don't have a car seat, but would you like a ride home? I have my car since I worked today." The younger woman leaned over to pickup her daughter and the toys. "No, but thanks. I'm sure we'll see you again soon."

The air was humid, heavy as Callie took a cup of coffee to the front porch. Luke was in Charlotte helping his mother. Melony had decided to downsize to a smaller condo following Tony's death several months ago. It was in the same development she and Tony lived in. Her condo was in a four-unit quadraplex.

Wish Luke was home. He's so good at helping me snap out of these moods., keeping me from being so serious. I hate this business of getting older. Everything just takes longer' 'cause I get so tired. Callie shook her head slowly. *But he needs to be there for his mother.*

Max seems lost without Louise at home. Glad Danny has been able to take over buying the seafood and supervising out new driver. Draining the last of her coffee, Callie went inside to freshen up before going to see Louise.

She pulled into the parking lot of the assisted living facility, Louise's home for the last three years. Max found it after the last time Louise had gone for a walk in the middle of the night. Callie checked in at the receptionist's desk. *It always smells fresh and clean. Not like some of the places Max toured.* She hesitated at the door to Louise's room. Some days Louise knew who she was. Others not.

Knocking softly, Callie called out as she entered the room."Hi, Louise. It's Callie."

Yet again, Callie marveled at the compact space and how homey Max had made it. You entered into a sitting room/dining area. There was enough room for a small dining table and four chairs. as well as a couple of armchairs and a loveseat. Just off this room was a small bedroom and bathroom. Except for the bed, everything had come from their home.

Louise was sitting a chair looking out the window at birds on the feeder Max had placed nearby. "Oh, hi," Louise said.

"I brought you some asters from my garden." She brought them over so Louise could look at them closely. "Do you want them here or in the bedroom?"

A crease flickered across Louise's brow. "They're so pretty. Just put them on the table there." She pointed to the right side of the room.

"We had a rain shower earlier," Callie said in an armchair after putting the flowers in a vase. "It just made it muggier."

"Yeah, we dud, too." She peered at Callie. "So how'd it go at the store?"

"It was a good day. The gallery was really busy." Callie smiled at her friend. "I meet the new people who moved into Brenda's old place."

Louise's eyes clouded over momentarily. "That's right. She's renting it out."

Over the last few years, Callie had learned to meet Louise wherever she might be at the time, rather than correct her. *She doesn't remember that Brenda put the house on the market several months ago.* "Right. Her name's Stella and she has a four year-old daughter."

"That's wonderful. Good to have young people on the island again." She shifted in her seat. "When's Max getting home. I missed him at supper."

"I expect he'll get in pretty soon. Would you like to watch TV until then?" Louise usually liked to watch "Wheel of Fortune", even though she no longer tried to solve the puzzles. She was always so happy for the winners.

"That's fine." Louise relaxed against her chair as she stared at the television.

Callie settled in the armchair again and hid a yawn behind her hand. *I'll stay until the next commercial. Max'll be here soon to help her get ready for bed.*

"Louise, I'll see you later," Callie said as the program took a break. She stood before hugging her friend.

"Good night, Callie," Louise said and turned her attention back to the television.

She met Max in the lobby and frowned slightly as she hugged her friend. *Wow he's shrunk. He still stands so straight I hadn't noticed before.* They chatted a few minutes before going their separate ways.

I can't believe that at eighty-nine Max still drives over here twice a day. He gets her ready for the day. Doing her hair the way she likes and eating breakfast together. Then he's back every night after supper to get her ready for bed. He sits reading to her until she's nearly asleep before going home.

Encountering little traffic as she drove from Mount Pleasant, Callie was soon home. After changing into a nightgown, she took a glass of iced tea to the porch and called Luke. With his sister's help he managed to get his mother settled in the new condo. Things left in the old place would be picked up by an auction house in the next few days. His sister agreed to oversee that so he'd be home tomorrow. Feeling relieved, Callie crawled into bed and drifted off to sleep.

Coming 2027

Seventeen years ago, Sherry and her husband, Keith, returned to the South and made Burlington, NC their home. She began writing as she retired from nursing. Sherry spent her early years on Johns Island SC or in nearby Charleston. Even though her family moved away from the coastal area when she was eight, Sherry was left with a deep love of the ocean and all the life surrounding it. When not writing she enjoys volunteering in her community, gardening and spending time with her children and grandchildren.